PERCY

Lessons Learned in a Gentler Time

by
Michael Shure

Published by Alexander Dare Publishing Company -
www.alexanderdarepublishing.com
First printed in 2004

ISBN:0 -9762542-6-3 (Dust Jacket)
ISBN:0-9762542-5-5 (Paperback)
ISBN:0-9762542-4-7 (E-Book)

Printed in the United States of America
and England.

Thank you Percy
for all the wonderful stories.

Chapter 1

I was staring over a ledge, concentrating on the river. A small gang of young boys was looking dumbly down at me. They were perched precariously on an overhang, clutching sprigs of scrub oak and bunches of Johnson grass. I was twenty feet or more from the water, but I could hear it lapping against the base rock like a pack of thirsty dogs. The boys dug their toes into the soil and hunched backward against the slope, taking a fresh hold.

"See anything?" one of them asked me.

I didn't answer. I was watching. That's all. If I had seen something, I would have said so. Then there would be more than enough to do.

Their eyes followed mine up to the great bend, through the near channel, into the shallows, and then onto a rolling expanse of gliding water and muddy slicks. On the margins were clusters of sagging trees and willows washed over by the current. The river was rising. I figured it wouldn't be long now.

I felt for the noose around my waist and fingered the knot, hoping it would release at the right instant. The handle of my knife protruded from my waistband. I rested an elbow on it and began coiling and uncoiling a length of rope the way I'd seen them do with the lading hooks down at the wharf. Tangling could be a problem; there was too much brush for a clear throw. Still, the rope was good, freshly-oiled hemp. I needed at least a hundred feet of play, and probably two hundred. I couldn't get more than that, not if the boys hung on to it – and heaven help me if they didn't.

"Hang on!" I warned, bringing the boys to attention a little prematurely.

They braced themselves against the incline, throwing their weight back on their heels and tightening their grip on the rope. Their sudden move yanked me off balance. It pissed me off, and I yanked back, yelling, "Watch it, stupid!"

I felt disdain when I saw their dark, skinny forearms, corded and trembling with exertion, and their innocent, dutiful faces full of anxiety, and shining with sweat. They weren't going to be as much help as I'd hoped.

"Not yet!" I said irritably. *Dumb little niggers*, I thought. *All I can get is a bunch of scared, dumb little niggers.*

The sounds from the river began to change. The water had risen almost five feet in five minutes, and I could see from the swollen hump at the bend that it was coming up more – maybe too much more.

"No matter what, keep outta the water! Take the rope. Take it to the ridge if you have to. If it tangles, let go. Don't worry 'bout me. But keep out the water. The devil is in this flood. Folks be going to hell today, and the devil wants you with 'em. I can see him there now. There… there's his face all toothy, just below the water. See it? He's saying, *Come on in here and see me, boys. I think I'll just take you right now.* He's saying that. Can you hear it?"

There was a low, indistinct vibration. I knew the boys felt it in their feet through the ground, because they were too scared to answer me. Boulders were beginning to tumble beneath the surface. The mighty river was reshaping itself. Then, from the bend came a higher-pitched sound, almost like muskets in warfare; the first wave of trees were clashing and grinding like charging bulls. They were mostly full-grown oaks and sycamores torn from their moorings. A white oak bore down on the boys from the narrows, then veered away, swinging tamely into a series of whirlpools and eddies. More trunks came rocking crossways just beneath the surface, with shattered limbs gesturing. Out in the main current, the debris passed in an orderly flotilla but, toward the shore, turned into a tangle of broken logs and discarded branches. It was worrisome but inevitable. Working through *that* was the trick.

I knew from the size of the sycamores that some of the big islands had given way, with their shoreline sloughing off in boat-sized chunks. Just the fact the oaks were there meant the levees were breached. Sure enough, this would be a bountiful flood, a harvest of misery wrought upstream where men and women were most likely crying out for each other and their belongings. But now they were sweeping toward me, and I would be fetching them. They, in turn, would be fetching the thing I needed: money.

Soon the wreckage appeared – shattered houses, bent and cockeyed, breaking off in pieces. One house came on down the river with a man and two children holding onto a pipe as it pitched and bucked, sometimes submerging, then bursting back onto the surface with its passengers securely attached. I couldn't hear them, but I knew they were praying. I also knew God probably wouldn't do anything, and *He* would just let it pass on them for bad luck.

Reverend Tollman, a preacher friend of my mother's, once told me God gave Satan power on the water, and that God pushed Satan off the land but let him have one domain, the water. My mother believed Satan held dominion over the Mississippi. That gave me good cause to be ashamed to tell her I was spending time in the river. She never knew I could swim, and for the most part, I didn't – unless, of course, I had to. And there were times I had to, because I lived by the river, and the river was always coming between me and the things I wanted.

I kept my eyes peeled upriver, and soon I could see what I wanted, little gray forms tossed about, almost invisible in the froth. Cargo! It was time. I stood on the ledge and calculated how far I'd have to leap to clear the tangle of snags and flotsam. I would have to carry some slack rope on my arm to make it. Otherwise, the weight would jerk me back and maybe spear me on a snag. In any event, I would have to pull hard to get myself into position.

"When I jump, let go the rope. Play it out 'til you get to the end. Then hold on. It'll swing me back over the bank. Don't let me go under a log. If you see me down under a tangle, you pull with everything you got. Don't wait, 'cause if I go under any trees, I'm not coming out."

"Go 'head, jump!" Meat looked straight down at me, braced like an anchor. The other boys were looking at Meat, then back at me. They seemed somewhat revived.

Meat had a broad face with deep-set, steady eyes. His neck was thick and set on stout shoulders. With all the clamoring around him, he stood as steady as an oak. With all his strength engaged, anything the others offered would be incidental.

Meat's intractability gave me hope. He had always been there when I needed him. I called out, "Let it play out with the current."

Meat smiled broadly. "Do what you do. I take care the rest."

I had never seen the Mississippi run so strong. I thought about what I was feeling. I had to make sure I wasn't fooling myself. I wanted to be certain I wasn't giving way to impatience or to the boys, who might just have wanted to see me make a bloody spectacle, then drag my corpse back to town. I've never known what people really want from me, but I have always known what I wanted for myself: I wanted it all.

A lot of fellows would risk their reputation on a dare, but I wasn't into casual betting, nor casual thinking. It was part of the way I presented myself to the world. I always relied on my own judgment. To anyone else, one time to jump might seem as good as the next, but to me it all had to feel right. There were no clear rules. I would jump when I was ready, and when I did, I would know the inner thrill – the instant when courage, purpose, and good sense come together. "All things come to him that waits on the Lord," I'd heard a preacher say, and I was waiting for the Lord to tell me when to jump. That would be the voice I would listen for, and that would make me different.

I didn't hear a voice that day, but I did feel an urge, and I jumped. There was no grace or beauty to it. My legs kicked out in great strides, and my arms spread to keep me and the ropes separated. My head was cocked, my eyes fixed on the spot I had singled out, and I tried desperately to hit it square, though I knew the instant I hit that I could be swept away in an eddy.

I smacked the water and turned toward the first spilled load: a net of hogsheads bobbing just above the surface like hippos. I kicked my way to an intervening log and clambered over it, glancing at the ledge to see how fast I was moving downstream. The rope began to tighten, so I let go three coils to give myself a chance to tie off the cargo. Using the smaller ropes in my belt, I tied off the barrels of wine that would fetch a handsome price in the Quarter, and began to pull toward what looked like a capsized keelboat. Its fore and aft rudders rose skyward like broken arms.

I felt a strong pull on the rope, and then I was suddenly darting to shore. I got a lesson about friendship that day, as I fought to keep my head above water. The boys were holding onto the rope as best they could, but Meat had done one better. He'd put the rope around his own waist and tied it off. If I had gone down river, I wouldn't have been alone.

There were some hard times on the river, and making a living was always tough. But I was lucky that day. Not only did I survive, I got a big haul from the river. I made sure that everyone shared in my good fortune. But the moment passed, and though I should have been happy, I wasn't. I had been living with a terrible sadness deep inside me. It was a feeling I couldn't shake, ever since my mother was murdered.

It all began when I was thirteen years old and a man named Louis La Pointe came to our house. He said he was a friend of my father's, and he had come to let us know that my father had been hanged for murder. He talked my mother into renting him a room while he was in New Orleans. One day when I was out, La Pointe stabbed my mother to death. To my everlasting shame, I saw the commotion at the house and I hid out. Afterwards, I tried to convince myself that I was young and didn't know any better, but that brought me no comfort. It still doesn't.

After my mother passed over, I lived on my own. I wasn't the only boy who felt the hardships of those times. There were others in similar circumstances back then in New Orleans. If an orphan boy was young enough and white, families took him in, because he was good help around the farm. That's not the way it was for colored boys. We were left to our own devices. You were from either one group or the other, and you didn't ever cross the line... I mean *ever*! And be sure, there was a line. That's the way it was in 1887, and it was just fine with me.

I turned to spending my time in the streets and the alleys of the French Quarter, hustling the goods I took from the river. Most people didn't want to be seen dealing for river goods, so I did my business at night. The night became my time. The locals didn't like any of us boys around there, but there wasn't much they could do short of killing us. Sometimes they ran us off for a night, and other times they kept after us for days at a time. Some of the boys disappeared for good. Even so, I always went back, because that's where the money was, and nobody was going to take what was rightfully mine. And when things were going right, I made a good living off the river. The Mississippi always held a lot of opportunity for those who had the nerve to go after it.

Michael Shure

Chapter 2

Commerce crowded the narrow streets of the French Quarter, and created a perfect environment for pimps and hustlers. There were times that I danced on the sidewalk in front of the clubs there, and when the crowds were good, I'd make some money. Dancing was a cover for the hustling I was doing. At the end of a particularly unprofitable day, I was tap dancing on the corner of Toulouse and Bourbon Streets, in front of Lafitte's Bar. It was late, and I was ready to call it quits, when I saw a buggy pull up in front of Miss Jeannie's Place. Miss Jeannie's Place had been a fashionable home that she converted to accommodate her hospitality business. She had a traditional bar, a lounge with a piano player, and a gaming room; but the big draw was the rooms upstairs that provided her working girls and their patrons a measure of privacy.

Money had been tight in New Orleans in the years after the War Between the States, and Miss Jeannie turned to making her living by using her good looks. She took paid dates with wealthy white men. Early on, she cultivated a friendship with a man from a socially prominent family. Their intimate relationship ended ten years later, when his wife died and he remarried a young woman from a rich family. He limited his contact with Miss Jeannie, but never stopped seeing her. He even helped her get her own house with his newly-acquired wealth.

My mother warned me about Miss Jeannie before she passed. "Miss Jeannie is a fallen woman," she would say, "a woman who's been known to cavort with the devil. Son, all you have to do is look at her to see she's pure evil. Best you leave her to herself."

My mother was jealous of Miss Jeannie, but I didn't think she had reason to be. Many men considered Miss Jeannie the finest-looking woman in the Quarter, but of course those men never saw my mother.

I stopped dancing to get a better look at what was going on at Miss Jeannie's. I saw Tiny, the greeter at Miss Jeannie's, open a carriage door for a finely-dressed white man.

Tiny was a large colored man that my friend Meat told me had helped him get a job upriver. I figured that was something a father would do for a son. I had always suspected Tiny was Meat's father, and I teased him about it, but he never owned up to it. When Meat left New Orleans, I figured he would be back after the cotton crop was in, like the boys who had gone upriver in other years. But I was wrong.

The man stood next to the carriage and talked to Tiny. I whispered, "Miss Jeannie's a-goin' tah be making some coin offin' that man this evening."

I half expected Meat to answer me with his usual, "You full of shit, Hey Boy." But he didn't answer. It would never be "Hey Boy" and "Meat" again. His real name was Joe Wallace. He got his nickname because his hands were so big. One of the older boys started calling him "Meat Hooks," and then another boy shortened it to just "Meat." After a time, the name just stuck.

My given name is Jean Percival Hays. My mother called me Jean and I hated that. I wanted to be called Percy. I got my nickname one night when a man called out, "Hey, boy." A group of us were standing on a corner, but I was the only one who answered. I started answering to anything resembling *Hey Boy*, figuring there might be a profit in it for me. My friends picked up on it and started calling me *Hey Boy*.

I kept an eye on what was happening at Miss Jeannie's place, while I tap danced to the music coming from the barroom. I saw Tiny point over at me. The man nodded his head *yes*, and started walking in my direction.

"Hey Boy, get over here!" he shouted.

Something inside me told me to ignore him.

He called out again, "I be talking to you, Hey Boy."

I backed further into the darkness of an alley.

"Come out here," he said. I could see him, but he couldn't see me.

"What if I ain't him?" I shouted.

"Then I be looking for Jean Hays? You know where that boy be?"

"There ain't no 'Jean' around here, mister."

"You know 'bout a 'Percy'?"

"Why you asking?"

"Get out here, boy! Out here where I can get a good look at you!"

I could have gotten away. I was a fast runner back then, and I knew every nook and cranny of the Quarter. And running wasn't new to me either. I had run many times before, but for reasons known only to God, I stayed this time. "You don't need to see me!"

"Get yourself out here, boy!"

"Why should I?" I said defiantly. Most colored boys were afraid to act proud in Louisiana back then. They feared there would be hell to pay if they did, but that didn't bother me. In the French Quarter, there was a band of young coloreds who were known to speak up, and I was the leader of that group.

"To see what you look like, boy."

"What you need to see for?" I backed still farther into the alley.

"To see if you be that boy."

"What then?"

"Then, I be looking for your momma," he said good-naturedly.

"Got no momma!"

"I need to talk to you, boy!"

I wasn't going to answer any questions about my mother.

"Come to the light, boy!"

I wasn't scared of him. I walked out to the end of the alley where he could see me.

"Come on. Come on over here, boy." He smiled.

That's how I met my father for the first time. He came looking for my mother, and he found me instead. Good Lord Almighty, my mother told me some things about my father before she died, but one thing she never told me was that he was a white man.

He grabbed me up by my shirt, held me out at arm's length, and looked me in the eye. He said, "Boy, where your momma be?"

"None of your business!" I said as bravely as I could.

"Percy, I come to see your momma." He put me down, smiled and looked down his nose at me. "Been awhile since I be in New Orleans."

I didn't give him the satisfaction of letting him know he hurt my arms. I asked, "How you know my momma?"

"I knew your momma 'fore you born." He held me by my shoulders. "Where she be?"

Tears welled up in my eyes. "My momma passed."

He was startled. "When?"

"A year ago."

"How'd she die?"

"She was murdered by a man called Louis La Pointe!"

"Son-of-a-bitch!" he yelled. His eyes took on a crazy look. "What happened?"

My whole body was shaking. "He stabbed her!"

"Not how!" He looked at me like I was stupid. "Why?"

"He said my momma took up with a man…" I stopped. I fought back angry tears. I didn't like to talk about my momma.

My father asked, "What man?"

"There was no man!"

"And what'd they do with La Pointe? Let him go?"

I nodded, *yes.*

He shook his head. "There be new folks in your momma's house," he paused. "Did you know that, boy?"

"Yes, sir!"

"You know where her stuff be?"

I only told him what I wanted him to know. "La Pointe took some stuff. The rest was put out on the stoop," I said.

"What happened to it?"

"It got stolen."

"All of it?"

"Except what he took."

"Where he be?"

"Don't know!" I said, but I knew what he was looking for. He was looking for what my mother hid in the cemetery. I followed her there one evening several weeks before she died. When I asked her about it, she told me never to tell anyone that she had been there, and that I should never go there by myself. I didn't know what she

13

hid, but it had to be valuable, because she was so worried about it. I listened to her, and never went anywhere near the cemetery ever again.

The smile left my father's face. He grabbed me by my hand and pulled me over to his carriage. He pushed me into the carriage, and got in behind me. After a minute, he asked, "Boy, what your momma say 'bout your father?"

I was nervous. I said, "That my father would come for us some day."

"Ever wonder why you be so white, boy?"

I took offense and said viciously, "It's my nature."

"*Your nature*, my ass! I be your father, Percy!"

He said it just like that – *I be your father, Percy*. He didn't catch me by surprise though. I didn't get skin as white as his, but I got his green eyes. Folks in Orleans Parish call my eyes *devil eyes*. And for sure, both Mr. Beau Monet and his son, Jean Percival Hays, had the very same eyes.

My father rode with the outlaw gangs in the border country for several years after the War Between the States. The illegal things he did back then were his undoing in the end. Those were rough times – not to say he was a victim of those times, because even under different circumstances, he would have ended up just the same.

The truth is, my father was always more lucky than he ever was smart. He shot a man dead in front of witnesses in broad daylight at the Palace Hotel in Jefferson City. A federal circuit court judge, leaving the hotel after lunch, witnessed the shooting. He had my father brought into his courtroom. He dispensed with a jury, waived testimony, and relied on his own recollections to come to a verdict. My father was tried and sentenced to die, all within an hour of the shooting.

The night before he was to be hanged, the deputy guarding him sat up all night and drank. Before the hangman got to the jail, a federal marshal came to pick up a prisoner bound for the federal penitentiary. The deputy, in a drunken stupor, gave the marshal my father to him by mistake. The hangman came soon after the marshal removed my father and took the man who was left behind and dragged him out to the gallows. The man yelled and claimed he was the wrong man. He carried on so that the hangman had to have him gagged.

Two men helped the hangman carry the man face-down to the gallows. They couldn't get him to stand on his own. The hangman put a sack over the man's head and secured a rope around his throat, while he was still on the deck. No one got to hear him or see him. The hangman had them pitch him through the trap door. His neck didn't break, and he dangled there and choked to death, while my father and the marshal watched from a buckboard.

When the man finally went limp, the marshal cracked the reins, and the buckboard lurched forward. My father was on his way to prison for a crime he didn't commit. He never acknowledged how lucky he was. Even after all that happened, because he had to serve time, he came away figuring that he had been wronged.

He thought he could do whatever he wanted, and nothing would ever happen to him. He would tell stories of how tough he was, but I think it was to scare people so they wouldn't mess with him. He said he was too old to fight in the war, but I didn't believe him. He was much older than my mother, but he wasn't *that* old. I knew a lot of men older than him who served on one side or the other. I figured that if he had joined up, he would have had to face his demons. My father killed more than one man. He never told me directly that he did, but you pick up on things. I believe that killing was in his nature – but not like a soldier kills in battle. He was never a soldier, and he didn't kill to protect himself or anything remotely

15

noble like that. He did it without any provocation or warning.

The silence in the carriage, the first night I was with my father, seemed like it would never end. I looked at him, but when he looked my way, I turned my eyes away from him. I was confused and I was afraid. After all, I was just a boy, and a lot of things happened in a real hurry. The one thing I remember most about that night was wondering what my momma would have thought of me, being there with my father. I didn't want to talk about my mother. I just didn't want to do that.

My father tapped on the window and the carriage moved, slowly at first, and then it raced along. It was my first carriage ride – inside a carriage, anyway. My life changed that night. But one thing has never changed: I miss my mother. Only God knows how much I loved my mother.

Chapter 3

Late on the first night we were together, I asked my father, "Are you looking for La Pointe?"

"You know where he be, boy?"

"No, sir!"

"Then why you ask?" He sat back and lit a cigar. The smoke filled the carriage, and created a halo around his head. It magnified the evil I saw in him – in my own mind, anyway. I didn't answer; I had already said too much.

"I asked you a question, boy!"

I thought fast. "It would be easier during the day."

He glared at me. "I go at night. I be finding the bastard *my* way."

"Yes, sir." I let the topic drop.

On the third night with my father, he made the driver stop the carriage. "Get your ass down offa there!"

The man pretended not to hear.

My father screamed, "Descendez!"

"Pourquoi?"

"Off the fucking rig!" my father hollered. He held the team with one hand and pointed his Derringer at the driver with the other.

"Votre mère est une putain, Monet!" the driver said. He climbed down.

"Fuck you!" my father screamed. He fired a shot over the driver's head. The man backed up and edged off to the side. My father fired another shot over his head. The driver ran into the brush and disappeared into the darkness.

"*Nobody* messes with Beau Monet," my father shouted. I took careful note of what he said. I never found out what happened between my father and the driver, but it was obvious there was no love lost between them.

After the altercation with the driver, my father drove the carriage at night. He had me stand watch during the day while he slept. I spent that time daydreaming about the ways I would kill La Pointe. I wanted to shoot him, hit him in the head with an ax, or stick him with a blade. Even when I slept, I dreamt of killing La Pointe – and when it came to that, I would let him know I was the one killing him, and why he had to die. I decided the best way for me to kill him was in a duel. He was the kind of man who would fight a boy, but maybe the surprise would be on him. I had fought in the streets in the French Quarter. I was proficient with a knife and knew what the business end of a blade felt like. If he chose swords, I was okay with that too. I had dueled with sticks, pipes, and everything else you could use to hurt someone, for as long as I could remember. I wanted to tell my father about my plan, but I had to wait for him to speak to me first. When he finished talking, I would say my piece.

Before dawn on the fifth night out from New Orleans, my father stopped at a stable near a crossroads that I knew we'd passed before. He climbed down from the carriage and motioned to me to get out. I jumped out and stood next to him in front of a big barn. Behind it was a little shack of a house with an outhouse in the back. I waited for him to say something to me – but he didn't. Instead, he shouted for the liveryman.

The liveryman came out of his shack in his nightclothes with a rifle pointed at us. "You got balls coming here, Monet," he shouted. He lowered the rifle and took hold of it by the barrel. He walked toward us. My father motioned me away. When I was out of earshot, he spoke quietly to the man. They made a deal. My father received a new team and also got some money in the bargain.

My father motioned me over. I started toward him, but I didn't move quickly enough. He made a fist and shook it at me. "Move it, boy!"

"Yes, sir," I said. I moved in behind him as he counted the money. It was thirty-five dollars, half what his team was worth. I helped switch the horses and then stood back from the carriage. The man took the horses he traded for and went into the barn.

"Hold these horses. Don't be letting them go, 'cause they'll bolt for the barn," my father said.

"I can get La Pointe!" I blurted out.

"How you going to did that?" he laughed. He thought it was funny.

"I'm going to call him out."

"Call him out!"

"Yeah! A duel!"

"You can't did that!"

"With a blade! At dawn!"

"It ain't that easy, boy. In the first place, you can't be calling a white man out." He slapped his thighs and laughed. "And at dawn! You plain silly, boy! He'll likely shoot you on the spot," he laughed again. "La Pointe, called out by a pickaninny!"

I wasn't laughing. "You wait and see!"

He grabbed me. "You be watching you own damn self, boy. Don't never be talking to me like that again!"

I stood motionless.

"You hear me, boy?" He shook me.

I nodded. I thought about running, but there was no place to run to.

"Understand? It will be me, if there be any calling out did!" He smiled a strange, forced smile. "Everything in its time, boy."

I nodded, but after the morning at the livery stable, I kept my thoughts to myself. The following day, I stood watch while he slept. The next morning we didn't stop as we had on the other nights. He changed direction, and we headed southwest toward the Delta. At midday, he pulled the team up at Bayou Lafourche, near Thibodaux, Louisiana. He took his bags from the back of the carriage and handed them to me. He unhitched the horses and slapped one of them on the rump, and they both took off running.

He lit a cigar, stood on the bank of the river and puffed away. It was a damp, overcast day, and the air hung like a moist curtain and made everything wet. I put the bags down and turned and looked out into the swamp. I stood in the dense brush that grew right down into the water, and waited for my father to say something. I heard glass breaking behind me and turned back to see my father smash the running lamps on the side of the carriage. He set the carriage on fire, and when it was engulfed in flames, he steered it down an embankment and right into the water.

"Pick them bags up outta the dirt, boy!" He walked quickly and I fell behind. "And stay close!" He stopped and waited for me to catch up, and then laid his fist on my shoulder. "I'll call you only once, boy!" he said.

I walked along the edge of the bayou, directly behind him. He tried to find a path along the edge of the bayou where the ground was firm, but couldn't. We were in the swamp and the footing was poor. Suddenly there was a loud splash and a squawk. I was startled and jumped back. I got a glimpse of a big alligator slipping under the water. I stayed close to my father the rest of the way.

We followed the bayou to the main channel, and were soon out of sight of the carriage. We came to a clearing where a dirt road from the west edged near the water. As we got closer to the road, I saw a flat-bottomed boat tied to a sapling on the bank, where the road turned north just before it ran into the water. My father headed straight for the boat and climbed in. He motioned me to join him.

He stood on the back of the boat and guided it through the overgrowth with a long pole. He showed me how to maneuver the boat with the pole. As soon as I got the hang of it, he sat down in the front and shouted directions at me. It was hard work and I tired quickly. He made his stints at the helm longer and longer as the day wore on. He was stronger than me, and the boat moved faster with him poling. I saw no reason to improve my poling skills, and I sat back and enjoyed the ride.

In the early evening, we reached a clearing. I saw a house in the dim light that looked like it was sitting right in the water. "We be at my momma's house now, you stay in the boat, understand me, boy?"

I nodded.

My father didn't say anything. He steered the boat to the front porch of the house, which also served as a makeshift pier. The boat bumped hard against the pilings, and the whole structure shook. He grabbed hold of a post and tied the boat off. Finally, he turned to me and said angrily, "Don't be acting up none!"

I nodded and settled down in the boat.

"You stay there. You ain't white enough to pass around here, boy, so you be keeping your head down!" My father jumped onto the porch and took his bags.

The house was a weather-worn clapboard structure with a patched tin roof and a metal stove pipe sticking up from it. It had two rooms, and to the side of the house was a shed for curing alligator meat, with alligator hides tacked to the outside walls.

My grandparents emerged from the house. My grandmother was clearly displeased that my father was there, and shouted in Cajun French that she thought he was dead, and she'd already mourned him, so he should go off somewhere else and die. I understood what she said; I had learned French in the Quarter. I had a gift with languages and picked them up quickly. I could even read and write in English better than most folks back then.

My father swung his arm around and took a bow like an actor would after a performance. "Je vais vivre pour jamais, momma," he said with a rakish laugh. I wondered what made him think he was going to live forever.

"Juste ma chance," she muttered, shaking her head.

My grandfather shook his head too, and kept shaking his, long after his wife stopped shaking hers. Then he grunted like he was clearing his throat. They all went into the house without a look in my direction.

From the greeting my father received, it was clear his folks weren't pleased he was back. I heard them through the walls, arguing in a mixture of Cajun French and bad English, most of which I couldn't understand because they were talking over one another. But one thing was very obvious; there were some serious disagreements among the members of the Monet family.

My grandparents didn't venture from their home in the swamp. They depended on their other son Henri for survival. He hadn't come out of the house to greet my father the day we arrived. When Henri and my father finally talked, they argued. There were serious, hard feelings between the two of them, and they didn't try to hide how they felt about each other.

The first time Henri saw me, he asked. "What you doing here, boy?"

"I'm with Mr. Beau, sir."

"I'm thinking you be his boy."

I didn't say anything.

"That's alright boy. You don't need to say nothing," he smiled a knowing smile. "Your secret be safe with me."

I spent considerable time with Henri, but he never spoke of his infirmity. His legs were stiff and he had to manipulate them in order to get up and down, and he had to use a crutch when he walked. Sometimes we would sit in the boat and eat and he would tell me stories of when he was a boy, and about the war. And other times, I would pole us through the bayou as we looked for alligators along the way. One time when we were in the boat, I got up the nerve to ask Henri, "What happened to your legs?"

"It was the War," he told me." After a minute, while we listened to the distant splash that could have been a 'gator, he started to tell me his whole story. He said that his father made him join the Confederate Army when he was fifteen years old. He had fought in the battle of New Orleans, and after the city fell to the Union Forces, he went with his unit to Virginia. And all of this happened before his sixteenth birthday. He was shot in the spine by a sniper and captured by the North in the spring of 1863. He was held for several months and then was released to fend for himself, as part of a prisoner exchange. With his injuries, it was nothing short of a miracle that he made his way back home. He stayed on and lived with his parents.

Uncle Henri let me stay in the curing shed, and regularly brought me food. He made me feel comfortable when he was around, and I liked him. Some evenings he would come out on the porch and play his banjo. He taught me how to strum a few chords, and I learned a couple of songs.

After I had been in the swamp several months, Henri let me help him load his boat some of the time when he was going to the trading post. But there were still other times when he would tell me to leave it to him. I attributed his erratic behavior to his being a proud man who didn't want anyone to know he accepted help. But even so, it was hard for me to see the way everyone treated Henri. I watched as his infirmity quickly worsened until he had no use of his left leg. But he got into a pirogue every Monday and went to the Houma Trading Post in Terrebonne Parish. I admired Uncle Henri for the way he never gave in to his disability.

Henri didn't like my father and would have run him off if he could've. He called my father a lazy, no-good, side-winding, back-shooting, whoremongering, Yankee-loving son-of-bitch, and said that it was a sad day for him when he found out that his brother wasn't dead after all.

I confided in Henri and told him I didn't like my father, and that I was feeling more hostility toward him every day I had contact with him. Henri told me that all the people he knew around the bayou didn't like my father, either.

I never had any use for my father, but there was one thing that I enjoyed doing with him in the bayou: going into the swamp with him and shooting alligators. He showed me how to shoot from the boat with a two-shot Derringer. My father was a great shot with his pistol. He taught me to shoot quick and aim for the eyes. The day I killed my first alligator, I shouted, "Got him!"

"Too slow! Don't never be hesitating; don't never do that! If there be trouble, you gotta act fast. Life be a deadly game, and only the winners play on."

I could never please him, and I told Uncle Henri about it. He said, "Boy, don't be taking it to heart. My brother is what he is. It ain't about you."

I asked, "Is he really my father?" Before he could answer, I said, "I can't never allow myself to see him with my mother!"

"He be your father all right. When my momma asked about your eyes, Beau told her that you be his son. He said that even though you look white, you be a colored."

"What'd she say?"

"She said she didn't want no niggers 'round the place. She wanted you off 'en her property." He looked at me and patted me on the back. "Listen boy, you don't owe them shit. I like it you be here. You stay on as long as you please. Take no mind to them looking at you like they do. They ain't gonna do nothin'. Rest assured, I'll see to that."

I thanked him for the way he treated me, and I started calling him Uncle when no one was around. He was pleased. One night, after I'd been in the swamp for about six months, my Uncle Henri came out to see me. He said he was feeling ill and needed some air, and wanted to talk.

I asked him, "What's got you feelin' so bad?"

"It's nothing for you to worry yourself 'bout, boy. I get some pains in my chest from time to time."

"Is there something I can do?"

"Yeah, just keep me company for a while, is all."

"Want me to get the banjo?"

He put his arm around my shoulders and said, "No. Let's just sit here a while."

"Are you sure you're alright?"

"Yeah," he said. He tightened his grip on me. "I want you to know how pleased I am to have met you."

"I'm glad I met you too, sir."

"Always remember, that I'm…" He grabbed his chest and lurched forward. His left arm was still around my shoulders. "Percy, get…" He released his hold on me and slumped down onto the porch.

"Uncle...." I yelled. I was struck dumb for a second; before I called out, "Help! Henri's sick!"

My father came out and dragged Henri back into the house. Henri died that night. I was sad for him in one way, but in another way I thought he was better off being dead. His family didn't care a lick about him. They never helped him, and they didn't care that he was living in terrible pain. I chose to believe he had gone on to a better place, and I prayed for the salvation of his eternal soul.

My father loaded Henri's body into a boat. My grandfather carried Henri's banjo as he got into the boat with Henri's body. "Why you got that?" my father asked.

"Mettre dans la terre, avec mon fils," my grandfather said.

My father grabbed the banjo from his father. "Give me that. You're not going to bury that next to Henri." He handed me Henri's banjo. "Boy, occupy yourself with this."

I knew my father gave me the banjo just to spite his father, but I was glad to have it. While they were gone, I played the tunes that Henri taught me. The banjo music scared the critters off, and sometimes I ended up playing all night long. I annoyed the hell out of my grandmother, but I didn't care. I had my fishing pole and enough food stored up to take care of myself for a long time. Hardtack and smoked alligator were tough on the teeth, but it helped me make do when the fish weren't biting.

Chapter 9

The *Iowa Princess* ran aground south of the crescent, while my father was in New Orleans to bury Henri. The captain was fired for being drunk at the helm. Louis La Pointe got the job, and he was profiled in *The Picayune* newspaper. He was hired, based on being an erstwhile river captain before the war. He was scheduled to be in Memphis with the *Iowa Princess* for her final repairs in the spring of 1889.

As soon as my father returned from New Orleans, we left the swamp in the flat-bottomed boat that brought us there. He gave me one of his pistols and told me there could be a time I would need it to cover his back. I wanted to talk about his plans as we made our way upriver to a sugar plantation in Lafourche Parish, but he wouldn't listen, and I let it go at that.

From Bayou Lafourche, my father booked us passage on a paddle-wheeler hauling cotton to Memphis. In Memphis, he rented a room for himself at a fine hotel overlooking the Mississippi. He arranged for me to work for my keep at a stable three blocks from his hotel. In bartering for my job, he got himself the occasional use of a horse, and me the privilege of sleeping in the barn.

My father told me he'd be waiting a time before he called La Pointe out. He said that because dueling was against the law in

Tennessee, there could be repercussions. But he said that no matter what, he wasn't going to let anything stop him from doing what he had to do. My part in the whole scheme was to take a carriage from the stable for our getaway. I didn't trust him, and I wasn't going to let myself get caught. If there was trouble and any came after me, there would be some shooting. I kept my pistol on me at all times.

My father had me follow him at a distance. He was a slow walker and would procrastinate along his way, so I would let myself fall a good distance behind, and then if I needed to catch up, I would run. He never called me on it.

Nothing was happening in Memphis, and I considered taking matters into my own hands. Before I could act, my father came by the stable late one afternoon and said, "Come on, boy. We be takin' a walk!"

I left my work just as it was and followed him. He walked to the levee and turned south, toward some deserted warehouses near the docks. I fell behind, but I could see my father clearly. He climbed up to the top of the levee, and walked at his usual slow pace. After a few minutes he stopped and looked around, like he was expecting someone. He paced back and forth a few minutes, looked at his watch several times, and then turned and started back in my direction.

I stopped to wait for him to come back, and looked out over the river. I thought about my father's riding in the gang with La Pointe in the border country after the war. Together with another man, Hiram Coles, they bushwhacked the men who had held up the First National Bank of St. Louis in 1878. My father and his cohorts separated and were supposed to meet up and split their loot. After my father stashed the loot at my mother's house, he met up with Coles and killed him. He planned to kill La Pointe too, but he was arrested before he could do it.

La Pointe heard my father was hanged in Missouri, and he went on a search for the loot. My father told him that he had kept company with my mother in the French Quarter, and he put two and two together and headed for New Orleans.

My father thought that La Pointe found the loot at my mother's house, and I let him think that. I figured that was the only reason why he was following La Pointe. My father paid informants, hired a detective, and bribed a policeman to get information about La Pointe. He had made some dangerous people suspicious with his questions.

I had lost track of time. When I turned to see where my father was, he was nowhere to be seen. I ran up the levee where I'd last seen him. I looked down each street as I went by. It was four blocks before I saw him walking between two warehouses. As I watched from the levee, a man with a gun stepped out of the shadows behind my father. I ran toward them. I tried to shout, but nothing came out. I saw a puff of smoke and heard a shot, then another puff of smoke and another cracking sound. I saw my father fall face-down in the street.

When I got close enough, I saw that it was Louis La Pointe who'd shot him. A feeling of exhaustion overcame me, and I found it hard to breathe. La Pointe turned and faced me. He looked right through me as if I weren't there. I stood still for a second, and then moved to within a few of feet of where my father lay.

My father never knew what hit him. When I regained my wits, my first inclination was to run away. Then I thought about my mother, and when I did, a rage welled up inside me. I hated La Pointe, and if he didn't die right then, I would never know any peace.

La Pointe didn't seem to care that I was there. When I put my hand in my pocket to get my pistol, he turned and looked at me. "Move on, boy!" he said. "This don't concern you!"

I lowered my head, nodded, and slowly turned away.

"I said *move it*, boy!"

I moved away, keeping an eye on him as I did. He turned back and looked at my father. "You dumb shit, Monet!" he said. He shook his head and knelt down.

As soon as his back was to me, I pulled the Derringer out of my pocket and ran as fast as I could toward him. "Louis La Pointe!" I shouted.

He was startled. "What the hell?" he turned his head and looked up at me. His gun was still in his hand but down at his side. He had let me get too close; it was his fatal mistake.

"This is for my momma" were the last words he ever heard. I put my pistol right up to his face and shot him in his right eye. He didn't have a chance. He fell over and rolled onto his back. I knelt down and shot him in the left eye. I got sick, but within seconds, I regained my composure. My mother had been avenged! And as for my father, well, he would have to answer to God for the life he'd lived.

Chapter 5

As the smoke was clearing, I heard, "You done a good job!" coming from a warehouse across the road. I looked up and saw a colored fancy man standing in front of the building. He was wearing a black derby and carrying an ivory-handled cane.

"What'd you say?" I glared at him, and then turned back to where La Pointe and my father lay dead in front of me.

"I said, you done a good job!"

I felt his eyes on me. I looked away for an instant. When I looked back, he smiled and waved. I waved back like some kind of a fool.

"Did you hear me?"

I looked for La Pointe's gun, but it was underneath his body.

"Cat got your tongue?" the man laughed.

I mustered all my courage. "You got no business with me, mister!" I said.

He came closer. "That's not altogether true, son."

"I ain't your son!" I yelled, "My father's dead!"

"Uh huh," he laughed. "One of them boys lying down there at your feet, I suppose?"

I was really scared. "Who's asking?" I said as bravely as I could.

"Tone it down," he said.

I backed away from the bodies, and looked at him.

"Tell me, which one of them boys is your father?"

"What's it to you?" I snapped.

"I'd like to think it ain't the one you shot," he snickered.

If he heard everything like he said, then he heard me call La Pointe by name. "Who's asking?" I said forcefully.

"Pappy Smathers."

"You're not my pappy."

"I'm not saying I'm *your* pappy. I'm saying I am Pappy." He came nearer. "Don't you be worrying none 'bout old Pappy now. I don't mean you no harm at all."

"How do I know that?" I took a slow step toward him.

"Because if I meant you any harm, you'd be lying next to them boys over there," he said. Before I could move, he said, "With this gift given to me by my good friend, Mr. Colt." He pulled a large revolver from under his coat as he spoke. He motioned me over to the bodies. "Now check 'em, son?"

"They're both dead!"

"For Christ's sake, boy, go see if they got any money on them." He came and stood next to me. "Come on now, let's check these boys out." He knelt and opened La Pointe's jacket and pulled out a money belt. It had a wad of paper money in it. He also found a gold watch and some coins in his pockets, too.

I bent down next to my father. It gave me an uncomfortable feeling. I pulled his jacket and his shirt up and exposed a knotted sash. Sixty 20-dollar gold pieces were neatly sewn into it. I was surprised by it. "I got no money! I need money," is what he would say to me all the time. I believed him. But there he lay, dead in a puddle of his own blood, all because he was hunting more money.

I stopped my search when I found the gold. Pappy nudged me out of the way, and turned my father over. He checked my father's

32

pockets and found a Derringer, a watch, and some loose coins. My father was on his back with his eyes wide open. "Well, there 'ain't any doubt which one's your father!" He stood and looked at me. "You know, son, most folk would've figured it was that one," he said, pointing to La Pointe, "him being darker and all." He smiled.

I reached over and closed my father's eyes. I said, "My momma was of the colored race."

Pappy patted my shoulder. "It'll be alright, son." He motioned me to follow him. "We got to be movin' right quick now, before someone comes," he said.

I followed him around the warehouse, where he had a horse and carriage waiting. When we were clear of the warehouses, we stopped and split up the money and the valuables. I kept my father's pistol and his store-bought cartridges.

Pappy asked me if I had anyplace to go. I told him I didn't, and he invited me to join him. He was heading to Galveston. I agreed, and along the way, I met people who knew him. They told me that he was quick and deadly with a gun, and all the men in Galveston who were of a mind to challenge him, already had. It seemed funny to me, because a fellow could easily mistake him for a pansy. But he was no pansy. I would find out what lots of other people already knew – and that was, that there was a good bit of safety in being his friend.

Galveston in the summer of 1889 was one hell-raising place. There was money floating all around town, and most of it ended up in the bars, gambling halls, and whorehouses. Pappy had told me to be careful and not to spend the money I got in Memphis. He said it was best that I save it. He arranged to pay me to run errands for him until I got a real job. He imposed on some friends, and got me a job on the docks. I didn't like being confined, and my mind would drift as I watched the ships sail off into the Gulf of Mexico. I wanted to work on the water, and so I got myself a job on a fishing boat. And when the fishing got slow, I would take work on an oyster boat for the season. When there were no jobs on the water, I was able to go back and run errands for Pappy.

There were men in Galveston making big money on the hustle. They were running the same games and scams I had seen being run in New Orleans. I wanted to get my own thing going in Galveston. My friendship with Pappy gave me an entree to the rich and powerful men around town. But I had to give up my ideas when he got wind of it and told me not to mess things up for him.

He was heavily involved in local politics, and he made his political statement with cash. Luckily for him he did, because when there were crackdowns on the gaming in town, they didn't affect him at all. It was known around town that he was into questionable enterprises, but it was also known that he suffered no interference from the local constabulary.

His chief political benefactor was Norris Cuney. Norris was a mulatto who looked a lot like me. His mother had been owned by his father, Jonathan Cuney, and he freed her before Norris was born. One time when Norris was running for office in Galveston, I heard him say, "I am by an accident of birth forced to live in a black uniform that by the laws of nature should have been of a different pigmentation. This and this alone sets me apart from the men with whom I must deal." He lost the race – but it was a close election in a predominantly white city.

Pappy's father was born a slave on the Jonson farm and was never had a given name; he was just known as Boy. When Pappy was born, his father named him Young Boy. He was put to work in the master's house, alongside his father, when he was just eight years old. He grew up around his master's children until he was twelve years old, then the master wanted him out of the main house. Pappy was made an apprentice in the stables, and his small size made him a perfect candidate to be a jockey and he was winning horse races within a year.

Mr. Jonson took him to Texas to ride in some important match races. He was fifteen years old and a proven winner. Mr. Jonson wanted to motivate him to win, and they made a deal: if he won three races in a row, he would get his freedom. After that, he had to continue to ride exclusively for his master, but as a free man. It didn't take long for him to win his freedom. He won the first three races he rode in Texas.

His first act as a free man was to take a new name. He called himself Freeman Smathers. And he chose the name for no other reason than he liked the way it sounded. He won twelve races out of sixteen starts on his Maryland mount, before the horse tried to kick down his stall one night and broke a leg. It had to be destroyed. When Mr. Jonson returned to Maryland, Pappy stayed on in Galveston to live as a free man.

In the years right before the War Between the States, he involved himself with the plight of runaway slaves. His first experience with the abolitionists was when he helped four colored boys evade the law. The boys had run off from their masters in the Brazos River country near the town of Richmond, Texas.

One of the boys, Sidney, was still working for Pappy when I got to Galveston. He had been the property of Norris Cuney's father, on his farm north of the main fork of the Brazos. The elder Cuney had some unusual ways of dealing with his slaves. He fathered children with some of them, and he kept some of the children as slaves on his plantation, sold others at auction, and gave others their freedom. He took protection money from the children he freed and sold protection to other free colored men. Freed slaves paid for protection from landowners; it was a necessity back then in Texas.

The runaways had headed for the Gulf – a route that took them to Galveston. They had stolen guns, which was a hanging offense. They made their way to Galveston Harbor and hid out near the docks, looking to get out by ship. A freed colored dockworker put them in touch with Norris Cuney, and Norris enlisted Pappy to help hide the boys.

A bounty hunter came looking to collect the reward offered for the boys. He confronted Pappy about where the boys were hiding. Pappy wouldn't talk. The bounty hunter had made a deal with a deputy while the sheriff was out of town. The deputy locked Pappy up, knowingly mistaking him for one of the runaways, in an effort to scare him into telling where the boys were.

Jed Robinson, an overseer from the Cuney plantation, joined in the conspiracy. Pappy still refused to tell anyone where the boys were. Robinson decided to get him out of jail to make him talk. Before he got the release, the sheriff returned. The sheriff was informed by Norris Cuney that Pappy was paying protection money to his father, Harley Cuney. He let Pappy go, and locked up Robinson, the bounty hunter, and the deputy for falsely imprisoning him.

The sheriff held the men in jail for their own protection, fearing Pappy would retaliate against them. With the men in jail, there was no one looking for the boys. Pappy was then able to negotiate the runaways' freedom with the sheriff. The deal let three of the boys get on the Underground Railroad, headed for New England. The fourth boy, Sidney, stayed hidden in Galveston and worked as a conductor on the Underground Railroad.

The sheriff became involved with the abolitionists for the money he could make. The tie to the sheriff was important for Pappy, and they worked together until the sheriff's untimely death, resulting from a fall from a horse a week before Lee's surrender at Appomattox.

I wanted to be like Pappy and Norris, but I wasn't. I got involved with some women, and started drinking heavily. Pappy told me I was too young to be using alcohol, and he didn't want me drunk at his saloon. He said he wanted nothing to do with me while I was drinking. I didn't listen. I spent all my money in the bars and the whorehouses that lined the Galveston beachfront. I liked drinking and I liked womanizing, and no one in the bars cared how much I drank, so long as I paid for it.

I went through all the money I got in Memphis. When I tried to go back to work on the water, I found out they weren't hiring. I swallowed my pride and went to see Pappy. He said I had to learn my lesson. He gave me fifty dollars and sent me away. I didn't let him know how scared I was. I left Galveston that day, and headed out with the purpose of a new life in California.

Several days into my travels, I learned of a place that was perfect for me. I got directions from a Mexican with whom I'd drank some very good cactus whiskey. I made a left turn south of San Antonio, and headed across the Mexican border toward Monterrey.

Michael Shure

Chapter 6

It turned out that shooting gators lazing in a swamp with a pistol is a lot different from shooting less confident prey out in the open. My ineptitude forced me to consume some vile things on that trip to Mexico – hunter-gatherers usually do – but I managed to survive, and I did it without spending the money I'd borrowed from Pappy.

I saw my first bullring on the main highway to the center of Monterrey City. It was there I saw an old man leaning on a pitchfork, near the holding pens outside the main arena. He looked sickly, and I took the pitchfork from him and worked his load while he sat on a bale of hay and feigned a complaint. When I was done, the old man took his pitchfork and left without as much as a "thank you."

The manager of the bullring saw the whole thing and came over to me. He said that the old man didn't speak English, and he thought it was a nice thing I had done. He started to walk away. I called after him, "I could use some work!"

He turned and looked me over. "A job, huh?"

"I could use one, sir."

"Be back here at first light."

"Thanks, I will."

As he walked away he turned back and said, "By the way, you'll be doing stalls."

It didn't matter to me. I was glad to get a job, and it turned out to be okay. The work wasn't too bad, and I was allowed to sleep in the stables.

It didn't take me long to find out that Monterrey was a good place for bad men, and a bad place for lawmen. Outlaws passed though town, one step ahead of the law, and I found a way to make money in the information business. The bounty hunters paid me for what I remembered, and the fugitives paid me even more for what I would forget.

I lived and worked in the stables for three years, before getting on the security force at the arena. With the promotion came an increase in my salary. I used the extra money to get a small place of my own. I was proud of my new job and happy with what it afforded me. I prayed that my mother was aware of my advancement, and that she was pleased by the way I was living my life.

One Sunday, during a bullfight, a novice matador tripped in the arena and froze on the ground where he fell. The picadors couldn't distract the bull in time. I had been driving spikes to hold tie-downs for a broken railing. I was using a sixteen-pound sledgehammer. I jumped over the fence and stood between the matador and the bull with the sledgehammer in my hand. I distracted the bull and he pulled up short. I didn't have to use the hammer that day, but the matadors encouraged me to keep it by my side during their fights.

The fighting bulls in Mexico are among the meanest critters in God's creation, and I can say the same for most of the people who went to watch them fight. Every Sunday, at least half the crowd was rooting for the bulls. On one wet Sunday evening, they got their wish. On the Saturday night before the fight, a group of drunken gringos had hassled people around the arena. The manager rounded up the security crew and told us to run off the hooligans, and we did. They snuck back in later that night and rigged the gate on the holding pen so when it was opened, it wouldn't close.

The next day, when the gates were opened to let in the first bull, the boys in the ring turned their backs to the gates. The gates didn't lock, and all the rest of the bulls in the holding pen came charging in behind them. Two of the men, picadors, were badly gored. One of them was dead before he'd even hit the ground.

I grabbed my sledgehammer and jumped into the ring. One of the bulls charged me. I could feel sweat beading my brow and I felt a tightness in my chest. I took a deep breath, and I stood my ground. The bull never veered from his course. I timed my swing and laid the head of the sledgehammer right on the bull's temple, with all my might. The force of the blow spun his head around. He fell and rolled up against me, and pushed me backward, causing me to stumble. I regained my balance, and hit him again. I left him stunned on the ground.

A novice I had worked with in the stables was running from another bull. I waved and called out, "Acá, diablo, acá!" as I ran toward them. I motioned to the boy. He turned and ran past me with the bull in close pursuit. The bull lowered his head and took aim at me. I jumped out of the range of his horns and swung downward with the sledgehammer; it landed on the top of his head. The bull fell to his knees. I hit him with a series of blows to the head. It was a bloody mess. The crowd went wild; they loved it.

A matador in the center of the ring was occupying another bull. He was one of the older boys and it seemed he knew what he was doing. But it didn't matter to me; I lifted the sledgehammer behind my head and ran at the bull. I swung the hammer and hit the bull in the side of the head from behind, stunning him. I hit him again, and he rolled to the ground. I finished him off by burying the hammer in his skull. The boys grabbed me and hoisted me on their shoulders and marched around the arena. My hands were covered with blood, and I felt a rush go though me.

For my efforts that day, I earned the respect of everyone in the arena. From that day forward, the matadors and picadors gave me pesos to ensure that I would watch their fights. They believed there was a safety in that for them. But I tried to keep everything that happened that day in its proper perspective. After *el día de la muerte*, the bullfights drew record crowds for the rest of the season. Bullfighting fans came, hoping for another *day of death*. The manager made me the *profesor de la seguridad* on fight days, and with it came a raise.

My life settled into a quiet routine, and stayed that way until the days before my twenty-first birthday. That's when I saw the most beautiful Yellow Rose I had ever seen. She was attending a May Day parade that passed through the plaza in front of the cathedral. I caught glimpses of her standing across the square as the procession passed. I made my way across the plaza to get a better look, but when I got to where I'd seen her standing, she was gone.

Later that same day at the bullfights, I saw her sitting alone in the stands. She saw me staring at her, and she turned her eyes away. I kept getting glimpses of her as I patrolled the arena. She was all I could think about. I asked around, to see if anyone knew her. One of the refreshment-stand cooks at the arena told me her name was Thelma. He said that he saw her at the market a lot of times when he went there in the morning. He said he thought she came by herself. Needless to say, I went to the market first thing Monday morning. She was there. I caught her eye and she smiled at me. It was an *I got you smile*, the kind that women often give you when they know they've put one over on you. I smiled back but kept myself at a distance from her that day.

I waited for a couple of days and then went to the market in the morning, looking for her. She was there, but I kept my distance. I went there five more times over a span of two weeks, before I worked up the nerve to introduce myself. Then it took me another week before I mustered the courage to ask her to join me for a walk around the market. She was receptive, and each day after that, I went to the market and we spent time together as she shopped.

She told me all about herself, and asked questions about me. I told her a lot about me, but I left out the part about what had happened in Memphis. I was looking over my shoulder because of that, and I was still expecting that one day someone would come to town hunting me. She picked up on the way I acted around strangers. I explained to her that a lot of outlaws passed through Monterrey, and I had the responsibility of keeping my eye on them for the arena. She said she understood.

I felt that fate had a big hand in our meeting each other, because we had shared a very similar life experience. Her father was a white man who had nothing to do with her or her mother, just as my father had nothing to do with my mother or me. But what was even more strange was that her mother died a violent death at the hands of a man when Thelma was young, just like my mother had when I was young. But Thelma was luckier than I was; she was raised by her grandparents.

Her grandfather was a sharecropper in Mississippi who quit after his wife died, and headed to Utah with Thelma. He worked for a short time in Ogden as a handyman for a Mormon family headed by Walter Smith, before he caught the gold fever. He then left Thelma in the care of the Smiths and went to prospect for gold in Cripple Creek, Colorado. It was 1892. Thelma lived with the family and helped with the work in their household. She never heard from her grandfather again, and she moved to Monterrey with the Smith family in 1896. There was a large number of expatriate American Mormon polygamists living there at the time. She told me that there wasn't a finer gentleman in the whole world than her benefactor, Walter Smith.

I had learned a lot about her, and it made me feel really close to her. There were things I felt that I wanted to tell her, but I was afraid to. Then one day, completely out of the blue, Thelma said, "Percy, do you find me attractive?"

I nervously said, "Yes, I do!"

She smiled and said, "Do you know that I like the way you look?" She touched my face.

I got a hot flash. "Thelma, I...."

She interrupted, "Look at you! You're blushing! That is so cute." She touched my face again and said, "I like it that you have light skin, Percy. I wasn't sure you were colored when I first saw you."

I was surprised by her boldness, and was confused by what she had said. I asked her, "You like me only for the color of my skin?"

"No, you're being silly! I like you for a lot of reasons. And besides, I had heard about your exploits in the bullring. I was anxious to meet you – I wanted to see what everyone was talking about. You're famous around here," she laughed. "Then I saw you, and after all, look at you, you're so big and strong."

"You're embarrassing me," I said coyly.

"Oh, really! Don't you think that women think about things like that?"

"I guess they do."

"Well yes, we do. And we think about what our children will look like if a man is the father. And one thing I've always wanted is to have light-skinned children. And I believe that if we had kids together, they would be light-skinned enough to live however they choose, just like you."

"All this talk about children, I...."

"Relax, Percy; don't you want to keep company with me?"

"Of course I do, but...."

"No buts! I'll be in church Sunday morning. I hope you have the presence of mind to be there too."

"I'll be there, all right. You can count on it."

She walked a short distance away, then turned and said, "I'll meet you in front and we'll go in together."

I was the first person in Monterrey to show up at the cathedral that next Sunday morning. I waited on the steps for Thelma to arrive. When I saw her in her Sunday best, I could hardly catch my breath. She was beautiful, and I wanted her to be mine.

When the church services were over, she surprised me by inviting herself over to my apartment for lunch. After we ate, she stayed and talked until it was time for me to work at the arena. I thought she was going back to work at the Smiths' when she left, but instead she went to the bullfights. I saw her there, and I spoke to her each time I passed where she was sitting as I made my rounds.

We met again the next Sunday at church, and then the Sunday after that too. After the fights, the third Sunday we met, I invited her back to my room. As soon as we were alone, I grabbed her and kissed her. She gently pushed back, "Isn't there something you'd like to say to me?"

"That you're pretty?"

"You're not doing very well!"

She was upset. I didn't know what to say. I looked up and closed my eyes, and then the answer came to me in a flash. I remembered that my mother had once asked me, "Son, do you love your momma?"

I had answered her without hesitation. I said, "Of course I do, momma!"

In my mind, I heard my momma tell me, "You need to tell me everyday that you love me. Remember son, a woman needs to hear she's loved."

I blurted out, "I love you, Thelma!"

She jumped into my arms, and I held her tightly and pulled her down onto my bed. We spent the night wrapped in each other's embrace. The next morning she awoke early, and got herself together to leave. I got between her and the door. When she tried to press by me, I held her and asked her not to go.

"I have to go," she said, "I have my work at the house. Sunday is my only day off."

"You don't need a job. I'll take care of you."

"You mean keep me?"

"No, I mean marry you."

"I would like that, but right now I have to keep my job until we can afford a better place for us to live."

"Is that a 'yes'?"

"Of course it's a 'yes'; that is if I hear you say something I want to hear."

"Okay! I'll take care of you. I'll get a better job. I'll take care of everything."

"No! How about, *I love you, Thelma!*"

"I told you before I love you."

"It's not enough. I want to hear it again."

My mother was right. "I love you, Thelma," I said, and added, "I didn't know what love was until I met you."

"That's much better, Percy. Now come back here!"

I was pleased with myself. She held me close to her, and tears ran down her cheeks. I said, "I love you, and I will always take care of you."

She whispered in my ear, "I love you."

I whispered back, "One day I'm going to make a lot of money, and we'll live in a big house. Important people will call on us, and we will be respected by everyone."

"That would be nice, Percy. But for now, I'd be satisfied just having a place we could call our own, a place where we could raise a family." She kissed me on the cheek and opened the door. "It's getting late and I want to be back before Mr. Smith gets up. I'd best be on my way right now."

"Okay, but don't worry yourself none! I'll find a way for us to be together."

"I love you, Percy Hays! I have to go now. I'll see you Sunday."

After she left, my mind raced. I wanted to provide her with the fine things in life, and to do it right away. She was used to living in style with the Smiths. In Monterrey, there were only two ways I knew of to make the kind of money I needed: I had to either ride guard on the mine shipments, or join up and ride with the outlaws. Both were dangerous, and both paid well, but only one was legal.

The mining company demanded that their guards have reputations for toughness, and required them to supply their own weapons. I had a reputation for fearlessness, so that was no problem. All I needed for the job was a high-powered rifle.

I told Thelma of my plans; she was pleased that I wanted to improve my station. She told her boss about what I wanted to do, and he said he knew an arms dealer who could get me the latest generation repeating rifle. He told her the rifle was very expensive, and he would need proof that I had the money. She arranged for me to meet him, and at the meeting I showed him my gold. He was satisfied and agreed to arrange for me to get the rifle from a dealer he knew.

It took three weeks for the dealer to get to Monterrey. The rifle was a special model, and he had to go to San Antonio to get it. The evening the rifle was to arrive, I went to Walter Smith's store. He was waiting for me out front. I was led through the store and into a back room. We walked through the dimly-lit storage area. I asked him why we were going in there. He said he didn't want anyone to know he was arranging for me to get a repeating rifle. I didn't like his tone. I waited there with him, but we didn't speak. A short time later the dealer knocked on the door, and Smith went outside. I tried to follow him. He told me to wait inside.

The two men walked several yards down the street and stood a distance from me while they talked. I couldn't hear what they were saying, but they were in agreement on whatever they were talking about. Smith called me over and then left me alone with the trader.

"Let me see the money," the trader said.

I handed him a leather sack containing the price of the rifle in gold coins. He took the coins out and looked them over. He put them back in the sack and put the sack in his pocket without counting the money. He turned and walked to his wagon. I followed him. He stood next to his buckboard and looked at me. He didn't say anything.

I waited a moment for him to say something, and when he didn't, I said, "I'll be thanking you for my rifle now!"

"What rifle?"

"The rifle I paid you for!"

"You must be mistaken, boy."

"I want the rifle or my gold!" I put my hand in my pocket.

He looked at me and laughed. "What gold?"

"My rifle or my gold!"

"There's no rifle for the likes of you," he laughed.

"You'd best be giving me one or the other!"

"Move on," he shouted, "And consider yourself lucky to get out of here at all. I don't like niggers."

He had a six-shooter in his hand pointed at me before I could react. I turned as if I were going to go, but I wasn't going to let him steal my gold. I was going to double back on him. Before I took a step, I heard him cock his gun. I dove head first onto the ground, and a shot buzzed by my head. I felt the sting. It nicked me and drew blood. I rolled over and came up shooting. One bullet hit him in the left eye, and the other one hit him in the chest. He put his hand to his heart, slumped forward, and fell face first to the ground.

I reached into his pocket and took out my gold. I heard some men coming. I grabbed the repeating rifle and mounted the trader's horse and rode out of Monterrey. I made it out just ahead of some men who came running down the alley in the back of the store. I was headed east, ducking down under a hail of bullets.

When things settled down, and my head cleared, my first thought was of Thelma. I didn't want to leave her, but I had no choice. I was on the run. In one instant, Thelma had become a part of my past, and I had left behind a piece of myself with her. There can only be one first and best love.

I thank God for it having been a moonless night, and that the horse I took was a fine one. A lesser animal wouldn't have gotten me clear of town in time. I had shot a white man in Monterrey, Mexico, but what was worse, I stole his horse. For the shooting, they would have held me for trial, but they would have hanged me on the spot for stealing the horse.

The land was tough heading northeast, and traveling fast was hard. Three days out of Monterrey I was resting on the road to San Antonio, when I decided that I would go back and get Thelma. But the fates were against me. When I tried to remount my horse, it was lame. I pulled on its lead and it took off running, as best it could, with me hanging onto the reins. It dragged me a distance before I was able to run it around in a circle by maintaining my hold on it. I finally calmed it down, and looked at its right front leg. There was no way that it could carry my weight. I turned it loose to fend for itself.

Without a horse, I had to give up any hope of going back for Thelma. I headed northeast on foot. As I walked, my thoughts were of Thelma. I longed for her to be once again in my arms. There were tears in my eyes every step of the way. I traveled at night and hid out during the day. On the Houston road northeast of San Antonio, I encountered a sundry trader with a damaged wagon wheel. I helped him lift the axle and replace the wheel. The man reciprocated by giving me a ride all the way to Galveston. I gave him the repeating rifle for his trouble. I didn't want it anymore because it held bad memories, and I would have had a whole lot of explaining to do if I were caught with the weapon anyway.

Chapter 7

I found Pappy seated at his favorite table in the back of the gaming room of his saloon, playing five-card stud. I was nervous as I walked over to the table to watch him play. I wondered – *What if he didn't want me around?*

Five men were sitting at the table with him. He was dealing the cards, and he never looked up at me, but he said, "Been quite a while, boy." He kept his eyes fixed on the card table. "You've grown."

"Yes, sir."

"What brings you to these parts?"

I didn't know what to say. I just stood there for a minute. He asked me if the cat had gotten my tongue. I told him I needed to talk to him alone. He won the hand, and swept the pot in and stacked his chips. He stood up and waved to Sidney. "I need you here!" he said.

Sidney came over to the table and stood next to Pappy. "Cash me out, Sidney," he said, and turned back to the table. "Good luck to all you boys."

Pappy had won a lot of money. A white man sitting next to him stood up and asked, "You coming back, boy?"

"Nope!" Pappy turned to face the man. He was mad. "I'm done for the day!"

Another man said, "Let it go, Hiram!"

"The nigger can leave," Hiram said in a threatening manner, "but the money stays on the table."

"Sit down!" Pappy said. "I don't want no trouble 'round here."

"The money stays!"

Sidney stepped in between Pappy and the man. I found myself right behind the man. I saw his hand inching toward his holstered gun. I grabbed his hand, twisted it and forced his arm behind his back, and put my other arm around his neck. I held him tight. The other men stood up and moved away from the table.

"Get the fuck off me!" the man shouted. I tightened my grip around his neck and cut his air off. He tried to talk, but it came out as a muted whisper.

Pappy walked over and took the man's gun from his holster. He removed the cartridges and put it back. "Percy, let loose of him."

I let the man go, and two bouncers were there to take him away.

"Come on with me," Pappy said.

We went to his office. "Suppose that man comes back?" I asked.

"He won't be back for a good while."

"Why?"

"He'll have to wait 'til his legs heal," he laughed. "If you walk into Lone Star Saloon and go for your gun, you crawl home. I got a reputation to protect here. You did good out there," he said. "Now, tell your old friend what brings you back to these parts."

"I shot a man in Monterrey," I blurted out.

"I heard about it."

"You heard about it?"

"Some boys were through here a while ago looking for a Paper Bag. They said the boy robbed a gun trader and shot him in the eye. They were looking for a fancy repeating rifle that was taken, too."

"What made you think it was me?"

"I didn't have to think, they had your name, boy. They were offering a two hundred dollar reward for the rifle, and a fifty dollar reward for the boy who stole it." Pappy laughed. "Why in the hell didn't you finish the bastard off?"

"I thought I did. I just wanted to get away."

"He's alive and kicking because you still use that pea shooter of yours?"

"Yes, sir."

"Do you like shooting people, boy?"

"Why you ask a question like that?"

"Just wanted to know!"

"No, I don't. I had to. I felt scared!"

"And after you shot him, did you get a little thrill, maybe?"

"No!" I said. I didn't want Pappy to know that I had had a feeling of elation.

"You shouldn't have left a witness, son!"

"Maybe so, but I feel a little better that he lived!"

"Maybe, but you best get yourself a revolver."

"I don't want to get into gun fights."

"What happens if you run into the gun trader?" He opened his coat to show me his pistol. "Let me tell you something. I attribute the respect I get in Galveston to the probability that you ain't the only one that's seen this gun."

"The man today wasn't scared!"

"Maybe so and maybe I'm getting a little old," he laughed, "but that doesn't change nothing. We're going to put some things behind us now. You stay around Galveston if you like; but be careful who you talk to. I don't want no trouble around here!"

We had dinner in his saloon, and spent the rest of the evening together. He arranged for me to get a job on the Gulf as a working fisherman, and I was to stay out of sight until he sent for me.

It was three long months before he finally sent for me. I had just come back from a week on the Gulf, and I was so excited that I went to see him just as I was. He was gambling in his usual seat. When he caught a whiff of me, he stood up, shook his head and motioned for me to follow him to his office. "Don't ever come in my place smelling like you do!"

"But the message said, 'right away,' Pappy."

"Go get yourself fixed up. Don't come back 'til you're respectable." He shook his head as he walked back to the bar.

Pappy was in his office waiting for me when I got back. He told me to sit down across the desk from him. He looked at me for a few seconds, and said thoughtfully, "I'm going to need your help. I'll be leaving town and going back east. I want you to forward things to me without letting anyone know where I am. I'm going to give you the key to my box, and you're not to tell anyone where I am. Understand?"

"What about your partner?"

"Listen to me, Percy! I want you to do what I tell you to do. Norris knows I'm leaving, but I don't want him to know where I'm going. I'll tell him, if and when *I* choose to do so. Do you understand what I'm saying, son?"

"What about Sidney?"

"Are you listening to me?"

"Yes!"

"It doesn't sound like you are! Here's what I'm telling you. I don't want Norris to know anything. I don't want Sidney to know anything. I don't want *anyone* to know anything. Now do you understand?"

He was intense. I said, "Okay!"

"You be careful who you talk to. And be sure not to let any one know where you come from."

"I never tell nobody nothing."

"That's why I chose you." He paused. "But I want you to swear it!"

I stood up. "I swear to Almighty God!"

He stood up and pointed at me. "Swear on your mother's grave."

"I swear, Pappy," I said. "I won't let you down."

He looked at me and put his hand over his mouth and rubbed his lips. He spoke slowly; he was weighing his every word. "You know, they never found the money La Pointe stashed."

"How'd you know about La Pointe?" I said too loudly.

"Shush!" He pushed me into my chair by my shoulders. "Hold it down, son."

I shook my head in wild disbelief. "You knew La Pointe?"

He shook his head. "Listen! There'll be some men looking for me."

"Why are they looking for you?"

"Because they know I was in Memphis the day your father died."

"What the hell are you saying?"

"I'm saying I knew of your father, and I knew of you, too!"

"But how?"

"Miss Jeannie Wallace!"

"I don't understand." I looked at him. When he didn't say anything, I repeated, "I don't understand."

"Let's just say she was a friend of mine."

"Like a girlfriend?"

"No! Like a gambler from Galveston knows a madam from New Orleans." He sat down. "I think it's time for you to know everything. A while back, La Pointe spent time with one of Miss Jeannie's girls. One night he got real drunk. He wanted to impress her and told her he was hunting treasure in New Orleans, and when he

55

found it he'd be on his way. He wanted her to join him when he left. The girl told Jeannie." He stopped and poured two shots of whiskey, and handed me one. "When your momma was killed, and La Pointe left town, Jeannie figured La Pointe got his hands on the money."

I was shaking. "And you went to Memphis looking for La Pointe?" We downed our shots.

"I was tailing him when he shot your father."

"Why'd you never tell me?"

"Wouldn't have served any purpose."

"But...."

"No purpose!" he interrupted.

I started to leave.

"Are you alright, Percy?"

I turned to face him. "Did you know Tiny?"

He shook his head "yes."

"Did you know his son?"

"I knew of him, like I knew of you."

"You know what happened to him?"

"Miss Jeannie sent him to work with his uncle in Biloxi, Mississippi."

"His mother?"

"Miss Jeannie," Pappy shook his head. "She wanted him away from the Quarter. You boys were becoming lightning rods for trouble. She didn't want trouble around her place."

"Me? A lightning rod for trouble?"

"Don't flatter yourself. It's all about the loot. You'll be fine, son," he smiled. "You just do what I told you, and everything will be okay."

I shook my head. "Why didn't you ever ask me about the money?"

"There was no reason. Your mother, your father, and La Pointe were all dead. I gave up on the chase."

"You should've asked me."

"Jesus Christ!" He had a strange look on his face. "Well! Are you going to tell me or make me guess?"

I decided to trust him. I told him all about my mother and her trips to the cemetery to hide the loot. He said the money was probably still there, or there wouldn't be men still hunting it. He told me to be careful, he expected that they might come looking for him. We made a deal and he changed his plans and was going to go to Maryland by the way of New Orleans. He told me how to reach him in Baltimore by telegraph, under the name of Y. B. Jonson.

A month after Pappy left Galveston, two tough-looking men showed up, looking for him. They found out that he had left Sidney in charge, and they were seen taking him out of town. When they came back, Sidney wasn't with them. By the time I found out, there was nothing I could do. A barmaid I was familiar with told the men I was a friend of Pappy's. They found me at the Hornet's Nest Bar, and approached me. A shootist named Perry took the lead, "You the boy they call Percy?"

"I am!"

"You know where your friend, Freeman Smathers, is?"

"You mean Pappy?"

"Yeah. That's him. We was friends up in Missouri," the other man, a degenerate I later learned was named Lane, said.

"I thought Pappy was from here!"

Perry looked me up and down. "He's from Missouri."

"I didn't know that." I said. I was pretty sure that they had no idea who I was. I had to tell them something, and it had to be believable. I had to take the chance that Pappy had found the loot in New Orleans and was on his way back east.

Perry moved next to me at the bar. "Mind if I sit?"

"Suit your own self."

"Maybe you can help me find my old friend," he said.

"You're a little late," I said.

He leaned on the bar beside me. "What's you mean, boy?"

"Pappy's gone to New Orleans."

"New Orleans!" He looked at Lane. He asked me, "What makes you think that?"

"I was with him when he left."

Lane grabbed my shirt. "Don't shit me, boy."

Lane pressed himself against me, and I couldn't get my hand in my pocket. "No, sir, I'm telling the truth. He was with a man in his bar, and then he was gone. That quick."

Lane tightened his grip on my shirt, ripping it.

"Ease up, Lane! Let the boy talk." Perry pointed his finger at me and said, "Did he say anything?"

"No!" I straightened myself up. "He left without even a goodbye."

"What makes you think he went to New Orleans?"

"I overheard the conversation."

"Well, what'd you hear?" Lane asked impatiently.

"Miss Jeannie in the French Quarter had something he was looking for."

"What was that?"

"Don't know."

Lane pressed closer to me.

"Look guys! I don't want no trouble. I figured it had to be important, 'cause he left so quick!"

"When's he coming back?" Lane had his right hand on his gun.

"I don't know." I tried to pull away to get my right hand free.

"Let up on the boy, Jake," Perry said. "We don't need no rough stuff." He looked at me. "Ain't that right, boy?"

"Yes, sir." Lane let go of me.

"Tell me everything you know, boy," Perry said.

"When I asked Sidney about it, he said he'd be back."

"When did Sidney tell you that?" Perry asked.

"Right after Pappy left, I asked Sidney for my wages. He said I had to wait for Pappy to be back to get paid."

"He's coming back?" Lane asked.

"Yeah!"

"How you know?"

"Cause Sidney said he'd let me know when he's gonna get back."

"From where?"

"New Orleans!"

Lane stood up. "Let's go."

"Hold it a damn minute!" Perry said. He turned to me. "You best be telling the truth, boy."

Lane grabbed me by the shirt collar. He said, "If you're lying…!" He pushed me away.

I sent a wire to Pappy in Baltimore, telling him I was on my way out of town and that I'd sent Perry and Lane to Miss Jeannie's. I didn't owe Miss Jeannie anything, and whatever happened to her was her problem. She knew about my father and La Pointe, and never told my mother or me. She should have.

Michael Shure

Chapter 8

I left the Hornet's Nest in the direction of the waterfront. I took off running north toward the docks when I heard someone running behind me. When I reached the harbor road, I was moving at full-tilt. The first two piers were empty, but at the third pier I saw a steamer making ready to sail. A sailor standing at the top of the gangway waved me on.

"Over here, if you're coming," he called out. He motioned me to come on board.

I ran up the gangway. He asked me if there were any more coming. I looked back to see who was chasing me, and was happy to see it wasn't Perry and Lane. I called up to the sailor, "Yeah! Two!"

He looked at me and laughed. "Any more coming, José?"

"No!" one of the men behind me yelled.

"Hurry!" the mate shouted.

The mate looked at me and asked if I needed a special invitation. I said, "I want to sign on."

"Come on, if you're coming," he laughed. "Whoever's chasing you can't be too far behind."

The men pushed by me to get on board. "Come on! You'd better get on board before whoever's chasing you catches up!" The mate laughed again.

I asked, "Where you headed?"

"Does it matter?"

It didn't, and he knew it. He smiled his toothless smile and waved me on. "We're heading for La Habana," he said as I passed him on the gangway.

My job on the ship was food prep and cleanup in the galley. I liked the work because I could eat as much as I wanted, and I got to hear all the scuttlebutt on the ship. There was lots of talk of the island paradise right across the Gulf of Mexico, in the Caribbean, and I thought it would be the perfect place for me.

We arrived in Cuba several days after the *USS Maine* blew up in the Havana harbor. By the end of April 1898, the United States and Spain were at war. I didn't have a stake in the fight, and I already knew enough to keep my head down whenever there was shooting.

La Habana was everything the sailors said it would be, and more. I spent a lot of my time in the neighborhood cantinas. I acquired a taste for the local rum that lasted a lifetime. I also developed a penchant for shooting crap, but I had to give it up or face losing all my money. I never quite got the hang of the game, and gambling was never my thing. But I enjoyed the action, and until I had a couple of serious losses, I played on.

I met a scrawny white man named James Jefferson one evening while I was enjoying my favorite rum in the back of a busy cantina. A fight broke out between him and a large, colored hooker over the price she wanted to charge. Even though she was getting the best of it, three large colored boys rushed to her aid. They applied a severe ass-whipping to poor old James. When they were finished, the boys decided to elevate the altercation into a robbery. Unfortunately for them, they included me in their plans. They pulled out knives and said they were going to do some cutting if they didn't get a whole lot of cooperation from everyone.

I was wearing my life savings at the time, and I planned to exit the cantina through a window. I worked my way to a table near the window in the front of the barroom, but before I could break the window out, the biggest of the men called out to me. "¡Venga acá!"

"I don't understand," I said in English. I wasn't going near the man.

He didn't understand me, but he saw me inching closer and closer to the window. He came after me, waving his knife. I backed up and took hold of a chair. When he was no more than two feet from me, I stepped aside and steered him out the window with the chair. He was badly cut. His friends started for me, but I had my pistol in my hand. When they saw my Derringer, they had the good sense to stop.

I held them at bay while James stumbled to his feet. I went over to him and took hold of his arm. "Get the fuck off me!" he shouted. He steadied himself against the bar with his left hand and took a swing at one of the boys with his right. He missed completely and ended up back on the floor. I reached down to help him up again.

"Fuck off!" He pushed my hand away and struggled back to his feet. "I'll kill the fuckers!" he shouted in a Cockney accent.

"You'd better get your ass out of here," I said.

"Bum fuckers!" he shouted.

"That's enough," I said. "Get outta here!"

"Who the fuck are you?"

"The man who's going to get you out of here while you're still alive."

I held his arm and propped him up. Before I got him though the door, he turned and shouted, "I'll get all you fuckers!"

I got James outside the bar, and I stopped in the doorway and watched the action inside. The bartender was pounding the two boys with a club. I thought, *those boys are in excellent hands.*

James righted himself. He looked me square in the eye and said, "They're bung-holing pricks."

"Your mouth's going to get you in trouble!"

"Fuck you, too. I should've killed the bloody fuckers!" he shouted. He tried to push by me and go back into the bar. He was bleeding from a cut over his left eye and his lip was split wide open.

"I'd calm myself down if I were you," I said.

"You're not me," he snickered, "and what the fuck do you know anyway?"

"I know you didn't get a single punch in on her."

"Yeah, I did!" He walked a short distance and looked back at me. "I was beating 'er ass!" He took a few more steps. "Well?"

"Well, what?" I turned away and started across the street.

"Hey! Where the fuck you going? The night's young. Let's get a drink."

"You're in bad shape. You'd best be getting home."

"Come on with me." He pointed me in the direction of his place.

I didn't have anything going on, so I went with him. We sat in his kitchen and drank the last of his rum. He started to ask me something, but stopped short. I asked him if he had something he wanted to say.

He looked me over. "What kind of man are you?"

"What do you mean?"

"You look like you're from Brazil, but you speak good English."

"What the fuck makes you think I'm from Brazil?"

"The way you look."

"And how do I look?"

"I was thinking that you look like you're from Brazil, that's all."

"Just what the fuck you getting at?"

"You're not from here, so I was wondering...."

"If I'm of the colored race," I interrupted.

"Yeah!"

"What if I am?" I stood up.

"Nothing. Sit down!" he said, "I just wasn't sure."

"You are now!" I wondered where he was going with it.

"You got any questions for me?" he asked.

"Yeah! Where are you from?"

"London, but I've lived all over."

"Brazil?"

"Nope, never been there."

"Then what the fuck made you think I was from there?"

"I had a girlfriend from Brazil," he said. "She was damn near as light as you are."

"She was, was she?"

"Yeah! A Negress."

"Are you' trying to get yourself hurt worse than you already are?"

"It ain't a bad word, asshole. And who the fuck is going to do all the hurting – you, tough guy?" He laughed.

I set my drink down and clenched my hand into a fist. "Keep talking that kind of shit and you'll find out who!"

"Fuck you too," he laughed. "The name's James, Private James Jefferson, late of 'er Majesty's service." He held out his hand.

I looked him in the eye. "I don't like that shit."

"Hey, man, I was wondering if you were from Brazil, like she was. She was great," he said, "and I loved 'er to death."

"Don't fucking mess with me!"

"For Christ's sake!" He held out his hand again.

I hesitated for a second and ignored his hand. "Percy Hays, a sailor on extended shore leave." I gave him a quick salute.

James Jefferson was an arrogant man, and he had a big mouth. But we hit it off from the start. I stayed at his place, and after a time I made it my home. He was older and worldlier than I was, and he knew of ways to make large sums of money. He was involved in some risky businesses, but I was interested in getting involved myself.

James had come to Cuba to broker an arms deal with a rebel band in the mountains. His partners in Bermuda were to deliver rifles and ammunition by the end of February 1898. The trouble in Havana harbor attracted too much attention, and James' delivery had to be postponed. He was in Havana, waiting for things to cool down enough for him to complete his deal.

It didn't take long for James to go through his cash, and he had to take a job in construction. I found day work as a laborer on the docks. We both worked until the war slowed things down. I was willing to take any job I could get, and ended up working in a bar near the waterfront. James didn't try to find work, and spent his days drinking and carousing. One afternoon, while James was feeling no pain, he called a policeman's wife a *puta*. A fight ensued, and James pulled a blade and cut the policeman. The bartender held a rifle on James until the police came and took him away.

James was brought before a hearing judge and got a dose of macho Latin justice. The magistrate dismissed the charges arising out of the fight, and those for being drunk and disorderly. But he found James guilty of resisting arrest, and for that, he sentenced James to three years' labor in the sugarcane fields.

The Spanish were hiring anyone who would work in the sugar fields, with no questions asked. It was easy to get a job working near where James was being held. There were days that I was able to make my way to where Jim was working. He was shackled to other men, and I wasn't able to get right next to him. When I was able to get within earshot, James would beg me to find a way for him to escape.

Working in the cane fields was straight-out miserable. Battles with insurgents had destroyed the narrow-gauge railroad tracks that were used to haul the sugarcane from the fields. The cane had to be hauled out on our backs to the oxcarts that took it on to the mills. To further exacerbate things, they didn't fire up the fields to drive out the vermin, so we had to dodge rats and snakes as we worked.

James worked in the fields until the war ended, when American sugar companies took over. They didn't use convict labor; a paid labor force was cheaper for them. The prisoners were transferred from the fields to prison cells. I had to act quickly to spring James before he was sent away to serve out the balance of his sentence. My skin having darkened from working in the sun, I easily passed for a Haitian mulatto. I used that to my advantage when I made arrangements with a fisherman to take James and me to Haiti.

I bribed a guard, and he moved James to an isolated holding pen near the perimeter of the camp. Then I bribed another guard to let me into the area. I planned to bribe the remaining guards and be on my way with James. But the Americans had taken over and replaced a lot of the old guards with new recruits. One of the new men got curious and went to the hut to see what was going on. He walked in on us while I was removing James' chains. I tried to hold him off with my pistol, but he came at me. He was on me when I fired a shot. The bullet shattered his cheekbone. He put his hand to his face and saw the blood. He was enraged. He charged me, and his momentum knocked me down. We wrestled on the floor. James hit him in the head with a chair and knocked him senseless.

We got clear of the compound and crossed the sugar fields under the cover of darkness, and followed the main road to the inlet. Before first light, we made our rendezvous with the fisherman.

Michael Shure

Chapter 9

The city of Port-au-Prince was an open sewer populated by a hopeless, pitiful people. There was a small ruling class of mulattos who lived very well and maintained their ascendancy by force, and by keeping the memory of the bloody race riots in Haiti fresh in everyone's mind. By 1900, the French Créoles had lost all their influence on the island and were targets of the mulattos. The situation was further exacerbated by the United States' efforts to gain control of the island's commerce, and to secure a military presence in Haiti. I was glad that I got James out of Cuba, but for my efforts, I had gone from the frying pan right into the fire. I knew I wouldn't be staying very long.

Things didn't work out as I planned, and it was James' and my great misfortune to have to celebrate the turn of the century in Haiti. We ended up spending New Year's Eve in the company of a number of self-righteous missionaries. There were "foot soldiers for the Lord" from every corner of the world in Port-au-Prince, all claiming they would save the Haitians' miserable souls. Some of the more enterprising Haitians made a business of being saved, and were counted as converts by several of the denominations. Some of the missionaries brought in medical supplies, doctors, and nurses. But it was all a big waste, because Haitian witch doctors were the ones who tended to the people's ills, and if anyone was really sick, they just died.

It was terrible there and we were desperate to get off the island. I wanted to take the overland route to the Dominican Republic, and ship out from there. James wanted to leave by a faster route. He was able to sign on a private yacht headed for Bermuda. He planned to jump ship in Hamilton and make his way back to Cuba from there. He tried to get me on the yacht, but I didn't pass muster; I wasn't white enough. And I was too light to be hired on any of the commercial ships, because they suspected that I was a mulatto spy. James offered to stay with me in Haiti, but I told him not to be stupid and go take care of his business. I was going to cross the island on foot. To do so, I had to take a job to get some local currency. I couldn't risk exchanging any of my gold in Port-au-Prince and becoming a target for the mulatto' thugs.

I rented a cart from an injured worker, to haul wood in from the countryside to make charcoal. It was a job reserved for the darkest of the Haitians, and it paid only a couple of francs per load. I figured it would take three months to save enough for the journey to the Dominican Republic. I sold my loads through a German missionary named Fritz who was stranded on the island. He was earning his passage home reselling to the charcoal burners the wood he'd bought in bulk.

I became concerned about crossing the island, because of what was happening in the Dominican Republic. Sailors were carrying tales of recent political assassinations there. I started checking the port in the mornings before I went to work, in the hope of finding a ship that would take me off the island. I also tried to buy passage, but there was a waiting list to get off the island. People were flocking out of Port-au-Prince.

After several weeks, I found an ocean-going, commercial fisherman making ready to sail. I went to the gangplank and shouted for the captain. A burly man with a scruffy white beard came over to me and asked what I wanted with the captain. I told him I was looking for work. He looked at me and laughed.

"I got some money," I said, "and I want to leave this island."

"I don't haul passengers."

"Then I'll work!"

"Got a full crew."

"I'll pay for the passage and work too."

"You're a funny man," he said. Just to prove it really wasn't a joke, he moved his loose-fitting vest to the side, exposing a revolver in his belt.

I looked him straight in his eyes. "You're lucky I'm in a good mood this morning, scumbag." My hand was in my pocket and on my Derringer.

He laughed, but kept his hands away from his pistol.

"Have a safe trip, Captain." I smiled and walked away.

The captain called out, "You got some balls. I'll say that for you."

"Think so?" I shouted back.

"Yeah! Try me next time. Maybe then." He paused. "Yeah, maybe then! Ask for me. I'm Captain Reynard."

Later that same afternoon, I brought Fritz a load of wood. I was waiting to be paid when a drunken customs agent started shouting at Fritz. The man ran toward us, kicking up a cloud of dust as he raced down the dirt street. As he got closer, Fritz backed up, and I moved off to the side. The man kept right on coming. He was yelling something about the Germans sinking a Haitian ship. I thought he was just spoiling for a fight with a white man.

71

When the man got to me, he stopped and pulled a knife from his boot. He looked at me for an instant, and then started at Fritz again. I reached in my pocket and pulled out my Derringer. He was just about to go after Fritz when I shot him in his ass. He felt the bullet bite, and he stopped and looked back at me. I held the Derringer up so he could see it. He turned and came at me. He left me no choice; I shot him in the face. He dropped to his knees, holding the side of his head.

A couple of the Haitian's cronies saw what happened and started toward us. Fritz took off running, with me close behind. We reached the dock, just as the fishing trawler I tried to book passage on in the morning was making ready to sail. Fritz and I ran as fast as we could and jumped onto the gangplank as it was being pulled in. Somehow we both ended up on the ship's deck.

One of the men pursuing us had the sense to stop. The other man was younger and in better shape, and was obviously more committed to the chase. When he got to the edge of the pier he made a leap for the boat, and ended up in the water. Fritz and I watched from the deck and laughed.

Captain Reynard recognized me and said, "Didn't I tell you to see me *next* trip?"

I told him about the trouble on the dock and asked him to let us stay on the ship until his next port of call. Fritz asked to buy passage to Puerto Plata. The captain negotiated with Fritz, and made a deal to take him to the Dominican Republic, where his church had a mission. It cost Fritz everything he had.

Captain Reynard turned his attention to me, and asked if I had the fare to Puerto Plata. I told him I didn't want to go there. He said, "That's where you're going if you have the fare. If not, you can swim wherever you want."

"I'll work my passage!" I said grimly.

He thought for a minute. "I lost a couple of boys this trip, and you can work your way to San Martín. If you don't pull your load, you'll be put off at sea."

That was fine with me. But while the ship was a self-proclaimed island fisherman, she carried no nets and no lines. She was fitted out with oversized boilers and a reinforced steel hull. And she carried an extra-large load of coal and had two tanks full of diesel fuel for a motor launch that was towed behind her. There wasn't going to be any fishing done on *La Joya de Panamá*. I planned to get off at the first port of call.

The thing I enjoyed most about the trip to Puerto Plata was getting to spend time with Fritz before he was put ashore. He was grateful for my help, and he told me he was going to Germany. He gave me his mission headquarters' address, and he told me to be sure to look him up someday.

Michael Shure

Chapter 10

Several days out from the Dominican Republic, I heard the lookout shout, "Ship ahoy!" I couldn't make anything out and asked him what he saw. He called down to me, "Off the starboard bow!"

All I could see was a speck just below the horizon. The first mate came running on deck and rang the ship's bell to muster the crew. Captain Reynard went to a steel locker that served as the ship's armory. My hopes were dashed, that we would reach a port before any trouble occurred. I joined the line waiting to be issued rifles and ammunition.

"To your stations!" the mate ordered.

"Bring us to her!" the captain yelled at the helmsman. He sent two men to feed the furnace. "Full speed ahead!" he called down to the furnace room. He pointed to a group of us. "Get in the longboat!"

"Aye, aye, sir!" We said. I still hadn't seen the ship.

The captain ordered the first mate. "Go with them, Lorenzo!"

"My place is on the bridge!" the mate said.

"Your place is with the men."

"Aye, sir!" the mate said, but he couldn't hide his anger.

The captain spoke slowly to the mate. "Circle 'round and force her back. Wait 'til I'm in position. Then tie on."

"Aye, aye," the first mate said.

We shimmied down the ropes into the motor launch. I tried not to think of the risk I was taking; instead I thought of the money I would make. The launch circled out past the yacht and then came back on her. The yacht made a run for it in the direction of *La Joya de Panamá*. The captain of the yacht saw his predicament and surrendered without a fight. The passengers and crew gave up their valuables and some of the ship's stores. We loaded everything onto the ship and left enough food and water for them to make port safely.

We got cash, jewelry, silver tableware, weapons, clothes, and the ship's fancy bell. I saw one of our crew pocket some silver. When we finished loading the spoils, we let the yacht go on its way.

Back on the ship, after the armory was secure, the captain mustered the crew. He said he wanted the man who stole from the yacht to step forward. Two sailors pushed the man I saw stealing out in front of the captain.

"Empty your pockets!" the captain ordered.

The man didn't move. The captain hit him on the side of the head with his pistol. "I said, empty your pockets!"

The man took silver tableware out of his pocket and dropped it on the deck.

The captain had Lorenzo put him over the side with a small wooden float. We were four days out from the nearest port and running outside of the shipping lanes. It was a certain death sentence. I took notice of what transpired.

The tools of the trade on *La Joya de Panamá* were British Enfield rifles with fitted bayonets and twelve-inch daggers. The weapons were collected and locked away after each raid. I had to keep my Derringer out of sight, for fear of losing it.

The captain targeted private yachts. He outflanked them with the motor launch, and once he had his prey in his sights, when they gave up without a fight, he took what he wanted and let them go on about their business. If they fought, he sank their yacht and put any survivors out to sea in lifeboats.

The first mate wanted to kill everyone, and leave no witnesses. Most of the crew agreed with the mate, but not me. For me, piracy was one thing, but cold-blooded murder was another. I worked hard and I fought hard. After participating successfully in some tough encounters at sea, I felt that I'd been accepted by everyone as a rightful member of the crew.

The captain feared the British Navy, and he avoided their shipping lanes. He never went near any of their colonies, and he would turn tail and run if he got a glimpse of one of their patrols. Even though there was a ready market everywhere in the Caribbean for the goods we plundered, the captain believed French Guiana was the safest place for us. He had his concerns about the crew, because they were prone to leave their money in the bars, brothels, and casinos during shore leave. In the city of Cayenne, the men were rolled for their money before they had the chance to spend it – but it didn't make a difference, because the ones who weren't robbed usually came back to the ship penniless anyway. I was cautious and saved most of my money, but I had some good times on shore leave, too.

I was on the ship for a year when I heard we were headed for San Juan, Puerto Rico, where the captain had family. There was an air of excitement on the ship for several days after the word came. Then the captain turned the ship around and headed in the direction of San Martin, and everyone was on edge. En route, we plied the shipping lanes, but our luck ran bad. The British had increased their patrols and that made things difficult for us.

Some hard times led to talk of a mutiny, led by the first mate. The word was that the Dutch and Portuguese would pay us a lot more for our goods then the French. I listened, but I was content not to get involved. I believed that whatever would happen, would happen, without any help or hindrance from me.

Then, as quickly as things started, they settled down when the first mate announced that we were going to turn around and head straight for Puerto Rico. It stayed that way for several days, until the captain mustered the crew and surprised us with the news that he was relieving the first mate of his responsibilities. The first mate took exception to his demotion and pulled a pistol on the captain. He told the captain he was taking over the ship and then shot him at point-blank range. He held his gun on the crew and had two of them heave the captain overboard.

He tried to make me the next order of business. He said he wouldn't suffer any negroes on his ship, no matter how light they were. He told two sailors to throw me in after the captain. The men hesitated. The first mate shot and killed one of the sailors, affording me the time to go for my Derringer. I shot the mate in the face. He stumbled backwards, and I rushed him and grabbed his pistol. I pointed the mate's gun at the crew. I was angry, and I was scared. "Anybody want to throw me overboard?" I shouted.

There was no response.

"I'm asking you for the last time," I said. I was shaking. "Anybody want to throw me overboard?" There was still no answer. I turned my attention back to the first mate. I pointed the revolver at him and motioned him forward. He didn't move. He was holding his eye, but I didn't see any blood on his face. I walked up to him and grabbed his shirt, and he stumbled forward. I turned him to face me. He had killed the captain, the man who gave me the chance to be part of the crew, and the bastard wanted me dead because I was colored. This was highly unsatisfactory.

The mate struggled to get away from me. I let loose of him, and he ended up with his back against the railing. "What happened?" he said. He was unsteady on his feet.

I asked sarcastically, "How are you feeling, *sir?*"

"I feel like shit," he said. He had a hand over his right eye.

"That's too damn bad," I said. The crew snickered.

"What's going on?" the mate asked.

"He shot you, asshole," one of the crew shouted. There was a lot of laughter.

"I'm shot? I didn't hear a shot." His neck was twitching, and his head turned from side to side rapidly.

"I shot you in your damn eye."

He was having trouble standing. "Kill the fucking nigger!" he ordered.

No one made a move. The mate fell on one knee and threw up on the deck. I grabbed him by the collar and pulled him back to his feet.

A friend of the sailor that the first mate had shot came over to help me. He grabbed him. "I don't want you messing up the deck anymore, Lorenzo," he said. He gave him a hard shove, and Lorenzo went over the side and into the sea. He said to the crew, "The captain and his first mate are back together again."

Some men cheered, some laughed, and others yelled obscenities over the side at the captain and the first mate. One man shouted, "Don't mess with the nigger!"

"Fucking right," another man hollered.

The crew milled around on the main deck. I asked, "Who wants to be captain?" It brought them somewhat to attention. "Who wants to be captain?" I asked again.

A rough-looking English bloke with an eye patch shouted, "Aye, ye should be captain!"

I said, "C'mon, cut the shit! Who wants to be the captain?"

"You!" another man shouted.

A man pushed his way to the front and shouted. "You're the captain now!"

"What about the rest of you?" I asked.

There were a few *aye, ayes*.

The man worked his way to me. "Let me 'ear it!" he shouted.

A loud, "Aye, aye," was heard from the crew.

"It's done! You're the captain, mate," he said to me.

It wasn't unanimous, but it was done without objection.

Chapter 11

I liked being the captain, but I knew how some of the men felt about me, so I slept with one eye open and the first mate's revolving pistol in my hand. Reynard was dead, and we couldn't deal with the French anymore; I needed an ally in the Caribbean. The Dutch were at odds with the French and the British, and were openly hostile to them. I went to Philipsburg and negotiated a deal with the Dutch administrator there. He agreed to treat us like he treated other renegade crews, and he allowed us to base out of Sint Maarten. To seal the deal, I had to pledge that *La Joya de Panamá* would target only French, English and Spanish vessels plying the shipping lanes between Western Europe and the Caribbean. We would stand off at a distance and demand a ransom for their safe passage. We were lucky and never encountered a captain who chose to arm his crew and fight. Our ilk was known as "zee rovers" in the Nederlandse Antillen, and the captains would sooner take their chances with us than have to worry about their own men being armed.

We stalked the Caribbean, running contraband for the Dutch, and taking occasional British and French prizes on the water. Life settled into a dull routine that lasted until the spring of 1913. We were pushing off from Paramaribo, in Dutch Guiana, when I saw an African boy running toward the ship. We were several yards from the pier, so I ordered the first mate to heave him a line. The boy jumped into the water and grabbed the rope. He held on as we drifted into the channel.

A man on the dock yelled, "Get the murdering nigger!"

I went portside. I told the crew to get the boy out of the water quickly. I could see how big he really was when he climbed over the rail.

"He's black as the ace of spades," my first mate laughed.

It only took one look from me for the mate to get my message. When I was sure the boy was safe, I said, "Carry on, André." *How dumb could he be?* I thought, as I walked away from him.

Two men from the pier decided to pursue the boy in a motor skiff. I took a megaphone and called out, "Turn about!"

One man held up a rifle for me to see. "Put the nigger off," he shouted.

"Best be on your way!" I hollered into the megaphone. They didn't listen. I took my revolver from my belt and aimed at the skiff. I fired two shots close to their water line; they got the message.

It was fate that the African boy and I both joined the crew by being chased onto the deck of *La Joya de Panamá.* To the consternation of the low life scum that served under me on the ship, I made him a member of the crew right away. My instincts about him were right. He never shirked his responsibilities, and in time, he was accepted among us as an equal.

Soon after Matumbo joined us The United States changed its policies in the Caribbean, and fast American patrol boats began to ply the shipping lanes. There weren't many privateers like us left by 1913, and we became one of their main targets. We quickly felt the increased pressure and were forced to the waters southeast of the isle of Hispaniola. Times were tough and my crew grew restless. Near the port of Bridgetown, off the coast of Barbados, the night watch let a British ocean patrol craft get too close to us. At daybreak the British made their move. There were more than a dozen armed Royal Marines on board. We had no choice but to stand and fight. We all knew our fate if we were to be captured. I took my place on the bow, and readied for battle. As the patrol boat pulled alongside, it bumped *La Joya de Panamá*. She lurched forward, and I was thrown into the sea.

Most of my crew's eyes were focused on the patrol boat and they didn't see me fall. They stood peering at the British waiting for my order to attack. But Matumbo had been watching me, and he saw me go into the water. He swung down on a rope from the crow's nest, and he hit the deck of the British patrol boat on the run. My crew showed the limeys their weapons, and shots were exchanged. Matumbo made his way through the Marines, from the aft of their ship where he had landed, toward the bow. Shots were fired at him, but he only suffered one superficial wound on his left arm. He was covered with blood when he took on a British sailor manning the ship's mounted cannon. He wrestled the cannon from him and shoved him into the sea.

He turned the cannon on the British crew, and held them at bay while he motioned for the crew of La *Joya de Panamá* to cut her free and turn to pass by the bow of the patrol boat. Then he pointed the cannon straight down and fired a shot into the deck. The shell shattered the patrol boat's hull and it began taking on water. Matumbo jumped clear of the ship off our starboard bow. He swam toward me. The British stood their posts on their floundering craft, and shot at him as he swam away.

The crew of *La Joya* took aim at the patrol boat and fired a hail of bullets, drawing the Limey's fire. The crew then put her on a course that took her between the patrol boat and Matumbo and me. They threw us a line and towed us away from the patrol boat, under a curtain of bullets fired from the British ship. The firing continued until the British were forced to take to their life boats.

We suffered causalities, but fortunately no one was killed. The crew voted Matumbo an extra half share for the entire tour for his heroics that day. But I owed him more than that; I owed him the debt of my enduring gratitude. I swore on my mother's memory, that one day I would repay him.

The confrontation, with the British patrol, was only the first sign of things to come. Ancient hostilities among the European powers continued to contribute to the havoc in and around the islands in the Caribbean. Privateers from all the world's oceans streamed into the region to take advantage of the turmoil. The area became a killing ground as cutthroats maimed, raped, and killed their victims. Ships had to turn and fight; there was no longer any negotiating for safe passage. The increased presence of Americans and British patrol boats wasn't enough to handle the onslaught, and they were forced to send in heavy armed war ships.

The opportunistic French began to offer a premium for contraband, and they announced that they were granting amnesty for anyone who would deal with them. It presented us the chance to get back in their good graces after a long hiatus. But I didn't trust them and decided it was far too risky for us to deal with them. Instead, I put us into the cargo business with the Dutch. We made runs between their colonies. It didn't pay much, but it took us out of harms way.

The first mate was opposed to my decision and wanted to put it to a vote. Unfortunately for him, before the crew could hold the vote, he was decapitated in a freak accident. It happened while we were unloading at Paramaribo. A case of my favorite rum fell from the helm just as he was bending over the side of the ship. Under pressure from me, the crew voted Matumbo the new first mate. For the next three months the coloreds ran *La Joya de Panamá.*

Matumbo had only one goal; to get back to Africa and his family. His grandfather was the headman of a Zulu tribe, and he wanted to claim his rightful place in the hierarchy of his people. It was clear that he would get back to his people, or die in the trying.

After his elevation to first mate, we spent a lot of time together. We planned the ship's itinerary and dealt with issues pertaining to the crew. One day, after a discussion at lunch, I asked him about the leather talisman he was wearing around his neck.

He said, "I wear it for my protection."

"Does it work?"

"You've seen me in action. What do you think?"

"I think you should keep wearing it."

"I plan to," he pointed at me, "and it's also a reminder of my heritage."

"Yeah, well, it's also a fashion statement." I pointed to the talisman. "Where can I get one like it?"

"Captain, to have a talisman like this," he said holding out for me to see, "you have to be born to it, or earn it."

"I like the look it gives a man."

He patted the talisman against his chest. "This ugly thing, you don't need one. It's not worn for fashion."

"Yeah...well that may be so, but what about my buying one?"

"It's like I told you, you'd have to earn it."

"How can I earn one?"

"You wouldn't understand."

"Try me."

"No. It's a tribal thing," he said.

I asked if I could see it close up. He pulled the talisman over his head and handed it to me. It was made out of stitched leather and had something hard inside it. "What's in it?" I asked.

"Only a man who gets one knows."

"I want one. There has to be a way for me to get one."

"The only way I know of for you get one, is for you to go to Africa and fight for my people."

"The dreaded Zulu?" I teased.

"Yes, the dreaded Zulu," he laughed.

As a boy, Matumbo had been kidnapped by Arab traders, and pressed into service on a Liberian steamer. The ship that took him and five other young Zulu sailed right out of Durban under the knowing eyes of the British Navy. I wanted to help him get back to his people, but I didn't know how to do it. Things in the Caribbean were deteriorating rapidly, and my first concern was finding a way out for myself.

I contacted James Jefferson to see if he had anything for me. And as the fates would have it, he was going to South Africa to look for opportunities. I asked him if he could help Matumbo. He told me to get him to England as soon as possible. I couldn't risk having Matumbo go to England, but I was able to arrange his immediate departure on a Dutch ship bound for Morocco. James agreed to meet him there. I advanced Matumbo what he was short for his fare, and paid protection money to the captain of the ship for his safe passage.

After Matumbo was gone, things on the ship were different for me. I could have joined James in South Africa, but I was worried about the politics there. I felt better about the situation in Germany, where Fritz had asked me to come and join him. I decided on Germany.

I left the ship without saying goodbye. For all the crew knew, I fell overboard and drowned. As before, I had the clothes I was wearing on my back, the money I had strapped around my waist and my father's pistol in my pocket.

Chapter 12

I arrived in Hamburg on a passenger liner in July 1914, traveling under the name Percy Jefferson, on doctored papers that I arranged for in Sint Maarten. I went directly from the port to the train station. It was crowded and I joined in a line to board the train to Hamburg. I followed an elderly woman on the train, and waited behind her as she slowly made her way to a seat. Some of the men on the train were making jokes about killing Frenchmen. She stopped and asked them, "Are you all so anxious for your sons to die?"

No one answered her.

"There's something wrong with all of you," she said. She sat down in the aisle seat of the last empty row on the train. I took the window seat next to her.

An old man, bent over in his seat from the weight of his paunch, lifted his head and sang the German national anthem. Other passengers joined in with him. The woman hid her face in her hands for a moment, and then she looked over at me.

"Ignore them!" I said.

"I can't," she said haltingly, "I have two sons in the army."

The men on the train watched us. The more upset she got, the louder they sang.

"You must be proud of your sons," I said.

She smiled and nodded yes.

The men kept singing and laughing, even after the train stopped at her station and she got off. She waved and smiled at me as she left. I wanted to do more for her, but if I had engaged the zealots on the train, it would have only made things worse.

As the train pulled into the Frankfurt station, I saw Fritz waiting for me. I rushed out to meet him. My foot caught between the train and the platform, and I stumbled up to him. I steadied myself on a guardrail.

Fritz reached out and took my arm. "You alright, Percy?"

"I'm alright!"

He patted me on the back. "I bet you're glad to be here."

"Yeah, but what's all this talk of war?"

"Hey! It's just talk."

"Maybe, but I don't need to be in a country that's at war."

"Since when does a little saber-rattling bother you? It's nothing for you to worry about."

I ended the conversation with, "I don't want to get involved!"

Fritz said he planned for us to stay several nights with his mother. He told me on the train ride to Frankfurt that she was a widow who had never remarried. His father was a captain in the artillery, and he died a decorated war hero in combat several months after Fritz was born in 1871. Jewish leaders in his neighborhood were proud of him, and they honored his memory with a plaque placed on a stone wall in a small park in front of the synagogue. The park was less than a block from his mother's apartment that she had shared with her husband on Uhlandstraße. It was a quiet street in a Jewish neighborhood. I never again broached the topic of his father with him. I figured if he wanted me to know anything more, he would tell me.

When we got to her apartment, he insisted on carrying my bag. His mother confronted us at the front door of her third-floor apartment, which she had kept intact for forty-three years as her monument to her dead husband. "I'm Fritz's mother, Sarah Sonnenblick," she said forcefully. "Who are you?"

Fritz stepped in between us, "Mom, he's a friend who is going to stay with us a few days."

"Next time you're going to have guests, let me know!" She stepped aside and pointed for us to go in. "You should have let me know!"

Fritz made the appropriate apologies, and his mother seemed satisfied. At the dinner table later that first evening, to make conversation, I asked, "When do you think the war will start?"

Frau Sonnenblick asked, "What did you hear?"

"I heard that troops are massing along both sides of the borders with France and Belgium."

"It's only a little disturbance in the Balkans. I don't understand what's got everyone so worked up," she said.

"Mom, it's more than a small disturbance," Fritz challenged her.

"There is nothing to worry about, son; the Kaiser has everything under control." "That's just not true," he said.

"It's true!" she snapped. Sarah got up and went to the kitchen. She called out, "The Kaiser is a friend of the Jewish people. He will do the right thing. He always does the right thing. We have to support him."

Fritz leaned over toward me and whispered, "Don't get her started. She'll keep going on all night."

I shook my head. I didn't have to be a genius to figure out that religion was a major issue in the Sonnenblick household.

Frau Sonnenblick returned with a basket of sliced black bread and plate of butter. She offered it to me.

89

"Thank you." I said.

"Try dipping it in the soup. It's good when you dip it."

"Thanks, I will," I said.

Fritz reached for the plate, but his mother pulled it away. "It's a little disturbance in the Balkans. That's all it is!"

"And what makes you think that, Mom?"

She didn't offer the plate to Fritz, but put it on the table within his reach. "We have a treaty with Francis Joseph of Austria," she said as she sat down.

"And you think the Kaiser's going to honor it?" he replied.

"Yes, he is. He will do whatever he has to, to honor it," she snapped. I kept eating as I listened to the discussion accelerate into a serious debate between two stubborn people who couldn't agree on anything.

"Mom, if he honors the treaty, there'll be a war!"

"Kaiser Wilhelm will never do anything to endanger us. If there is to be a war, he'll limit the fallout and there'll be no war on German soil." She handed Fritz a newspaper from the credenza behind her. "Here, read about it yourself. It's right here," she said, pointing to the headlines.

"I read that this morning." Fritz said.

"You're just scared that you'll be called to serve in the army," she said angrily.

He turned to me and said, "Here we go!"

I smiled.

"Let me tell you something. Your father would already be with the troops at the front. He would have done it on the mere chance that there could be trouble. Germany is the only place in Europe where Jews can be real citizens. We all owe a debt to the Kaiser."

"I know, Mom, and now you're going to tell me that Dad carried a gun for the Fatherland," he mocked.

"And what do you do?" she asked sarcastically.

"I carry a cross for God."

"Yes, you do, and is there any mention of a cross in the Torah?" She stood up, crossed her arms, and shook her head at him.

"No, there isn't, and there's no mention of a gun in there, either."

"But it speaks of swords," she snapped. "And guns have replaced swords!"

"Okay, I'm sorry, Mom. But I think it's stupid to go to war over anything, especially over the assassination of a stupid Austrian in Serbia. It should be an internal Austrian matter."

She calmed herself and said, "You may be right about that, son. I do think the Archduke got just what he deserved." There was a hint of laughter in her voice. "I read where the Serbs tried to kill him in the morning and they missed. He ignored all the warnings he was given and went on about his business that day. He got shot that same afternoon for all his trouble. I can't have any sympathy for him or anyone else who's that stupid," she said

"Stupid or not, his dying could cause a lot of problems," Fritz said.

"I don't think we have anything to worry about," she said.

"I hope you're right," he backed off.

She turned to me, "So tell me, Mr. Hays, where are you from?"

"I was born in New Orleans, Louisiana."

"Is that where you met my Frederick?"

Before I could answer her, Fritz interrupted, "Mother, more strudel please."

"Just a second," she said. She looked at me.

I looked at Fritz. He nodded. I said, "In Haiti."

"Haiti?" She appeared puzzled. "How did the two of you meet, Mr. Hays?"

"I was waiting to ship out when I met Fritz."

"You're a sailor?"

"Of sorts. I've spent some time at sea."

She looked at Fritz. "Frederick, you never said you were in Haiti. Were you a sailor too?"

"No mother, I wasn't a sailor. But I made a stop in Haiti and met Percy there."

"Why didn't you tell me your friend was a sailor?"

Fritz satisfied her curiosity with a partially true story about his making a trip to Haiti to deliver medical supplies, and then leaving on the same ship as I did. Then he turned the conversation back to the war. Fritz said that it was all about national honor and international treaties. But that's not what I thought; I believed it was all about royal family feuds. All the crowned heads of Europe were related and always had been. It was like all families with lots of money and lots of power; there never seemed to be peace for any length of time.

I made a commitment to a new life in Germany, for the most part because I had no place else to go. I didn't want to chance traveling with my altered credentials while everyone in Europe was on heightened security, on account of the prospect of a war. But when the German army mobilized along the border with France, I was glad I had stayed. The way I felt about the damned French, being in Germany put me on the right side if there was going to be a conflict. And in any event, I wasn't a citizen and I wasn't going to have to fight in any war.

Chapter 13

We stayed at Frau Sonnenblick's home for a fortnight. By the time Fritz finished with his business in Frankfurt, most of Europe was at war. There was an air of confident expectation in Germany that the Great War would be of short duration. Most everyone in the homeland expected it to be over before the end of the first year.

On our trip south from his mother's home to Munich, I learned that before he went to Haiti, he had worked with Helga at the Lutheran mission in The Sudan for ten years. They had an intimate relationship that they kept secret from the church. He said that near the end of his tenure in The Sudan, an infant girl was brought to the mission after her family died of a river virus in nearby Ethiopia. Fritz and Helga decided to adopt the baby, and to satisfy the church requirements for the adoption, they got married. On the marriage documents, he changed his name from Frederick Sonnenblick to Fritz Erickson. By doing so, he hoped to improve his chances for advancement in the church.

Helga and Fritz planned to stay in The Sudan after their wedding, but within weeks he was called away to a mission in Haiti. When he left Africa, Helga stayed there to raise the child. The baby's given Muslim name was Sulayma. She renamed the baby Regina, and brought her into the Lutheran faith. By so doing, she had committed a crime punishable by death in The Sudan.

In 1901, when Regina was four years old, Helga transferred back to Germany and she took Regina with her. A year later, Fritz, returned to Germany, and joined his family. He said that the people close to the Lutheran community accepted Regina, but outside of the church group there were racial problems. Her skin was light, and except for a few diplomats and their staff, there were no other Africans in town. That's when he told me he had an ulterior motive for bringing me to Germany: he felt Regina was at a marrying age, and he wanted me to be her husband.

My mind raced. I still had an ache in my heart from when I left Thelma in Monterrey. I had never considered marrying anyone, and yet I was in a new country with a man whom I barely knew, and I was willing to consider marrying a woman before I'd even met her. My first thought was that I was getting old, but upon later reflection, I believe I experienced a moment of clairvoyance.

Regina was working with Helga at her church's world mission headquarters. Fritz made the headquarters our first stop when we got to town, and I met Regina there. She was very beautiful and very young.

Fritz told me that in her country, young girls customarily were married off to older men by their families. When they were pretty, they fetched a large dowry and either married tribal elders or became their concubines.

I asked him, "What kind of dowry are you expecting from me?"

"If I were to ask from you for what she's worth, you couldn't afford her!"

"Then what are you asking?"

"What I am asking for is your promise to take care of her, keep her with you, and protect her. It's dangerous for her here, and it could be for you, too, when people realize you're a Negro. So when you leave – and trust me, you'll leave – choose a place where you and she can be both be happy. Take her to America, my friend. That's what I'm asking."

I told him I needed some time to see how things went with her, because even though I understood that Regina was raised expecting her marriage to be arranged, it wasn't good enough for me.

Fritz understood, and he had me move into the basement of his house. He also arranged a job for me working in a youth program at the Lutheran church, next door to the mission headquarters where Regina worked.

At first, I was standoffish with her at the mission office, because I didn't want to feel pressured in anyway. But I greeted her everyday at the house, and we shared some polite pleasantries there. After a time, I began to stop by her workplace occasionally and talked to her. To my surprise, she came to the church school to visit me several times too. But I wasn't moving fast enough to suit old Fritz. He was growing impatient and wanted me to spend more time, and get to know her faster.

After speaking to him, I went to see her at the mission headquarters. As soon as she saw me, she came over and stood next to me. "What a nice surprise," she said.

"It is...I mean, I came here to ask you to go to church with me Sunday," I said. It had worked for me with Thelma, and I was hoping that it would trigger a response in Regina.

She looked at me for a minute, and then said, "I would like that. I would like that very much."

"I'll come upstairs from my room to meet you," I said laughingly, "and we'll walk together."

95

She smiled. "I'll be ready."

On Sunday morning, I felt as though I were walking on a cloud, as I climbed the stairs in Fritz's house to meet her.

"Morning, Mr. Jefferson, how are you?" she said politely.

"Morning, Miss Erickson. How are you today?"

"I'm fine, and thank you so very much for inquiring." She took my arm, and we left the house and we walked to church. As we were walking she said, "You know, Mr. Jefferson, people around the church are saying how well you work with the boys."

"I like working with the boys," I said.

"Helga told me that you met Fritz in Haiti. Were you working with children there?"

"No. This is the first time I've had the chance to work with boys. How is your work at the mission going?"

"It's okay, I like working there, but I would rather transfer and work with kids like you do."

"Why don't you? They're recruiting teachers."

"I've thought about it," she said, "but Helga depends on me too much in the mission office."

Helga kept her on a short leash. She made me feel as though she didn't want Regina to spend time with me. When I told Fritz about it, he said that he would talk to Helga, but that I should continue to pursue Regina.

We began spending time together at the house, and it wasn't long until we were taking walks in the evenings to be alone. She was curious about my past, and asked a lot of questions. I told her a lot, but I left out a lot, too. After the first Sunday that we went to church together, I got dressed up every Sunday morning, and I went to church services with Regina.

When Regina started talking in terms of *us* and *we*, I got cold feet. I was forty years old, and had concerns that my age would affect us later on. I finally took the initiative and said to her, "I don't think I'm the best thing for you. There are a lot of years between us, darling. One day, while you are still quite young, I will be an old man."

She said, with a bit of attitude, "I'm eighteen, Percy Jefferson, and I'll decide for my own self what's good for me!"

I gave her a hug, and she pulled me close to her and kissed me. From then on, she asserted herself and took over the direction of our relationship. I listened to her and took her lead on most things. I felt her strength, and I started thinking in terms of *us* and *we*. It wasn't long before *we* were planning *our* wedding.

The war in Europe was raging on, but I didn't let it affect our growing closeness. I steered our conversations to talk of happy things and to our plans for the future. Back then, even as casualties at the front were mounting and more soldiers had to be sent there, the German citizenry remained apathetic. Their apathy didn't stop the work force from becoming depleted, which created an opportunity for me to make money. A farmer at the church told me that whether there was war or not, Germans demanded their sweets and their brew. With his help, I stopped working at the mission and started brokering sugar through a contact I had in Cuba.

The business grew quickly, and I moved the operation from Fritz's basement to a rented shop in the center of town. From there, in addition to my sugar brokerage, I sold retail sweets to the public, which had been made from my sugar by local farmers. Fritz saw the money I was making and wanted to work with me. In order to join me, he gave up his position in the church – a decision that didn't sit well with Helga. After a time, she learned to live with his decision.

The war notwithstanding, Regina and I were happy. We spent all of our free time together. Regina had a thirst for knowledge, and she encouraged me to share it with her. We would sit together and read. I read about banking and world finance. I read about all the great swindlers, and how the scoundrels plied their trade. I read how most great fortunes started as the result of a great crime. It confirmed what I had always believed: that the world held riches for those who dared to go after them.

I gained insight into how Regina thought and what her hopes for the future were. Her big dream was for us to go to Africa together one day. She wanted me to join in the fight for Ethiopian independence. She envisioned me as a leader, a man's man, but that was mostly because of the stories I told her about my past. She believed that I was the kind of man who could some day help her countrymen become free. I felt compelled to tell her that I had no such lofty goals for myself, but she insisted that it was going to be my destiny. I went along with her, half because it made her happy, and half because I was intrigued by the very thought of the adventure. We agreed that the final decision on Africa would wait until after we were married and the war was over.

We went together to tell Helga of our plans to marry. Regina said, "Mom, I love Percy and we want to get married."

"Are you sure that you are not just trying to please your father?"

Regina was upset. "No," she said, "we love each other!" She looked at me and said, "Help me here, Percy!"

"I love Regina and I'll take care of her." I took Regina's hand in mine. "I'll make her happy," I said.

"I hope you two know what you're getting yourselves into," Helga said and turned to leave.

"We do...." Regina and I said in almost perfect unison as Helga left the room.

It was clear that I wasn't Helga's first preference for Regina, but she soon put on a good face. She arranged for our wedding at the Lutheran church, and even insisted that we continue to live with her and Fritz after the wedding.

I was in love – something I never thought would be possible for me after losing Thelma. I married Regina, and even as The War to End Wars pressed on, the days that followed our wedding were the most wonderful days of my life. Regina was radiant, and we lived for the moment.

Rationing became a way of life for everyone. Sugar supplies dried up and I was almost put out of business. But the Germans still demanded their confections, and they were willing to lower their standards and accept substitutes. I altered my business plan. Since there was ersatz coffee, they needed ersatz sugar to go in it. I turned to a new trade and got the ersatz sweeteners needed to satisfy the demand for sugar. I was told about alternative sweeteners by an agricultural expert at Ludwig-Maximilians Universität München, who had worked as a volunteer in the youth program at the church. He taught me to cook beets and crystallize the beet sugar. Beets were plentiful, and even with the war on, they were feeding them to the pigs.

We bartered our beet sugar for flour and other ingredients from local farmers on the black market. We enlarged our shop and manufactured candies and other confections. We sold our goods to shopkeepers for resale to the public.

In the spring of 1916, Regina found she was pregnant. We celebrated the news by buying a house on a quiet street near the mission headquarters. With the war on, I couldn't access my money; Fritz lent us his life savings to help make the purchase.

My beautiful pregnant wife became radiant with joy whenever she spoke of our future together. She told me the stories that Fritz had told her about being the daughter of an Ethiopian princess. I wasn't surprised when she came to me several weeks before the baby was due, and said, "I pray that if we have a boy, he will grow up to be a king. And if she's a girl, I want to raise her to be a leader who will work to free her people."

I said to her, "Ginny, you know something, girl? All I really want is for our child to be healthy." But in my heart I really wanted a son that I could give the love that only a father can give a son. He would be heir to the kind of love that was absent from my life. My son would have a father and a mother to watch over him, and love him.

"Don't worry yourself about that, my husband. Our child will be healthy. And look at me, for goodness sake," she laughed, "you know it'll be big too!"

The doctor said she had gained too much weight during the pregnancy. He put her on a strict but healthy diet, and had her limit her activities. I had stayed with her all day everyday for several days after she saw the doctor. But then I let Fritz talk me into going with him to a local Biergarten. I went into her room where she was resting in bed, and said, "Ginny, Fritz is going to buy me a drink. Okay?"

She started to cry, "How can you leave me?"

I said to her, "I'm not leaving you, sweetheart. I'm just going for drink with Fritz is all. I'll be home before you know I'm even gone."

She gave me a smile, and I went over to the bed and gave her a kiss. That was the last time I saw her alive. Our happiness was all too short-lived. My darling wife Regina died giving birth to our son. When I first saw him, with his blonde hair and blue eyes, I had trouble dealing with it. But fortunately there was something inside me that kept me under control. My suspicions be damn, I put it out of my mind and let it pass. I allowed Helga to take the boy in and care for him, but I avoided all contact with the child.

I had loved my wife with everything that was in me, and I didn't want to go forward feeling in my heart that the baby wasn't mine. But I couldn't help myself at the time. I was angry, and didn't speak to anyone at Regina's funeral. It turned out to be the most difficult day of my life.

I avoided Fritz and Helga, and I shunned the boy. It was the only way I could deal with it. They named my son Percy Jefferson Junior. Fritz hadn't told Helga my real name, because Captain Percy Hays was still a wanted man in countries on both sides of the Great War. They called the boy, Schätze, *their little treasure*. I left them to themselves to raise the boy as their own.

In 1917, America declared war on Germany. Boatload after boatload of American soldiers landed in France, and the tide of war shifted from a stalemate to a certain Allied victory. The Great War had taken its toll on Germany, and its people were worn out. Things were changing quickly, and so were people's attitudes. My business was struggling, but at times got even worse. Woodrow Wilson's idea of "peace with honor" didn't sit well with his allies. The Europeans wanted their pound of flesh and got it with the Treaty of Versailles, designed to ensure the destruction of the German nation.

By the winter of 1918, the diplomacy of violence had turned against Germany. In their view, inferior nations had smashed through the fronts at the Somme and on the Marne, and Alsace had fallen. The Munich newspaper's headlines screamed, "The barbarians are at the gates!" Clearly the gates were only meagerly attended. What wasn't clear was whether God was at fault or not, but I thought *He* hadn't been much help.

The Kaiser's great scheme failed badly. A creeping sense of some great misdeed began to overtake the country, under which her shaken pride stood up poorly. Now the victors' judgment prevailed in an unvarnished and uncensored dictate. There was no appeal. The impossible had happened. The regime of steel was broken, and the national character was the greatest single casualty of the war.

I'm a man of the streets, and I had seen an empire of warriors become a nation of peddlers and barterers. I understood that basic economy. It suited me, even though there was no room for innovation or even dedication in a country stripped of its character. Nothing was fresh or nice. There were no dreams to dream, only nights to endure and days of destitution and complacency. The war was lost. So what! The Kaiser was gone. So what! I had lived through worse – much worse.

The two years after my wife died were torturous for me and dangerous for Fritz. Every time I thought about the boy, I got angry with Fritz. When I thought about Fritz, I got angry with my dead wife. Once the war was over, I had to deal with the situation. The boy looked white, but the people in the church knew his mother was Ethiopian. He was at risk if he stayed in Germany.

I needed to find a place for Fritz and Helga to take Schätze where he would be safe. I took a chance and sent a wire to Pappy Smathers in care of Y. B. Jonson in Baltimore. I gave him my address in Munich.

He wrote back that I should have contacted him sooner. He said that when he got to New Orleans, back in 1898, he looked for the loot where I told him to, in the Papineau family tomb, but found nothing there. Several weeks later, while he was still searching in the cemetery, Perry and Lane showed up in town looking for Miss Jeannie. Pappy said that, coincidently, Miss Jeannie's place had burnt down right after they got to town. She left town in a hurry with Tiny, and they were never heard from again.

And as to Perry and Lane, they were both back shot. Pappy said that they died at the hand of an unknown assailant. After Perry and

Lane's demise, he said he returned to his search, and in time figured out that the loot was in the bottom of the tomb with the bones of several generations of the Papineau family. He assured me that the coast was now clear, and that I could come back.

I took Pappy's letter as an omen. I wrote him and arranged for Fritz and Helga to migrate to the United States with Schätze. I told them that he would have a chance at a good life there. They agreed to go. I wired Pappy Smathers and had him arrange a place for them to stay. I asked him to use some of my money from my share of the loot to get Fritz set up. The money more than repaid Fritz for what he had lent me to buy my house. Pappy sent me the rest of the money that he was holding for me.

Pappy was getting old and he wanted me to come to America to help him in his business. I wrote him that I had business of my own that needed attention, and that I couldn't come.

I quit the confection business as soon as Fritz left Germany. I had been using it as a front for a new business that I had developed near the end of the war: smuggling diamonds. I started the business after I read about South African diamonds in a book about Cecil John Rhodes. I formulated a plan and contacted James Jefferson in Pretoria. Matumbo joined in, and we became partners in a dangerous criminal enterprise.

We handled uncut diamonds stolen from mines in South Africa, and sold them to diamond cutters in Germany and Holland. James and Matumbo smuggled the diamonds to me, hidden in chocolate. It was easy money, and with the wartime inflation, the diamond traffic boomed. Neither buyers nor sellers wanted paper currency. Diamonds and gold were in demand.

Shortly after the war, I got a wire from Matumbo. He said he needed help getting guns. De Beers' agents, British mercenaries, and Afrikaners took turns raiding his village, slaughtering his people. He asked me to come join him, and his timing was right. All it took to get me to go to South Africa then was my knowing that there was a place for me to live.

I left for Africa with a small suitcase, and some of the gold I had earned from the diamond trade tied around my waist. I put the rest of my money in my Swiss account.

Chapter 14

A courier, who delivered goods to Amsterdam for me, said that a Dutch diamond cutter had given my name to Interpol when he was caught with smuggled diamonds. Interpol forwarded the information to De Beers. They had agents in Europe pursuing diamond smugglers like me. I heeded his warning and left right away. Leaving several days sooner than I had planned, I got out of Germany just in the nick of time. I went through France to Marseilles on the Mediterranean coast, where I shipped out as a seaman on a tramp steamer to South Africa. Once again, I was starting my life over, and I was on my way to a new life in Durban.

When I arrived in South Africa in 1919, the British had solidified their hold on their colonies in sub-Saharan Africa. They had crushed the native rebellions. The French, along with the British, were trying to expand their influence on the so-called Dark Continent, but the Portuguese, Italians, Belgians, and Dutch weren't conceding anything to them. But the United States expressed no interest in Africa. It wouldn't have mattered if they had, because the Europeans had no intention of sharing their spoils with their former ally. They treated the United States' involvement in the war as a historical footnote and nothing more.

I found South Africa to my liking. For well over a decade, I passed for white and lived as I pleased. I was the go-between on numerous arms deals with James, and I traded in diamonds and gold with Matumbo. During the Great War, the Xhosa tribesmen, who had support from one side or the other, started taking diamonds from the mines where they were working. They continued taking the diamonds, and things remained pretty much the same all through the 1920's. With the world depression – which started with the stock market crash in October 1929 – the price of diamonds fell drastically. To try and support the diamond market and control prices, De Beers began a crackdown on all illegal diamond transactions. High on their priority list were the Xhosa miners who had been supplying us with diamonds. After the crackdown by De Beers, any miner suspected of taking a diamond was dealt with harshly. Many were summarily executed.

My business was effectively shut down, and it was the same for James and Matumbo. We met in the Natal and decided to join our forces. The first order of business for my new partnership with Matumbo and James was to neutralize the De Beers Company's grip over the region. Before the crackdown, everyone in the business was making a lot of money. Everyone, that is, except the miners. I believed that the best way to motivate the miners and rekindle their interest in dealing with us was to pay them more for their diamonds. The price had to be high enough to give the miners enough cash to leave the mines. The Oppenheimer Cartel countered us by making the assumption that any miner who left was guilty of stealing. Then they treated other men in the suspected thief's family as accomplices. In the homelands, things reached the point where even if a miner died of natural causes, his family contacted the De Beers representatives to examine the body before burial.

The best way to regenerate our diamond business was to make a deal with the Xhosa miners with whom we had always dealt. But there were two problems besides the crackdown by De Beers. First, was the Xhosa's natural hatred of the Zulu, and second was that they suspected James Jefferson of having betrayed them in several deals. James tried to ingratiate himself with the Xhosa by breaking off his ties with Matumbo, and dealing directly with De Beers. I warned him that it would create problems for Matumbo and me, but he didn't listen. It all came crashing down for him when the Xhosa caught him short-changing them. To further compound his problems, it was discovered that he mishandled several arms deals, and that put him at odds with the English and the Boers. He was at risk, but he refused to leave the country. He moved to Johannesburg among his old friends – the pimps and whores – there. He was lucky to have escaped with his life.

Matumbo had been using his share profits from our diamond trade to arm his people, but they needed more weapons. The Cartel's scheme was working and the Xhosa tribesmen had slowed down their dealing in diamonds. Matumbo needed to find another source for diamonds. He asked for my help. But the only way I knew of to get more diamonds was to raid De Beers' outposts, and hijack their diamond transports.

It didn't take much for Matumbo to talk me into putting what I had made up for a deal that would afford me half of the profits of future raids. What made things more attractive was that Matumbo's father was a very powerful man, and he could afford us protection among the tribes. Not only was he the headman of the largest tribe in the Zulu Nation, but he also served as the right hand man of the King. His position was akin to that of the Prime Minister of England, and that made him the most powerful man in the nation. He had resisted our plan at first, but when I pledged my fortune and assured him that there would be guns for the Zulu no matter what happened on the raids: he changed his mind.

It was my job to put the factions back together. Getting James to agree was easy; he wanted back in the action. He insisted on working out of his flat in Johannesburg, and he refused to stop associating with his friends in the bawdy district. That didn't sit well with Matumbo. I couldn't get him to agree to James' continued participation. When I argued with him, he brought up the fact that I had reunited with a woman that I had an on and off relationship with in Durban for years. He didn't trust her. He gave me an ultimatum not to see her, which I rejected. He got angry and said his father wouldn't approve of it, and it could cause us serious problems. I was upfront with him and told him that his father didn't have to know about it. I insisted that I needed the cover she could provide me. I assured him that if his father ever found out, I would shoulder all the blame. He relented; I wanted to believe it was all because he valued our relationship, but, I knew money played a roll in it too.

I had met the woman, Floris Willingham, when I was traveling from Durban to Cape Town to negotiate for some weapons soon after I got to Africa. I went to the dining car to have my lunch and there were no empty tables. I looked around and saw her sitting at a table for two, dining alone. She saw me, and motioned me over.

"May I join you?"

"Certainly," she said in a very gracious manner.

"Thank you." I started to introduce my self, "I'm Percy...." I stumbled over my last name by saying, "Hay...." and then clearing my throat I said, "Jefferson."

"Pardon me," she said.

I thought quickly, "Excuse me. Something got caught in my throat. My name is Hayden Percival Jefferson, but my friends call me Percy."

"It is nice to make your acquaintance, Mr. Jefferson," she held out her hand, "I'm Mrs. Floris Willingham. Won't you please join me?"

I thanked her and sat down across from her. She smiled and nodded. She was a contemporary of mine, and I found her to be very attractive. I had seen her on the train from Johannesburg before, and had thought about striking up a conversation with her then, but never did. I had been staying out of the sun and that kept my skin quite light, but I was never sure if I would be mistaken for one of the Coloreds.

She handed me a menu. "I already decided on what I'm having, won't you make your selection?"

"Thank you," I said. We ordered lunch and we made some small talk. I told her I was a retired seaman looking for business opportunities in South Africa. She told me she was a widow, and that her husband had been a member of the Foreign Service and died quite young of a seizure. We stayed there two hours, sipping tea and having conversation.

I saw her look at her watch, and realized she probably wanted to leave. I said, "Excuse me if I am being too bold, but I want to ask you if you'll join me for dinner this evening here in the dining car?"

"I would consider it a pleasure, Mr. Jefferson."

We met for dinner that evening, and then for breakfast the next day. We shared the rest of the ride to Durban, where she resided. She also had a second residence in Cape Town, where she was originally from. She had family living there, and she made the long trip between the two cities on a regular basis.

I called on her in Durban, and after a short time, I moved in with her. I took her on many of my trips though South Africa and Rhodesia, and that enabled me to travel freely. For several years, I spent most of my time with her, and only left her when I went on raids with Matumbo and his men.

Financially things were going well for Matumbo and me – that is, until rumors surfaced that a white man was leading the Zulu raids. That was unacceptable for Matumbo's father. Making a political statement was as important to him as profits from the raids. To cover my identity on a raid on a De Beers station in the interior, I darkened my skin with an unguent I got from a Zulu healer. After the raid, I found out that the stain wouldn't come off for weeks. I couldn't go back to Floris – she would demand the truth, and I feared she might turn me in. Also there was always the possibility I would get caught and she would be in trouble for being with me.

I sent her a telegraph, telling her that I had to return to America on business, and I wouldn't be back for some time. I moved into the Zulu village, and I took a Zulu woman as a companion. Matumbo felt better about my new situation.

During the time I lived at the village, Matumbo and his father had a falling out. His father decided he didn't want to risk the British getting involved in our war with the Oppenheimer Cartel. He instituted a policy of non-aggression. He made us wait until there was an attack on a Zulu village before we could initiate a retaliatory raid. We also had to limit our attacks to Afrikaner compounds and De Beers' outposts. Matumbo, on the other hand, wanted all-out war against everyone including the British, but couldn't get his father to even consider it.

Matumbo's father died suddenly in 1922 after suffering a massive heart attack. Matumbo became the tribe's headman and took his father's place at the side of the king. He began lobbying the king immediately for authority to initiate his own raids. He quickly got the kings approval for a more aggressive war, and then there was nothing holding us back. He went to war with the Xhosa, the Afrikaners, the English, the Dutch, the Portuguese, the Coloureds, and the Hottentots alike.

Matumbo hated the Afrikaners and the British, but he held a special kind of hatred for any man who worked for De Beers. After five years of successful diamond raids and limited violence, Matumbo inexplicably ordered a reign of terror. His first order of business was to direct his men to execute any De Beers' employees that were captured. I could have condoned punishing men who were known to have wronged the Zulu, but I couldn't agree with his decision to kill all captives. I took a strong stand and refused to lead any more raiding parties for him. He expressed his disappointment with me, and told me that I had to leave the village.

I went to Durban, and I stayed in a safe-house outside of town. I couldn't stay there forever, so I made a call on Floris. She let me back in, but things were different. We slept in different rooms, and she wouldn't allow any intimacy between us.

While I was staying at Floris', the newspapers were filled with reports of an accelerated number of Zulu raids. There was a heightened level of violence in the encounters, and that brought British troops to assist the cartel. Things turned bleak for the Zulu. Matumbo's father had been right, and now the days of big profits and low risk were over. My relationship with Floris was over too; she wanted me to stop traveling and live with her off her inheritance. She said I had to prove to her that things would change for the better between us. I couldn't perform the penance she required of me. I packed my things, and was ready to leave Africa for Germany.

I still considered Matumbo my best friend in the whole world, and I sent a message to him, telling him of my plans to leave. He sent me a message back asking me to come to see him before I left. He said that all was forgiven, and he wanted my counsel.

I left immediately to see him. I managed a ride from Durban that dropped me off several miles from Matumbo's village. Near the village, I ran into a group of teenage Zulu boys. I knew some of them and we started toward the village together, the boys walking up ahead.

We hadn't gotten far when a drunken Boer confronted us. "Today's my lucky day," the man laughed.

I stepped in front of the boys. "Let us pass!" I was dressed like a British civil servant in khaki pants, a white shirt, and red striped tie.

He shouted. "I'm going to kill some Kaffirs today."

I stood my ground, and told him to go on about his business. He pulled out a pistol and pointed it at me and shouted for me to move. I kept the boys behind me. He waved his pistol threateningly, and said, "I'll shoot through you if I have to!"

I said, "These boys mean you no harm!"

"You're going to get dead!" he said. He pulled the hammer back on his revolver. "You fucking Kaffir lover!"

The boys stayed behind me. "You got 'til three!" He waved his revolver again. "One," he pointed the gun, "two!"

I let out a blood-curdling yell and drew my knife from my pocket as I charged him. He fired. The bullet struck my upper arm. I was on him before he could get off a second shot. I knocked the gun from his hand as I swung wildly with my knife. The force of the blade severed several fingers on his right hand. I was hurt. I had to finish him off quickly. I grabbed his hair and stretched his neck back. In an uncontrollable rage, I cut his neck clean though. I stood holding his severed head in my hand. I dropped his head next to his lifeless body.

There was a moment of quiet, and then all hell broke loose. One of the boys grabbed the man's pistol, another took his head, and the rest of them dragged the man's lifeless body toward the village, yelling and screaming as they went along. I tied a tourniquet around my arm to stop the bleeding and joined the procession. When we got to the village, a crowd gathered.

The story of how I beheaded the Boer grew with each telling, from village to village. There were men in the village who didn't like the notoriety I received. Some of the elders had resented my influence on the tribe, even before the incident with the Boer. Their resentment grew as my perceived power grew. There were threats made against me, but I managed to avoid any confrontations with them. They complained to Matumbo, but he only compounded the situation by proclaiming me an invincible warrior with magical powers.

He confided in me that he wanted to use me to draw attention away from himself, for political reasons. He loved the fact that I had reacted with such brutality. He said that when he compared himself to me, he considered himself a gentle man. I disagreed.

He arranged a meeting for me with the elders and Naruto the diviner, the tribe's spiritual leader. Naruto said he had a vision of me leading the Zulu into war. He was the Dreamhouse, and his visions were truths. As a result of his revelations I was awarded the highest warrior status in the tribe. I became Matumbo's brother and protector, and what pleased me the most, was that I received my own talisman. The Dreamhouse recited a praise song in my honor:

He excels over all others with a spear
He wins all battles with his small gun
He who brings death to his enemies
He is the protector of the young

He will walk forever with the great warriors
He is strong and he is wise
He who is called Balaa Dekua Baa.

The Dreamhouse ended the ceremony by holding up a vial of liquid. He said, "When death is near, Balaa Dekua Baa, drink this potion. You will join the great Zulu warriors who preceded you into the unknown." He put the potion in my talisman and secured it with a leather tie.

I said, "You honor me." I bowed my head.

Matumbo came over to me. "I'm proud, my brother," he said. He embraced me.

The legend of Balaa Dekua Baa spread all over the African sub-continent. Every raid, whether or not I was involved, was credited to me, and the embellished tales of a white Zulu devil filled the local papers. I was the Oppenheimers' worst nightmare. A few of the older men in the village resented my growing status, and they made no effort to hide their animus. Their behavior emboldened a young warrior who attacked me. He came at me from behind, but somehow, I felt him coming and ducked in the nick of time. His stabbing spear gashed my back and glanced off my shoulder blade. I pulled my knife and spun around. I stuck my knife into the man's abdomen and disemboweled him with one move. The warriors who saw what happened spread the word of my deed among the tribes.

I rejoined Matumbo, and led raids against De Beers for him. The Oppenheimer Cartel increased its security and we had to use more force – and so, we caused more casualties. Each encounter became a fight to the death. Those who ran, faced a fate worse than death if they were caught.

It was a war of independence for the Zulu, but it was business for me. The raids ranged farther and farther into the heart of South Africa, and then spread to neighboring countries.

The world was changing, but not politics in South Africa. I found it was possible to do business with all sides. I took De Beers' diamonds, and had James Jefferson sell them right back to them. They knew the diamonds were stolen from their agents, but they bought them anyway to keep them off the open market.

In November 1932, I led a small raiding party into Lesotho. Early one evening, we came upon a De Beers armored payroll truck, broken down on the side of the road to Buthe-Buthe. The guards were relaxing by the truck and looked to be easy prey. I posted sentries and waited for nightfall.

We had traveled in three groups for safety. I traveled out in the open with three colored soldiers of fortune who were dressed like men from the townships. The rest of the men traveled out of sight. One group of eight men was in combat attire with rifles, and the other group of nine men was in traditional war-dress, with stabbing spears and shields. The men with spears were of little value, but Matumbo still wanted to make sure the world knew the Zulu were fighting a revolution.

The warriors wanted a chance to fight, and I thought they could handle an ambush. I had them surround the truck at a distance, and told them they would have the battle they wanted in the morning.

At first light, the Zulu crept forward. The guards didn't move. My riflemen watched from a distance as I advanced with the warriors armed only with stabbing spears and shields. When we were ten feet from the truck, the four guards jumped up with their rifles in their hands. Then twelve uniformed soldiers jumped out of the truck and encircled us. I ordered my men to stand down and drop their weapons. With the Afrikaners closing in on us, I told my men in Swahili to fall to the ground when I hollered *shoot!*

"Stabbing spears against guns? Good thing you gave it up, Kaffir," the commandant, Jacques Vanderlip, shouted to me. He was a middle-aged Afrikaner officer, and had been a known adversary of the Zulu for many years. He looked me up and down. "Goddamn! I caught me the white savage!

I nodded deferentially. "Seems that way," I said.

He was suspicious. "Without a fight?" he asked.

I shouted, "Shoot!" I dove to the ground. My riflemen opened fire on the guards taking them by surprise. The Afrikaners turned and returned their fire. When the guard's' backs were to us, we were on them. My men used their stabbing spears to slaughter the Afrikaners. When the carnage was done, I said to the dying Jacques Vanderlip, "Don't you just love knives? I do!"

Chapter 15

Jarred Skidmore, an English soldier of fortune, had been a paid mercenary, informing on the Afrikaners for Matumbo's father. Matumbo never trusted Skidmore, and he severed relations with him soon after his father died. I hadn't heard from Skidmore for years until he contacted me in late November 1932. He said he had valuable information for me, and would meet with me in any place of my choosing. I had him brought blindfolded to a safe-house near Ulundi. He claimed he was working for the Afrikaners, and that he had contacts all the way up the chain of command. He wanted to get back on the payroll. I told him if what he had to offer was important, I might arrange it.

He reported that James Jefferson's drinking had gotten completely out of control. He said that James had gone on a bender, and got involved with an undercover Afrikaner agent who was posing as a gun dealer. The man persuaded James that he could get him small arms on the cheap. James supposedly came to Skidmore for funding, and he told James he smelled a rat. Skidmore said he turned the deal down.

I asked Skidmore why he thought I would pay for the information he had. He said because James had gotten real cozy with the agent and let him stay at his place. And what was more, he said that the agent took a picture of me that was in James' apartment. It was the only photo of me that I knew existed. Skidmore speculated that wanted posters with my likeness would soon show up in South Africa. I made a deal with Skidmore to find out what he could about James, and to see if he could get his hands on the picture. I told him time was of the essence and to get back to me as soon as he could.

I had been forewarned, and I took it upon myself to arrange a meeting with James at a safe-house in Johannesburg. I told him of my plans to retire, and let him know that Matumbo viewed him as a threat. He copped an attitude with me, but I assured him that I was his only friend in the Natal, and that the only thing saving him from the Zulu was me. I told him he should leave South Africa right away. He told me to mind my own business, and that he was staying in South Africa. I tried to reason with him, but he said that I wasn't his keeper. He said he wasn't afraid of Matumbo, and never had been.

There wasn't much I could do at that point for James, and I went about finalizing my plans to leave. Right after the New Year, Skidmore came to me again. He reported back to me that things were dire for James. He said James had struck up a conversation with a woman at a pub in Johannesburg. She was an Afrikaner agent who was sent to get close to him. She steered their conversation to the reports of the latest Zulu raids, and the light-skinned man who led them.

James asked her, "So you heard about the white Kaffir, did you?"

"Everyone has heard of him," she said with a laugh. "I'd like to get part of the reward they have out on him."

"Really?" James looked around to make sure no one was listening. "I know him."

"You know where he is now?"

"I might. What's in for me?"

She told her handler that she promised James half the reward, and he was all ears. She kept him at the bar until her associates got there. Then she lured James out of the bar and into a waiting lorry. He was taken to an Afrikaner compound in Johannesburg, and held there until late February. From there, he was then taken to the Afrikaners' militia stronghold in Pretoria. It was a drab, gray stone building in the center of the city, which once had served as the British Army's regional headquarters. The Afrikaners, with the knowledge of the Hertzog government, ran their vigilante activities from where they were to have an Afrikaner awareness center. As long as the Afrikaners directed their attacks against tribesmen and Coloureds, the British turned their heads and winked.

The Afrikaners interrogated James for two days and two nights, and then put him in solitary confinement for three days; he didn't talk. He was then taken to an office on the second floor and chained to a chair. James was to be interviewed by Lieutenant Hans Vanderlip, the son of the officer I killed in my failed Buthe-Buthe raid. Skidmore had arranged to be in on the interrogation, by convincing his superiors that he would be useful. Vanderlip wanted to be alone with James, because he knew that James and I knew about him being a major dealer in guns and diamonds. He needed to get rid of both of us before we fell into the hands of the British.

Vanderlip stared at James. "What's it going to take, Jefferson?"

"Take?"

"Cut the shit! Where's the white Kaffir?"

"I don't know anything."

He said to James, "Just tell 'em what they want to hear and get it over with."

"I don't know nothing!"

Vanderlip said to Skidmore, "I'll handle this!" He went over to

James, "I know you know where Percy is." He paused. "Yeah, you know!"

"Can't help you!"

Vanderlip moved back from the chair. "You will." He said angrily. "I want that fucker, and you're going to tell me where he is."

"I can't tell you what I don't know."

"For argument's sake, let's say I believe you, and you don't know anything. And then, let's say, you're not stupid enough to die for a fucking Kaffir." Vanderlip looked at James and shook his head. "Then what?"

"Christ, I did a little business with the Kaffir, and that's all."

"What business?"

"I got him guns from Angola."

"Where is he now?"

"He's here. He's there. He's everywhere."

Vanderlip pounded his fist on his desk. "You fucking jerk!"

"No, I swear! I don't know where he is."

"Then I'm talking to a dead man!" Vanderlip turned away. "You fucking jokester."

"You....you don't understand."

"I understand. He's here. He's there. He's everywhere."

"But...."

"No buts!" Vanderlip moved toward the door. "You dumb fuck."

"I don't know where he is, but I know where he's going to be!"

Vanderlip stopped in his tracks. "Where's that?"

"You have to get me to a safe place before I tell."

"What the fuck are you talking about?"

"If I tell you, there'll be no place for me to hide. If he doesn't get me, the Zulu will. For Christ's sake, his friends are everywhere. You have to get me out of South Africa!"

"I've had it with your shit!" Vanderlip shouted.

"We can work something out!"

"'Work something out'? What does that mean?"

"There's Percy, and then there's me."

"Yeah?"

"And then there's the Congo! When I'm safe in the Congo, I'll tell you who knows where Percy is, and give you the list you want."

After Skidmore told me about the Congo, I knew he was telling the truth and James was putting our contingency plan into play. It was simple: he was to get his captors to take him to Durban, Cape Town, or Léopoldville. He would then send them to a house in the homeland that corresponded to where he was being held. Each house in each homeland sent a different message. We designated houses in the townships of people who were sympathetic to various political groups.

Vanderlip took the bait. He opened the door; as he left, he told Skidmore to watch him, and if he moved, to shoot him. He turned to James and said, "Don't do anything stupid!"

When Vanderlip left the room, James asked Skidmore, "What the fuck are you doing here, you son of a bitch?"

Skidmore grabbed him and spoke directly into his ear, "Covering your fat ass, you stupid fuck! And you'd better keep your big mouth shut!"

Vanderlip wasted no time setting things into motion. Skidmore said that he went with Vanderlip, James, and two guards, all dressed in old clothes, and they flew to Brazzaville. From there, he drove in an unmarked lorry to the border with the Belgian Congo. The border crossing was held by rebels, who were demanding tribute from anyone who passed. They took money and weapons and then let them through. When they were out of sight of the rebels, twelve heavily-armed Afrikaner militiamen met them. Vanderlip rearmed his group and had two of the men join him for the rest of the trip.

In Léopoldville, James gave Vanderlip the address. Vanderlip sent the message back to his superiors at the command center in South Africa with Skidmore. Within hours, Afrikaner agents showed up at a British loyalist's house in the homeland. The man living there claimed he knew nothing of me. The agents beat him sense-less in front of his family. They ran the family off and destroyed the house. Three armed men stayed at what remained of the house, waiting for me. The neighbors saw the commotion, and the news of the Afrikaner's foray spread through the townships.

After hearing the whole story from Skidmore, I had a decision to make. James, as usual, had created problems for himself, but I also had problems of my own. I decided to go on with my own business. I was dealing with the loss of six of my best men, and De Beers' agents were closing in on me.

The Xhosa, whom I'd always been able to depend on, turned on me and refused to help with my wounded. My men demanded re-venge against the Xhosa. We buried our dead, and I sent two riflemen back with the wounded. The remainder of the raiding party stayed in Buthe-Buthe to hunt down the Xhosa who refused them aid.

I made my final plans to leave South Africa. I went to a safe-house in Soweto to arrange for my departure. No sooner than I got there, the news of the Afrikaner attack on the British loyalist reached me. I had a change of heart; it wasn't in me to leave James in Vanderlip's hands.

Chapter 16

The pilot landed in a field near the Congo River, and taxied to a road ten miles from Léopoldville. From there it was a short distance to the city on the main road. I didn't see any activity, but I hid in the bushes to make certain that no one saw the plane, and that the coast was clear. It was a good thing I did, because it wasn't. I saw a contingent of Tutsi rebels marching Hutu captives away from Léopoldville. The Tutsi guards hacked with their blades at prisoners who stumbled. The only thing that was keeping rival tribes from killing each other off completely was the presence of Belgian troops. But there were none around that day; they had all been called back to Léopoldville.

I had had to deal with James' incarcerations over the years, but I promised myself that this was going to be the last time I was ever going to get involved. The more he drank, the less dependable he became.

It was easy to find out where six white men who couldn't speak a word of French were hiding in Léopoldville. I put a few francs in a boy's palm, and in minutes I was looking at the building where they were holding James. Neither Vanderlip, nor any of his crew, had an inkling I was anywhere nearby. They were waiting for news that I was captured in South Africa, so they could dispose of James.

There was no way for me to finesse the deal. I had to get inside to free James, and there was no easy access into the building. It was a dilapidated, two-storey structure with a food market on the ground floor and rooms to let on the second. Guards were posted at the front and back. It was one of only two buildings that survived a recent fire which had leveled two square blocks. The other building, right next to the building where they were holding James, stood unoccupied. There was a space between the buildings that looked wide enough for a man of my size to squirm through and get to the roof. I needed a diversion to get close to the building without being seen. From the roof, I planned to lower myself to a window on the second floor. For that, I needed fifteen feet of strong rope, which I had a young street hustler get me for a few francs.

I paid some boys to toss rocks at the building and shout obscenities at the guards when it got dark. A guard was hit in the head with a rock, and when he fell, it was fortunate that his gun went off. The noise drew a crowd. In the confusion, I slipped into the opening between the buildings. I put one hand on each side of the buildings' outer walls and shimmied slowly up to the roof. When I got to the roof, there was a large hole through which I spotted two guards in the hallway below. The shot had unnerved them, and they were looking out the window. I moved to the edge of the roof, and bent down behind a small façade that concealed me from the people on the street below.

I waited for two hours to make sure the crowd in the street had dispersed, and then leaned over the edge. There I saw that all the windows were open to the room below where James was being held.

There was no time for planning. I tied the rope off on an exposed roof support beam and climbed down the rope to the side of the window. I edged over and looked in. James was sitting in a chair near the back wall of the room. One man stood behind him, and another sat at a table in front of him with his back to me. He heard something and turned toward the door. I saw it was my old nemesis, Hans Vanderlip.

I didn't hesitate. I pushed out and away from the side of the building as hard as I could. My momentum brought me back through the window and onto the floor in the middle of the room. The guard standing behind James was startled. James threw himself on the floor, giving me a clear path to the guard behind him. I jumped up with a revolver in my right hand and a dagger in my left. I thrust my blade up to the hilt into the guard's abdomen. The force of my forward motion lifted the guard off the ground. I pulled the knife out, spun around, and confronted Vanderlip. We were face to face. Before he could react, I stabbed him in the chest. He slumped backward and fell the floor.

James was waiting for my lead. There were two guards in the hall that heard the commotion, and I pointed to the window. James nodded his head and started for it. Before he could get out the window, the doorknob turned and the door opened. I slammed it back with all my weight, knocking one of the guards down. I pulled the door open and went into the hall. I stabbed the guard standing by the door in the neck. I quickly pulled the knife out and stabbed the other guard in the heart with it.

James pointed his finger at me. "The man who brings death to his enemies!" He shouted and pounded his chest.

"Hold it down!" I pushed him toward the door. "We're not out of here yet."

"What took you so long, you fucker?" James grabbed a gun from one of the dead guards and waved it back and forth.

"What do you plan to do with that?"

"Nothing! Let's get the fuck out of here."

"Slow down! We still have a problem downstairs."

"What's that?"

"More guards," I said.

"Shit! How many are there?"

"I saw at least one in front. And there has to be one in back, too."

"There probably is, but counting these guys, the most there can be is two. Why don't we sneak out? It's dark."

"There's no cover to get away," I said.

"Fuck it! We can make a run for it, they'll never catch us."

"Cut the shit, James. I'm going back to the roof and climbing down the way I got up. You go to the back door and wait for me. If there's a guard, wait for me to distract him and then take him from behind. And make damn sure there's no noise!"

"If 'e's there I'll get 'im."

"See that you do!"

"Stop the damn talk already!" James pushed me toward the window. "Get moving! I want out of 'ere!"

I wriggled down between the buildings the same way I came up and then circled slowly to the back of the building. I walked up to the guard. "I'm here for the prisoner."

The guard pulled his side arm and shouted, "Come into the light!"

I moved into a dim light coming from an oil lantern hanging on a nail. While I stood there, James came out the back door. He hit the guard hard with the butt of his gun.

"Let's go!"

"We have to get the other guard in front."

"Fuck the other guard! "'e could've 'eard us. Let's go!"

126

He was getting on my very last nerve. "I don't want to have to worry about being followed," I said.

We walked around the building. The guard was leaning against the entrance to the store, talking to the shopkeeper. The shopkeeper spotted us, but looked away. I kept my eyes on both men. I was uneasy about leaving a witness, but I walked away.

Michael Shure

Chapter 17

The De Beers interests blamed me for the direct loss of millions of pounds sterling over the years. They also blamed me for breaking the circle of fear they had exerted over the African miners. Their agents boasted that they would take me down, cut me up, and send each tribe a piece of me. A newspaper article claimed that I was an American expatriate wanted for piracy on the high seas. Handbills were circulated identifying me as Balaa Dekua Baa, and offering a large reward for my capture, dead or alive.

Communications in Africa were evolving, and cooperation between the countries in tracking fugitives was improving. I couldn't trust anyone. I learned while I was with my father that even the lowly alligator, with its little brain, knew enough to stay away from hunters. It was time for me to go.

James didn't share my concerns. He felt his exposure was limited, and that there were still opportunities for him in Africa. He had the advantage of having a valid British passport, and with Vanderlip dead, he thought he could travel anywhere on the Dark Continent. He wanted to try Angola, which was a short trip from the Congo. We parted ways. James headed east, and I headed north.

I started my trip with a paid guide in a stolen truck. He got me as far as Lake Victoria, and he left me there. I hired a boat at the headwaters of the Nile, and made my way to the Mediterranean at Alexandria. I dodged west along the coast of North Africa. Bad weather forced me to land at Tobruk, and I made the rest of the trip to Tripoli by land along the Libyan coast.

I quickly found out that looking like an Arab was one thing, but living like one was quite another – I didn't know which smelled worse, the camels or the women. There was water all around Tripoli, yet no one used any of it. I didn't like the people that populated North Africa, and wanted to get away as soon as possible.

I signed on a tramp steamer going to Europe with a bunch of other undocumented seamen. Most of the men in line in front of me begged off the trip when they found out they would be paid in Libyan currency when they got to France. The only place Libyan dinars were any good was Libya. I didn't give a tinker's damn about the money; I had money. All I wanted was a ride across the Mediterranean.

The captain was aware of why we all signed on his ship. He had guards loyal to him, stationed fore and aft, and had sentries walking the decks. The ship was a virtual prison. We made port in France at last light. I climbed over the rail on the starboard side, grabbed the deck overhang while the ship was being eased into her berth, took a deep breath, and let go. I fell feet first into the shipping channel. I maneuvered clear of the channel and swam to an empty slip two hundred yards away, disappearing into the growing darkness.

I crossed the French border twenty kilometers from Saarbrücken. From there, I took a train to my home in Munich. I went to the front door and forced it open. The house was a shambles. Four gypsy men, shielding women and children with their bodies, confronted me in the foyer, and my hands went immediately to my pockets for my weapons.

"What do you want here?" one of the men asked.

I took a step back and took my hands out of my pockets and held them, palms up. "It's my house!"

An old gypsy man stepped slowly forward. "There's been no one here."

"Where are they?" I asked.

"There was no one here when we came," a man came forward and said.

"You're the first person here since we came," a woman said.

Another man talked over them. "We didn't think anyone lived here. It's a broken-down old house."

A young boy stepped up and asked, "Are you one of them?"

"Of who?"

"Nazis?"

"Me, a Nazi!" I laughed.

"Are you going to turn us in?" the boy asked.

"Enough, boy," an old man said.

"No, that's alright," I said.

"Are you?" the boy asked again.

"I'm not turning anyone in." I patted his shoulder. He tried to stare me down. I liked that in the boy. "You all can stay," I said.

"Who are you to say we can stay?" a woman asked angrily.

I told her it had been my home. She asked me if I was going to stay. I told her I'd be on my way soon enough, and that Germany was no longer a place for me.

The next morning I smelled food cooking in the kitchen. Leo, the boy, greeted me at the foot of the stairs. He held his hand out, and led me to the kitchen table. His mother served me a bowl of beet juice with sour cream, a hard-boiled egg on a plate, and a cup of ersatz coffee. It was the lion's share of what the family had to eat for the day. I accepted their generosity.

When I finished eating, I called Leo over to me. He looked at his mother for approval. She nodded and he came over to me. I took his hand. "Boy, come to town with me?"

He asked his mother if he could go. She looked at me. I told her I would look after him. She smiled and looked to the old man for his consent. When she got it, she said yes, but I could see she was worried.

The old man spoke up as we were leaving. "Who are you?" He was a smallish man, balding, and wore his hair long and tied behind his head. He was wearing gold earrings and a heavy gold chain with a medallion around his neck.

"Percy Hays, Sir," I said, "a fellow traveler. And you?"

"I am Mikhail."

Leo's mother spoke up. "He is our Voivodes, our...."

"Shush, woman," Mikhail interrupted.

I knew that she had slipped and that he was their leader, or their king. "It's an honor, sir," I said.

He touched my shoulder. He turned to Leo. "You listen to Mr. Hays, and don't get into any mischief."

On the way to the store, Leo told me that gypsies, Jews, and homosexuals were being rounded up by the SS and sent to detainment centers. The SS was separating families and sending them to different camps. Leo said his family wanted to go back to Romania. I didn't think they would have much of a chance of making it. I took the boy to a greengrocer and to the butcher shop, and brought the food to his family.

I needed money. I called Otto Clemens, a Dutch diamond cutter who owed me money for a shipment I had sent from Africa. He was an Evangelical Christian, and I thought him to be a man above reproach. When I reached him on the phone, he said he no longer owed me any money. I got the message – I had always thought it was a Jewish diamond merchant that had turned the De Beers agents onto me when I left Germany after the war; I was wrong.

I arranged to have money wired to a Munich bank from my Swiss account. The next day I went to the bank and picked up the money. On the way back to the house, Leo stopped me. He was crying. He said the Brown Shirts had come looking for me. When they found his family, they tried to arrest them. A fight ensued, and his mother and two uncles were killed in the melee. The rest of the family scattered and ran in every direction.

I asked him where he was going. He said he wanted to find his family and asked me to join him. I shook my head no, and started toward my house.

"Don't go there!" Leo grabbed my arm. "There's a Brown Shirt that set your house on fire."

I pulled away and ran toward the house. I saw Leo's grandfather in the bushes. He called me over. I stopped. He was doubled over and there was blood running down the side of his head. I said, "I'll take care of this!"

"Don't go there. They're looking for you!" He called after me.

I stopped and looked back. Leo had followed me and joined his grandfather behind the hedge. I left them there and worked my way down the street. I saw the Brown Shirt leaning on his rifle, watching my house burn. I snuck up on him from behind and kicked the rifle from under him. He stumbled forward. I hit him in the head and knocked him down. He struggled to his feet and lunged at me with a knife. I dodged the blade and pushed him. He stumbled toward the house. I gave him a shove in the back and he fell into the fire he started.

I heard a neighbor shriek, and I beat a quick retreat back to where I had left Leo and his grandfather. I gave Leo three gold coins. I told him to go with his grandfather and get far away, as fast as he could. I decided to do the same.

Chapter 18

I took a train from Munich to Freiburg, knowing that it would take some time to get a search started. From Freiburg, I took a bus to within sight of the French border. There were armed soldiers on both sides of the border. I watched from a distance. The French were sending people back that the Germans had let through. For my part, it was a poor choice for a crossing.

I walked the German countryside for two days until I found an isolated border crossing at a bridge over a small river. I hid behind some bushes on a hill overlooking the border. A lone guard watched on the German side. On the French side there was an armed guard in a tower, but none on the bridge. I planned to sneak by the German guard and cross to the small island at night. Once I got across the river, it would be easy to climb unnoticed over the barrier on the French side.

I hid out behind a barn within sight of the border, until it was dark. A heavy fog rolled in, and I crept to the bridge. I cut branches to cover the barbed-wire fence and gathered them near a low spot on the border, out of sight of the French guard tower. I thought I was in the clear. Then suddenly a farmer came out of nowhere and confronted me. "Halt!" he shouted. He was wearing an armband with a swastika.

I stopped and pulled my Derringer. "Herr Nazi," I laughed, "stolz auf das Hakenkreuz!" I put a bullet through the center of his armband. He ran. I ran after him and brought him down from behind.

"Arschloch!" he screamed as he crawled away.

I silenced him with a blow to the head. I crouched down next to him and waited to make sure the coast was clear. I left him on the ground unconscious, and crept by the border station unnoticed, on a dark night shrouded with a fog.

In Paris, in the fall of 1936, colored people were very much in vogue, and Josephine Baker was the rage. It was a good place for me, and it was a place where a man with money was king. You could rub elbows with the rich, the powerful, and the royals. All you needed was the price of the cover charge. I found myself going, more and more, into my belt to buy myself a good time.

The good times, in *la ville de lumière*, came close to unraveling one night at the bar at the Moulin Rouge. I went there after getting a buzz on at the Lido Club, smoking a reefer with a fellow expatriate. I was still feeling the effects when I walked to the bar. Two women made room for me between them. One of the women, Neddi Loire, spoke to me. We were making small talk, when a redneck American wedged himself between us. "Move it!" he said.

I pushed him away and put enough distance between us so I could get my hand in my pocket and on my pistol. Neddi interceded. "Let the bouncer handle it!"

"Best you be on your way, boy," I said.

He backed away, and started to leave. Then he turned back to me, "I'll 'boy' you, nigger!" He pulled a switchblade from his pocket.

"Don't be stupid," I said. My hand went to my pistol.

"Fuck you!"

I cocked the hammer of the Derringer. Neddi stepped between us again. Her body pressed up against mine. "Relax, handsome," she whispered. "The bouncer is on his way."

I stayed behind her with my body pressed up against hers. The boy shouted, "Come out here, you asshole!"

Neddi kept herself between us. I felt myself swell as she drew deep breaths and leaned back hard against me. "I don't want any trouble, but I can handle it," I said in her ear.

"Just relax," she said. She reached her hand behind her and pressed it against my crotch. "Ooh! Or maybe you shouldn't."

The boy was shouting that he was going to cut me, and was waving his knife back and forth when the bouncer got there. He disarmed the boy and escorted him out of the bar.

I told Neddi that she could easily have gotten hurt. She said the boy was just showing off for the girls. That's why he picked the biggest man at the bar to start up with. She giggled and told me that boys had to do things to impress women when they're young. She said that they would do better if they saved their energy for other things, and she moved even closer to me.

I asked what made her so smart about those kinds of things. She said that I should find out for myself, and she kissed me on my cheek.

The manager came and apologized for the inconvenience, and asked if I wanted the bouncer to see me safely out of the club. I told him I would be staying with the ladies.

Neddi brushed up against me and touched my arms. I was careful and made sure I didn't touch her until she touched me first. She was wearing a sheer dress that drew more than just my gaze. She was elegant, and I felt good being with her. At the end of the evening, she invited me to take her home. We walked out of the Moulin Rouge together, arm in arm.

We had gone less than a block when I saw the boy come out of a doorway across the street from where we were. My hand went into my pocket, and I started toward him. Neddi grabbed me and quickly pulled me to a cab that was sitting at the curb. She hustled me in and climbed in behind me. "I want you tonight. He can't have you," she said.

At her place, she said, "Come on with me!" and tugged on my arm. I followed her into the building and onto the lift to her apartment. It was an elegant flat. She went to her bedroom and came out wearing a sheer robe. She poured two glasses of champagne and offered me one, then asked, "You know what I like?"

"No. What do you like?"

"I like big men, just like you."

I mumbled something like, "I was hoping you did." I felt stupid after I said it.

She started away from me. Then she turned quickly and swung her arm. Her hand bumped my crotch. "Oh! Excuse me." She smiled and looked up at me. "I'm so clumsy."

"I like clumsy!"

"You bad boy, you!" She pressed herself against me. "Ooh. What's this?"

"Just what you think it is."

She unbuttoned my pants, put her hand inside, and grabbed hold of me. She kissed me and pulled me to her bedroom, where I found paradise. It was dawn before I fell asleep, exhausted from a combination of sex and alcohol.

The next afternoon, I woke up to breakfast in bed. Neddi spent the day fulfilling my every desire. There was food and there was sex. In the late afternoon, she sent me back to my hotel to get my things. She wanted me to stay with her so she could show me Paris her way.

When I first saw Neddi's apartment, I thought a rich man was keeping her, but I was wrong. No man controlled Neddi. She was a successful designer and an innovator. She wouldn't be chosen; *she* did the choosing.

We went to the Louvre, and made love right there in the toilet. We went to la Rive Gauche and made love there. We went all over Paris. It got so that I got excited every time I saw a quiet little nook or cranny where we could be together.

I stayed with Neddi, in a state of euphoria, for four weeks. I liked it that she was uninhibited, and she taught me how to enjoy another person. I thought about how it would be if I never left. Before I could say anything to her about it, she told me she had to get back to work. She said I could stay the weekend, but on Monday morning I had to go. Bright and early, she had my things packed neatly in my suitcase, and she showed me the door. She kissed me on the cheek and said, "Maybe the next time you're in Paris we can get together again."

I wasn't sure what I had missed in our relationship, but clearly things between us were not as I assumed. Not wanting to let on how I felt, I said, "Maybe I will. I had a good a time, thanks for the hospitality."

She opened the door for me and said, "Goodbye, Percy."

I walked to the lift. She called after me. I turned and faced her.

"Maybe you could call me in a month or so?"

I smiled and waved goodbye.

I went across the street to a tobacco shop. I spent a few minutes in the store, picking out some Monte Cristo cigars. When I came out of the shop, my eyes were drawn across the street to Neddi's apartment building, and I saw the American boy from the Moulin Rouge. *That's trouble*, I thought. But then I realized that he knew where she lived. He was looking at his watch and pacing back and forth in front of the entrance. I watched from the side of a building, where I couldn't be seen. Neddi came out of her building and greeted him with a hug and kiss. I didn't like it, and I didn't know what was going on in her mind, but I wasn't finished with Miss Neddi Loire.

I took a room in a boarding house near the Lido club, and frequented the private rooms at the club with courtesans. It was an expensive diversion. But all the sex and drugs in Paris couldn't make me forget Neddi. Even with everything I knew, I wanted to be with her. I fought the urge to contact her.

I made myself known around the Paris hot spots, and let her friends know where I was. It took some time, but I was told she was coming to the Lido Club to see me. I was expecting a delivery of drugs the night I expected her to come. I trusted my dealer, but even so, I always checked things out in the manager's office before I paid.

When the dealer came, I followed him into the office. As the door closed, Neddi's young man stepped in behind me. He pressed a knife against my back.

"You have money for me?" the dealer asked.

I wasn't sure if it was a holdup or a murder. "For the goods, I do."

"Give it to me!" the dealer demanded.

"It's in my pocket." I started to move my hand.

The boy pressed the knife harder against my back. "Don't move."

"Let off the knife and I'll give you the fucking money."

"Give him some room, Carl," the dealer said.

That was his mistake. I brought out my Derringer, and spun around. I put it in right in Carl's face and fired a shot. I turned on the dealer. He was reaching for the knife that had fallen to the floor. I shot him at point-blank range. I took the bag with the drugs and exited the building by a side door. I left Paris in a hurry that evening. I headed west by rail, with no plan, and no feeling of studied purpose.

Michael Shure

Chapter 19

It was late summer in the summer of 1936, when I reached Spain. There were gallant foreigners serving on all sides of the Civil War, but there was no gallantry. They were doing their service to Spain by killing Spaniards. There was no *mano* à *mano* combat to the sound of clashing blades; there were only aviators cutting down the Republican cavalry from the sky, and tanks running down foot soldiers.

The Nationalists spouted off about the rule of law and how Franco was the answer to all the country's problems. They had the support of Germany and Italy, and that got them sophisticated weaponry. The Loyalists turned to invoking the name of God, but I didn't see any evidence that *He* cared what was happening on the Iberian Peninsula. Or perhaps the involvement of the Communists deflected *His* interest.

It was to be the first step in what was to come for all of Europe. France would be the biggest loser of all. All her holdings in the world were at risk. The Japanese invaded Indochina, and the French African colonies were as good as gone, too. In my mind, the French deserved whatever they got. Vive la France!

There were Americans serving in the International Brigade, and they tried to get me to join them, but they were on a suicide mission, and I wasn't about to join them or anyone else. The Spanish

Civil War was not a war for a man like me. And I was getting too old for that kind of thing. I'd heard it said that some people age from the outside in and others from the inside out. Even though I was in my early sixties, I felt fit; I figured I was one of the latter. The conflict held no profit for the fighters; the winners would only get to perpetuate their specific agenda of hatred. To me, it seemed that the war was about governments at their very worst, and nothing more. I would have solved part of the problem by kicking out all the newspapermen, and stopping a lot of the boys from pouring in from all over the world. They were lured by the stories in the press. The romantic bullshit the journalists spewed got an awful lot of young men killed. There was no romance in Spain – only carnage.

In Madrid, posters for bullfights were plastered everywhere. They were silent messengers, directing people to the Plaza de Toros. I followed the signs to the Plaza, walking on the cobblestone streets that Roman legions had traveled two thousand years before. I was told that the bullfights at Las Ventas were supposed to be nonpolitical; perhaps they were, but the streets that led to Las Ventas were certainly very political. The powerful wanted to control access, because Las Ventas was to bullfighting what Mecca was to Islam.

The walls of the Las Ventas arena rose higher with each step I took toward them. They blocked the sun and cast long shadows on the neighborhoods to the north. The arena's battlements were an architectural barrier against the forces that wanted to end the blood sport. But Las Ventas' very presence ensured the survival of its bloody culture.

In the center of the Plaza de Toros, a large statue of a matador fighting a bull presided over the courtyard. I saw a sign with an arrow pointing to the arena office. My clothes were ragged and soiled from my trip, but it was the perfect attire for me to wear for a job interview where my sole ambition was to muck stalls.

Through the office window I saw a fat, ugly woman sitting alone at her desk, facing the door. I opened the door and stood there with my suitcase in my hand, and waited for her to say something.

The woman looked up from her desk at me, made a face, and shook her head. "¡Vete!" she shrilled.

I wasn't leaving; I was there for a job. I told her in a soft voice that I wanted work; I was humble in tone, but purposeful. She looked up at me and said there was no work to be had, and asked me to leave. I stood my ground. "Realmente necesito trabajo, complazca la dama," I pled with her.

She stared at me. "¡Jesús!" she yelled.

She looked at me, wrinkled her nose, and sniffed several times. I got the message, and I backed up several paces. The general manager, Jesús Corvalán, came out of an adjoining office. He was a well-dressed, short, swarthy man, with thick, black hair combed straight back and parted in the middle. I bowed and said, "Complazca al señor, me gustaría obtener trabajo."

"¿Usted es Mejicano?" Jesús asked.

"No, señor. Soy Norte Americano."

"American. That's wonderful. Where in America are you from?" Jesús asked with a pronounced British accent.

"I'm from New Orleans – New Orleans, Louisiana!" I said proudly. Jesús didn't say anything. I waited a moment and then asked, "Are you from England?"

He told me he wasn't, but that he had lived in England with his parents when he was a boy. He was impatient with me, and asked what I was doing in Spain. I told him I was passing through and needed a job. He said he didn't have anything, and said I would find that things were tough around Madrid.

I told him I would take anything. He fiddled with his mustache and said, "You can hang around and eat staff leftovers tonight. There's always a little something left after everyone eats. And you can stay over in the barn for the night, if you choose."

I thanked him for his kindness. He smiled, pointed me to the door, and said, "The stable hands eat at the commissary. It's out the door and then to the right, Mr. Jefferson."

That evening I ate well and slept in an empty stable. The next day I stayed around Las Ventas and prospected for work with the keepers and the grooms. I got food and a place to sleep, in exchange for walking the horses and cleaning their stalls. I lived off the generosity of the people who worked around the stables. My life settled into a comfortable routine. I felt safe there in the sheltered world of Las Ventas, while the civil war raged on in Spain.

Two years into my stay, Jesús' wife of twenty years ran off with a matador's agent. He was devastated. He started to spend time with me around the stables. Jesús just needed a sympathetic ear, and I was there. As poor and down-and-out as he thought I was, he greeted me with a friendly smile whenever he saw me. He liked to speak in English, and he spent a lot of time with me. He said he wanted to give me a job, but he had no money to pay me. I understood, and any money he would have paid me would have been incidental to my circumstances, anyway.

Jesús had a taste for wine, and I liked rum, but it didn't take him long to acquire a taste for my drink. Rum and cigars were the things I spent my gold on, and Jesús was happy to share them with me. My drinking buddy let me commandeer a large shed and convert it into a residence. I viewed the rum and cigars I shared with him as a form of rent. I did, however, wonder where he thought I got the money to pay for it, but he never asked and I never made an issue of it.

Jesús had trouble getting past his wife's leaving him. I encouraged him to go out with some of the women who came to the fights, but he didn't handle that well. Then I fixed him up with some paid dates, but all he wanted to do was talk about his wife. The putas didn't mind the conversation, but it got to be very old with me. When I was with a woman, the last thing I wanted to do was talk about another woman. But he paid his money, and he was entitled to spend the time in any way he saw fit.

Early one morning, I was hung over from a night of heavy drinking, when Jesús showed up at my shed with a guitar. He was full of piss and vinegar and started to play. I asked him what he thought he was doing. He said, "Playing a tune, amigo."

I told him to cut the shit. He said it was time for him to start enjoying life again. He had met Carmelita and he was in love. I said, "You got laid, didn't you, you son of a bitch!"

He laughed. "Hey, I just thought you'd like to hear some music!"

"Not this early, Jesús!"

"I love the guitar any time, day or night." He strummed as he talked.

He fancied himself something of a virtuoso, but he wasn't very good. "Give me that thing, boy." I reached out for the guitar.

"Hey!"

"Just give it here! I took it, and played and sang, *Massa's in de Cold, Cold Ground.* When I finished, I handed the guitar back to Jesús. He looked at me funny, and told me he would be back in the evening around eight. I told him I would be around, as I didn't have anywhere to go.

Later that evening, he brought me an old guitar. After that, his visits always featured us playing the guitars. There were still times we drank too much rum, and we talked about our lost loves. He had had terrible luck with women. His wife wasn't the first to leave him. He started talking about going to England one day and finding his first love. I, on the other hand, was content to talk about finding my next love – or next *loves*, for that matter.

The war in Spain ended in March 1939, and I decided to stay on in Madrid. Jesús had supported the Nationalists, and he was reaping the benefits of their victory. I continued my friendship with him, and was happy at Las Ventas. But things changed when his broken heart mended. He grew distant, and a competition built between us, most noticeably where women were concerned. He tried to outdo me in little things, and I probably didn't help matters any by always rising to the challenge.

One Sunday afternoon in the summer of 1939, Jesús and I were drinking in my shed and swapping stories, when he unexpectedly stopped laughing. He said, "In a few minutes, some brave boys will face death in the ring."

"Yeah, so what's that got to do with anything?" I laughed.

"I was wondering what it would be like to be in the ring with a bull."

"Hell, there ain't nothing to it!" I said cavalierly.

He took exception to my joking, and said, "More of your big talk!"

I said, "Hell, I knocked bulls down in the ring with a sledgehammer back in Monterrey."

Jesús growled, "You're full of shit!"

I told him he was the one who was full of shit. Then he called me an asshole. I said, "If I say I can do something, I can do it."

He threw his hands up and said, "No one can do that!" I was going to let it drop right there. But he shouted at me, "Admit you're full of shit!"

I tried to make light of it. I told him that when I was a boy, I'd rope bulls and ride them. But he wouldn't let it go. He mumbled, "Riding some old bull in a pasture is easy."

"Easy, my ass! Maybe the bulls were a little smaller back in Mexico, but they were some mean critters," I said.

"All fucking talk," he sneered.

"If I tell you I can take a bull down with a sledgehammer, I can do it!"

"Bullshit!" he shouted at the top of his lungs.

He was mad. I credited his misbehavior to too much rum. But he kept on about it, and said I was full shit. I took a new tack and agreed that I may have been a little full of it.

He said angrily, "I want to see you knock a bull down!" He gulped down the last of my rum, and said, just as plain as you please, "You don't know shit, man!"

Then I got mad. "If I say I can bring down a bull with a sledge-hammer, I can bring down a bull with a sledgehammer!"

"Yeah! Yeah!" He laughed. "How much you want to bet?

I jumped right on it. "Loser pays for drinks for a year."

There we were, two drunks, making a wager to be settled with alcohol. The terms of the bet were that I had to knock a bull down. If he was still alive, I was to look at Jesús like he was a Caesar, and see if he wanted me to kill the bull. If I did it, he would buy the rum for a year.

If I lost the bet, Jesús wanted me to buy him wine for the same length of time. He said he was tired of drinking cheap rum. That pissed me off. I paid for that rum, and it was anything but cheap.

Jesús told the manager I was going into the ring. He said I was crazy and tried to reason with me. But I wouldn't budge, so he asked me to postpone the match so he could arrange for it properly. When that failed, he pled with me to reconsider for my own safety. Finally, he told me it was inappropriate to deviate from the program and he just couldn't do it.

Jesús pulled rank and told the manager to get things ready for me to go into the ring. I wanted to wear a matador's outfit and insisted on it. Jesús searched the lockers for an outfit, but he couldn't find one to fit me. I was much too big for anything they had.

Jesús accused me of trying to get out of going into the ring. I told him I wanted to look like I belonged there. He said the best he could do was a dark brown maintenance uniform. The pants were a little too short and the shirt was a little too small, but I wore the outfit anyway. I looked like a fool. The crowd buzzed when they realized I had a sledgehammer in my hand. I looked around the stands and waved at the crowd. There was silence until the trumpet sounded, and then the stands came alive with hoots and whistles.

A moment later, the gate opened and the cheers got louder when a big, reddish bull rushed into the ring. Then there was a hush in the arena as the picadors approached the bull. The bull pawed the ground, lowered his head, and charged one of the men on his horse.

"¡Olé!" the crowd roared. There was a pause, and then another "¡Olé!" Then still another pause as a picador stuck his pick deep into the bull's neck, then another roar of, "¡Olé!"

The bulls I had dealt with in Monterrey were smaller than the bulls in Spain, but they hadn't faced skilled picadors like they had at Las Ventas. The picadors dug their picks into the bull, and the crowd responded to each thrust. The bull was cagey and charged toward one picador, and then spun around and pinned another picador and his mount against the wall of the ring. The bull turned and charged again and again, and its only reward was cuts to its neck. The bull weakened, and my confidence grew as the picadors finished their job and the banderilleros came in and danced around the bull. The crowd responded "¡Olé!" as each of the banderillas found its place on the back of the bull's neck. I got more help when the novices rushed out, and they turned the bull around and around in wide circles with their capes. The crowd cheered after each pass by the bull.

I was in the ring with a sixteen-pound sledgehammer in my hand. I held my shoulders back and walked to the center of the ring. I looked around at the crowd, and held the hammer over my head with both hands for them to see. There was a hush when they realized I was going to fight the bull with a sledgehammer. There was a gasp when the bull started toward me. One of the banderilleros saw me and took it upon himself to distract the bull. The bull turned and made a pass at him.

"Back off," I shouted and I waved at the banderilleros to go away. I motioned to the picadors too, and they backed off.

The bull stood with its head down, pawing at the ground. Blood flowed from the wounds in its neck. He was breathless and seemed tired. The crowd hissed and whistled its disapproval of me; I loved it. I held my left hand up to still the crowd. The bull moved to face me. I stood motionless. In my uniform, I blended in with the retaining walls and he lost sight of me. I studied his every movement. He was different from the Mexican bulls in more than just size. The Mexican bulls charged straight ahead, but this guy moved to the right and then veered to the left.

I started toward the bull and he spotted me. Every time I moved, it turned to face me. I moved to the bull's left to keep its head turning to the left. Then it made a sudden start. The crowd jumped to its feet, screaming, but fell quiet when the bull stopped in its tracks. It started again and then stopped again. But each time it slowed up, it snapped its head to the left. It would dip its head to the right, and then snap it to the left. I kept walking slowly toward it. The crowd roared louder with my every step.

When I got to within five meters of the bull, it charged. I stopped in my tracks and readied myself, but the bull stopped when I stopped. I took a couple more steps toward it. The bull didn't move. The crowd whistled and catcalled. I heard, "¡Toro! ¡Toro!" *The crowd was rooting for that damn bull!*

I needed the bull to charge straight at me so I could get a clean swing at its head. I walked toward him again, and again he made a false start. I moved closer and it backed off. It spun around and charged a picador, ramming his horse. But it charged, true to its form. If it did that when it came at me, it was mine. But I needed it to charge me.

I made a false start toward him, and got his attention; then I turned and ran. He chased me, and things began to move fast. I could feel it gaining on me; I spun around and faced it. I raised the sledgehammer over my left shoulder and took a step toward the bull. I was ready. The bull was closing fast, and I started my swing just before it reached me. I stepped to the left and avoided its horns and swung the sledgehammer with all my might. Its head was exposed as it veered to the left and the hammer hit it with the combined force of my swing and its momentum. A loud cracking sound echoed through the stadium. The bull fell dead at my feet. There was pandemonium in the arena. There had to be some benefit to what I had just done, but *the orphans will eat well tonight*, was all I could think.

When I got to Jesús, he was shaking his head in disgust and wonder. I was an old man who had just bested one of his prized bulls. It made me feel like I did when I was 30. I pointed to the bull and laughed. The crowd's eyes were all on me, and they were cheering.

It turned out that General Franco had come to the fights, and was in the stands, cheering right along with the rest of the crowd.

Jesús pointed out Franco to me, and asked me to wave and then bow in his direction. I did, because I didn't want to give Jesús a reason to renege on our bet. The general nodded toward me and applauded.

A matador cut off the bull's ears and tail and held them up. The crowd roared its approval. He motioned me to the center of the ring. He handed me the ears and the tail. I held them up for the crowd to see.

Jesús wanted a show, and I was going to give him one. I climbed into the stands, and went to where General Franco was with his entourage. Nobody stopped me. I got close to him, and I stopped and held out the ears and the tail. An aide took them from me and handed them to the general. He held them up, and the crowd went wild.

General Franco took off his wristwatch and motioned me to come closer. I climbed the last three steps very slowly. Franco held my shoulders and kissed me on both cheeks. Then he smiled and offered me his hand. I had no choice, took it, and he handed me his watch with his other hand. I held the watch up and waved to the crowd.

I became a celebrity, and that changed things for Jesús. The time we spent together took on new importance for him, but for me, the balance in our relationship was gone. I felt different when I was drinking the rum he paid for, and he acted differently too. He started to keep track of how much each of us drank. The real topper, though, was the watch that Franco gave me; I think my having it drove him nuts.

My ring appearance created extra business for Las Ventas, and as the crowds grew, so did the tale of my exploit. People clamored for another match for me and my sledgehammer. The owners of the Las Ventas were eager to put it on and wanted to do it quickly. They told Jesús to arrange it. He tried to talk me into another match, and when I wouldn't go along with it, he said I would have to leave. It didn't matter to me. I was ready to move on anyway.

The world was still suffering from a catastrophic depression, and there was still a sense of hopelessness from the Spanish Civil War that still festered all around us at Las Ventas. I told everyone at Las Ventas that I liked my life in Madrid, and I entertained no thoughts of leaving. I stayed in contact with my friends in Africa, but I didn't conduct any business with them. I also told them I planned to stay in Spain. But I had been lying to myself and to everyone else. I found out in 1936 that Schätze really was my son, when I wired Fritz and got a wire back from my son. He told me I was a grandfather and that my granddaughter, Pearl, had my green eyes. That's all it took for me to realize that I had made a mistake. I wired Schätze and told him I was coming to the United States to be with him.

Three days after I sent the wire to my son, I got a cable from Helga telling me my son had been murdered. My joy turned to sorrow; my mother was murdered, my father was murdered, and now my son had been murdered. I was mad at God, and turned my back on *Him*. I didn't go to America. I'm not sure whether I was mourning the boy, or feeling sorry for myself. I never responded to the wire, or to any of the wires that followed. Helga wrote me letters about my granddaughter Pearl, and after a time, she wrote me about Fritz's deteriorating health. I read and reread the letters, but I couldn't bring myself to answer them. She stopped writing in the fall of 1938.

I wanted to leave behind all the hurt I felt about never knowing my son, and to move on. I reached out to James and found him in England. He offered me a deal in Portugal, and I planned to take it. As I was arranging to leave, the unexpected happened: I received a personal invitation to fight another bull, from none other than

Generalissimo Francisco Franco himself. I postponed my trip. Who was I to say no to El Caudillo? The stage was set for another match. I avoided Jesús; I wanted to be left to myself until the day of the fight.

The Las Ventas management went all-out to promote the contest. They put out posters and banners all over Spain. The radio covered the story, and it was headline news in all the papers. General Franco was quoted every day, and photographs of the first contest were everywhere. I was worried, because all the excitement and pictures of me was not a good thing. I was still a wanted man in some parts of the world. My appearance hadn't changed much, and I was worried that they were still looking for me.

As the time for the contest drew near, the detractors began with their theories. One reporter claimed that there was a gunshot fired just as the bull fell, and he quoted eyewitnesses in the paper. Believe me, the only person I knew who wanted that bull shot before he got to me, was me. Things were spiraling out of control. I kept a very low profile around the arena.

A week before the fight, I received a note from General Franco, together with a Spanish military uniform. The uniform was identical to the one he planned to wear to the arena. In place of his battle ribbons and military insignia, my uniform had plain epaulettes. In place of the service metals I was to wear two hand-cut silver pins, one saying *OLÉ* and the other, *MADRID*.

Franco thanked me for the service I was doing him in his effort to raise the morale of the Spanish people. He said that years of civil war had divided the nation, and he could envision the extravaganza reuniting his countrymen in sport. I saw it as something less noble, and would have been more committed if he had offered me money. But the only offer of any consequence that I had in quite a long time came from James Jefferson – his timing was uncanny. Even

155

though I had some trust issues with him, I allowed him to turn my head with talk of a golden opportunity he had for me in Lisbon.

By the day of the fight, I had decided to do the deal with James, and that made me even less committed to my task in the ring. When the crowd gathered at Las Ventas, I retired to my shed. I sat down with a glass of rum and I picked up my guitar and strummed a few chords. As I played, I reflected on the three years I'd spent in Spain – good years, but I knew that like everything else, they had to come to an end.

Time passed slowly, and I spent most of the day reviewing my options. I drank heavily, and when it was time to go into the ring, I was in no condition to face a bull. I never really intended to do it anyway. The special invitation from Franco was flattering, but that wasn't enough to motivate me. I didn't like his politics. And anyway, I knew I was lucky the first time, and I would never have done it then if I hadn't been so drunk. I wasn't about to tempt fate again.

I dug up the gold I had buried under my bed and put it in my money belt. I slipped a specially-fashioned 24-karat gold link necklace around my neck, and slipped into an old shirt to cover it up. I put on my old sandals and poured a final glass of rum. I stood to drink a final toast to my time in Madrid, and just as I did, a teenage boy with a knife broke into the shed. He had come with a group of Basque separatists who wanted to kill Franco.

The boy threatened me with the knife. I slowly raised my hands to show that all I had was a glass of rum. I told him I was on his side, and to just let me be. I offered him a drink.

He said I had an accent and was one of the men who fought the war against his people. I tried to reason with him. He would have nothing of it. I took a step toward him and held out the glass. The boy looked down at the glass, and as soon as he lowered his eyes, I was on him. I shook the knife from his hand and knocked him to the ground. He grabbed for the knife, but I had my Derringer out and fired a single shot. With all the noise outside the shed, no one heard it.

I felt bad for the boy. There was no reason he had to die that day. I had already made up my mind to leave the arena, and all I wanted to do was to slip out quietly. My instincts cost the boy his life – I couldn't avoid it. And he wasn't the only young Basque to die that day; he was only the first. Franco's men slaughtered the insurgents before they reached him in the stands.

I moved the boy's body over to the hole where I had dug up my gold. He was an unusually large boy, almost my size. I tried to put my uniform on him but it proved to be too difficult to do, so I laid the clothes across his body. I went to the garage, got a can of petrol, and brought it back. I took my watch off and put it on the boy's wrist, and then poured some of the petrol on him. I lit it and his clothes caught fire.

The sight of the boy's burning body made me think about when I was a boy, and when I got my pistol from my father. I thought about how happy it had made me then, but how sad it made me feel to have used it on the boy. I didn't want to be like my father, but sometimes I wondered if I was, in some ways. Not in the way he treated women – for sure, he treated my mother shamefully, and I will hate him for that through all of eternity. My father was a killer, a thief, and a liar, but that doesn't mean everything he told me was a lie. One thing he told me back then, that I believed, was that if someone suspects you have a hidden weapon on you, they won't let you get close enough to use it. So my rule was, never let anyone know you have it. And you always have it on you, or you'll never have it when you need it. Don't flash it, and when you bring it out, use it.

Smoke and a vile smell filled the shed. I threw gasoline on my bed and on the walls. I poured more on the boy, and it burst into flames. As I left the shed, I threw the can in behind me. The whole place burst into flames.

The guard at the service entrance left his post and headed for the shed, and I slipped out of Las Ventas unnoticed, just minutes before my fight was scheduled to start. I left behind what I couldn't carry to be burned in the fire. I walked slowly for several blocks down a narrow alley that led away from the arena, and then turned onto a tree-lined street that went past the city park. I looked up; it was a beautiful, sunny day – and the good *Lord* knows how I love sunny days.

Chapter 20

From the harbor I could see more than a dozen tar-covered ropes, each the thickness of a ballerina's leg, extending out into the water to pediments anchored in bedrock more than a mile out. Along the ties, a thousand small vessels of every size and description were tied off, forming an impromptu marina around which shallow-drafted landing vessels motored about, offering to taxi people and products ashore.

The ancient port bristled with portents of a sea-change in national dynamics that made the petty quarrels of the city Dons pale to nothing. Even the ancient relics were resonant with the sense of impending change. October 1939 was a perfect time for me to go to Lisbon.

It was the last great market of the year, and the Praia dos Marineiros teemed with humanity. Its semicircular colonnade, known to voyagers since the Saracen invasion, formed a boundary of steps and pillars separating the marketplace from the city proper. Here the National Guardsmen stood in twos, their carbines slung over their shoulders to ensure clear demarcation.

Beyond the guards, Lisbon arose pale pink, yellow, and blue, toward the top of a high plateau where the home guard was quartered and the government houses occupied positions of authority.

Further on was the modern city – the brick houses and concrete apartment buildings; the right angles and parallel causeways; the broad ways and auto-filled, tree-lined avenues; the brave, new, and ugly sections where almost everyone lived. Here also was the Arena Navigador – the bullring with its gloomy façade, withered bannerettes, and peculiar odor reminiscent of Las Ventas.

I had a corner room at the Pension Camões, overlooking the great market to the north and the harbor to the east. My room had three tall, shuttered windows that swung like narrow doorways onto a small wrought-iron balcony. I looked out at the market in the late evening and absorbed its exotic smells and intoxicating sounds. The pensioneer presented me with a bottle of sturdy port when I registered. Pieces of cork were scattered across the top of a small wooden lamp table as I sipped the wine and contemplated the spectacle of lights and sounds that came like a gentle breeze off the water. I would have preferred a fifth of rum, but by midnight my mood was mellow, and I raised my glass to a young gypsy woman below who glared at me, then disappeared into the darkness. Still, I waited for her. I spread out on my bed with no pillow and only a linen sheet drawn over my body.

I heard footsteps shuffling across the landing, people fumbling for keys, stifled coughs and occasional laughter. She never knocked, but I dreamt she did. She padded in and, without a word, removed her shift and lay it neatly across my feet. I felt its weight and the motion of the mattress as she settled beside me. She lay motionless, facing the ceiling, and we passed the night like two mannequins. When I awoke, she was gone. The windows were still open, and the shutters creaked on their hinges. It was cold, and I felt an ache in my soul.

I walked to the divided panes of the east window where the sunlight streamed in, warm against my skin. Far across the river I saw the towering cranes of Setubal unloading the big cargo ships and realized that the fortunes of Lisbon's ancient harbor had changed. Setubal was becoming Portugal's great commercial link with the rest of the world while Lisbon slipped into shady business built on three pillars of corruption – a declining empire, an insecure dictator, and war. I looked back into the room and caught a glimpse of myself in the mirror. I saw myself, as I was: an old man – an old man in an old city.

My mind did not run to great causes or intellectual musings. Those were the pastimes of the well-born, the idle educated and their wealthy patrons. Those were the preoccupations of university students who sipped coffee and munched hard bread at sidewalk cafés, who denounced governments and potentates and argued the merits of anarchy. I could see some of them clustered near the Restaurante Gallo. I wondered if I envied them in some way.

One held a placard with writing on it, but I didn't strain to read it. I instead felt a wave of disinterest and a sense of futility. I disliked them and the academic way they wanted to reshape the world. One day they would be old and realize that all they had done was carry signs, which accomplishes nothing. I wondered who paid for and profited from their ink. In the end, it would all be of no consequence.

I dressed and went casually down three flights of stairs. "I'm waiting for a gentleman who will ask for me by name," I said to Omar, the swarthy, rotund innkeeper who well understood both the importance of discretion and the advantages of not abiding by it. His children clambered noisily around the desk and chased themselves through the open porch that served as a lobby.

"Shall I fetch you then, sir?" Omar asked obsequiously.

"No. You will give him this letter."

Omar's nostrils quivered, and his eyes darkened with interest.

He stared at me until my contemptuous gaze cowed him. I turned and left the hotel. The sense of Omar fingering the envelope and his nearly irresistible urge to open it was palpable. I knew he would find some way to get at the contents. I also knew he would have no way to know what to make of them.

It wasn't just the money that drew me back, I had missed the action. On my way to meet my contact at a bar in Lisbon, I thought of the Portuguese I sailed with in the Caribbean. They were scruffy little fellows who would gamble on anything. By the end of each tour, more likely then not, they owed their whole pay to someone or other. Bamboozling them out of their ration of rum was easy, too.

James hated the Portuguese because of his dealings with them in Angola. He said that the little buggers would pay their hard-earned money to watch monkeys fuck. He once told me, "Take them for whatever you can, whenever you can – because if you don't get it from them, someone else will." He didn't hate them enough not to do business with them, but it was going to be easier for me to do the deal than him, because I held no animosity toward them.

I always wondered why the Portuguese didn't make new friends or seek companionship from anyone outside their own culture. Even as a nation, they formed no alliances. Before the German invasion of Poland in September 1939, Portugal had declared its neutrality and made Lisbon an open city. Within a month of the German attack on Poland, all the traffickers and traders from around the world came to Lisbon to move their goods. Diplomats, undercover agents and spies, all converged on Lisbon. Every kind of dirty dealing you could imagine went on there.

It was perfect in James' mind, but his deal was all about gold – I wanted more than that. I wanted to deal in diamonds, too. I would make James' gold deal happen, because it was big, but the side action in diamonds was to be all mine.

I found the bar on the waterfront. It was sleazy – just sleazy enough, I figured, to promise financial opportunity. As I entered the bar, I felt far removed from what I had felt in the morning at the hotel. Whatever melancholy had beset me there, was gone. I felt young and full of life. I was ready for action. I took a seat at the bar, "I'll have a bottle of rum."

The bartender ignored me. "I'll have rum!" I repeated. He still ignored me. "Get the fuckin' rum!" I shouted.

The bartender gestured for me to show him money. I took a link from my gold chain and put it on the bar. The bartender reached for it. I grabbed his arm and held onto him. "I'll have the rum first."

The bartender winced, but wouldn't let go of the link. I tightened my grip and twisted his arm. "Fuck you!" he shouted, as he let the gold link fall to the bar.

"If it's not too much trouble, would you be kind enough to bring my rum now?"

The hair on my neck stood up, and my hand went into my pocket. I felt the presence of a man next to me. "Is there a problem here?" he asked.

"What business is it of yours?"

"I'm the owner."

He was my contact. I took my hand off the pistol. "There's no problem," I said.

"What can I do for you, *viajante inglês?*"

He was looking for a password. He was to call James *the English traveler*, and James was to say *Greetings from the king*. But I said, "Get me some rum!" I wanted to feel the man out and see what kind of edge I could get. If these people wanted to do the deal with me, they would do it my way.

He said to the bartender, "Give my friend here some rum!" He moved away to the end of the bar.

The bartender poured a glass of rum and slid it in front of me. I drained the glass in one gulp. When I pushed it toward the bartender, I said, "I'll take a bottle. Make it island rum this time."

He looked to the owner for approval, and then put a bottle of Cuban rum on the bar. I took my gold link from the bar and grabbed the bottle of rum. I walked to the back of the cantina and sat down at an empty table.

I motioned to the owner, and called out, "We have to talk." I held up the gold link. He came to the table. "Sit down," I said.

"You're playing a dangerous game," he said. "Do you have my gold, *viajante inglês?*"

I shrugged. "Maybe," I said. He was still waiting for the password. I didn't cooperate. He jumped up from his chair and called the bouncer over. I turned my chair so I could see him. "This is Pepe. He's here, so you'll tell me if you have the gold you're supposed to have for me," the owner said.

"And why does Pepe want me to do that?"

I had pushed it, but it wouldn't have mattered if I hadn't. I had to change the deal, and I was sure the Germans had picked up my proposal from Omar at the hotel. There was no turning back. I couldn't let my contact think he was in control of anything.

Pepe reached for my shoulder. I grabbed his hand and spun around. I swung my arm over his, and had his arm extended and twisted. The speed and the force of my move threw him off balance. I pushed with all my weight against his extended arm until it snapped. He fell to the floor. I was on him in a flash, and held my Derringer to his temple.

"What kind of devil are you?" the owner screamed at me.

"Who's asking?" I said with my pistol pointed at Pepe's head.

"Paulo Méndez," he said nervously.

I introduced myself and told him James sent his regards from the king. He asked why James hadn't come himself. I told him that he was ill and I was his partner. He asked me to let his man go. I took the gun from Pepe's head and motioned to him to get up. Méndez waved him away.

"Any questions?" I asked.

"Why didn't you use the password?"

"I don't use passwords."

"It would have made things a lot easier if you had," he said.

"But I don't use passwords."

"We'll have to work around it. Let's start over. My friends call me Méndez." He held out his hand.

I didn't take it. "They call me Percy," I said.

"What about the gold you have for me?" he asked.

"There's a lot of gold," I said.

"When can I see it?"

"When I get money, you get gold."

"You get paid when you deliver the gold. That's the way it works," Méndez said. He was getting unnerved.

"I get paid first. Then I deliver the gold." I walked back to the table and sat down. I took the bottle of rum and filled a glass and offered the bottle to Méndez. He shook his head.

I set the bottle down. "When you prepay an account at my bank in Switzerland, then I deliver the gold."

"That's not how it was supposed to be," Méndez argued.

"If you want the gold, that's how it will be."

"I can't...."

"Am I to understand that the terms are unacceptable?"

He was nervous. "Not exactly...."

"What are you trying to say, Méndez?"

"Look around you. Does it look to you like I have that kind of money?" Méndez looked around his bar, then back at me.

"I suspect there's money someplace. There usually is."

"My people won't advance any money."

"How do you know that?"

"They say they won't front any money."

"I get my money deposited before I deliver."

"It's not like you think."

I shook my finger at Méndez. "I have come a long way to see you! I was told that a deal was going to happen here. You'd better say something I want to hear."

"There's nothing I can say!"

"You'd better say something," I said.

"You don't know these people. You don't want me to tell them about you!"

"You're going to have to tell someone, or the deal's dead."

Méndez glared at me.

"Where do they think the gold is coming from?" I asked.

"They don't want to know where it's from. It's cash on delivery."

"Cash through a third party!"

"We have the gold first," he said.

"You'll get the gold."

"Good, then we have a deal?" He held out a hand.

I took his hand and held it tight. "A deal! You think I'm going to be some place sitting on top of a ton of gold? No. I'll put the gold in the same bank you put the money in. Don't tell me the Swiss don't want to use their own bank. You'd best be careful what you say next, Méndez."

He made a face, but didn't say anything.

166

"I want to deal direct with your people!" I said. I knew from the size of the deal that I was dealing with the Swiss government. I was in with the Germans, and using their gold.

"That won't work," he said.

"You make it work!"

"I can't!" Méndez was sweating. "You're hurting my hand!"

"You will. You have to," I said.

"No. That will never happen."

"Call Pepe over here," I said.

"Why?"

"I want to ask him something."

"That's not a good idea."

I motioned Pepe over to me. He came over slowly, nursing his arm, and stood next to Méndez.

"I want you to tell Mr. Méndez just how bad your arm hurts."

"I think it's broken," Pepe said.

"I think you should go get it fixed." I turned to Méndez. "Right, Méndez?"

"Yeah, it's okay," Méndez said shakily.

Pepe left. Méndez was alone with me, and he was scared.

"What now?" he asked.

"We set up a meeting with your buyer."

"I can't do that. They won't meet with anyone but me."

"They'll have to."

Méndez wasn't a smuggler. It was obvious he had never dealt with any contraband, except maybe an occasional watch or ring. Méndez had become involved in the deal through a Swiss banker who had befriended his father-in-law in Lisbon. The banker put Méndez and his father-in-law together with James to handle a gold transaction with the Germans. The banker told them that no matter what happened, they were to keep his name out of it.

We stood looking at each other. "Let me call them and ask if they'll meet," he said. "That's the best I can do."

"No. Let's go see them."

"I can't do it."

"You don't have a choice! If you know how to call them, then you know how to find them," I said. I had my hand in my pocket. I motioned for him to leave.

Méndez was paralyzed with fear. I pushed him, and he moved stiffly toward the door. He looked around, hoping someone would see what was happening and help him. The bartender had his back to us; he had no intention of turning around until we were gone.

Outside the bar, I asked, "Which way?" I had the pistol stuck in his side.

He didn't move. I told him that if I didn't meet his partners by four o'clock, my gun was going off. He walked without saying a word, and soon we were standing in front of the Swiss Embassy.

Everything fell into place. The German diplomats picked up my letter from the hotel and contacted Berlin. My terms were agreed to. I had lived among them long enough to know how their minds work. I predicated the deal on the premise that they had no intention of fulfilling their end of the bargain. But my plan had built-in safeguards for me.

In Germany, *Sieg heil! Heil, Hitler Dir!* had replaced *Mit Gott für König und Vaterland*. Blind loyalty to Der Führer replaced blind loyalty to Kaiser Wilhelm. All of the suppressed, festering resentments of the last hundred years were boiling to the surface. They had to win at everything. They had to profit on every deal and to hell with everyone else. I would use their greed against them. In this deal, it was *I* who would get *das Geld*.

Getting the money was only one of my concerns. The deal was

also about the war in Africa. The Zulu were still fighting for their land and for their independence from South Africa and Rhodesia. Matumbo needed modern guns. He was desperate and asked me to help him. To complicate his situation further, the Germans, Italians, French, Portuguese, Belgians, and British all were jockeying for position in Africa, killing off the natives who resisted them.

The Zulu's enemies had modern weapons. The days of stabbing spears and Zulu war parties had been over for a long time. Every encounter was a fight to the death. Small bands of Zulu gunmen continued to raid the De Beers outposts for diamonds. With James and me out of business, Matumbo couldn't get market price for the diamonds anymore. The Oppenheimer Cartel was winning.

Things had deteriorated, and Matumbo feared that his total defeat was imminent. The British reinforced their garrisons in South Africa and Rhodesia, and were cracking down on the Zulu tribes. I wasn't in a position to go to Africa to help. When Matumbo told me that he had contacted James, I knew things were at a low point for him.

James agreed to help Matumbo, but he demanded a big slice of the profit. He had developed contacts in Portugal when he was dealing weapons in Angola, who could pull off a deal large enough to help Matumbo. His plan was simple. James arranged to trade African diamonds for German gold, and then sell the gold for Swiss cash. He would buy guns and ammunition with some of the cash and keep the rest for himself. He set the plan in motion, but when he got sick, he contacted me. Doing the deal James' way would have been a cakewalk for him, but there wasn't enough in it for me. And, just as importantly, I didn't trust James' contacts in Lisbon.

I reworked the deal. My plan was more involved than the original one. First, I arranged for Matumbo's weapons. Getting Czech guns right there in Lisbon was no trouble. An arms glut drove the price down, which was good. The Germans were eager to get in on the deal. Guns for Zulu aligned against the British suited them just fine. They also wanted to swap gold for international currency, especially Swiss francs and American dollars. They agreed to get the deal moving by trading their gold for my diamonds. The Swiss jumped on the deal. They wanted the gold without having to acknowledge it came from the Nazis. That was the easy part.

Still, after everything was said and done, there was no profit for me, the way things stood. I needed to twist the deal to make it all worth my while. Matumbo shipped the diamonds hidden in chocolate bars to me in Lisbon, with the help of the Swiss embassy in Pretoria. I swapped them with the Nazis for the gold. I got the help I needed from the German and Swiss consulates.

The Swiss had their gold, the Germans had their diamonds, and Matumbo had his arms. The Swiss paid James' money to me. My cut depended on the Nazis delivering the diamonds to the Dutch for their payoff. The Dutch would deposit the money in my Swiss bank when they got the diamonds. I split the money into my share and the Germans' share. Once the diamonds were delivered, the diamond merchants made a call and released the money. They were glad to get diamonds under market, and they threw caution to the wind. That would be the last deal they would ever do.

I didn't trust anyone in Portugal, so I kept the end game all to myself. I had no love for the Germans, and I was determined to beat them out of their money, too. I wanted to win, and win *big*. I would measure the victory by how much money I ended up with.

Being the greedy bastards they were, the Germans agreed to my deal with the Dutch. They wanted hard currency and agreed to sell the diamonds at a discount. After the dominoes fell, the only thing left to happen was the Germans delivering the diamonds to the Dutch.

I had my plan, and the Germans had theirs. They were happy to see the weapons going to dissidents in South Africa, so they let the weapons deal happen. They occupied Czechoslovakia, and that took care of the Czech weapons. And the Swiss were happy with their end of the deal, too.

The German plan was elementary. They had the diamonds, and they planned to get the money for them from the Dutch, and then keep them. They had no intention of giving the diamonds up.

I made a bargain with the devil – De Beers. They were determined to recover what they knew was theirs, and they agreed to deal with me if they had to. They paid rewards to anyone who led them to their diamonds. My planned diamond delivery in Amsterdam went well for me, but not for the Germans or the Dutch. The diamond dealers that I set up were the ones who had tried to turn me in to De Beers. Turnabout was fair play.

I notified the Germans, and they killed the Dutch diamond merchants. The Dutch police and the De Beers agents were waiting for the Germans to leave. The Germans chose to fight and were killed by the De Beers agents. The Dutch police stood aside and watched.

The Oppenheimer people wanted to do more business, but I worried they were trying to zero in on me. I took my reward from De Beers, and headed straight for England to settle up with James.

Michael Shure

Chapter 21

The captain of our aging ship, *The Miranda,* set a course that put us ahead of the storm. In the waters off the northern coast of Ireland, our fishing luck was good. But our good fortune was short-lived when the weather turned bad; the hold was less than half full when we pulled our nets and made for open water. The captain slipped in behind the front, which came from the north. That left us with only one safe heading: southeast. We deadheaded for Portsmouth.

The Miranda churned into Portsmouth harbor. She was a nasty-looking ship whose rusted yardarms and battered hull commanded no respect. The crew was a sorry looking lot, too – men who couldn't crew on any other ship.

The captain enticed the crew in Lisbon with the promise of payment in hard currency. Portugal was a nation of fishermen, and while they were never known to be smart, they understood pounds sterling. I signed on *The Miranda* to get to England, where the money was. I knew where she was headed, even though the captain wouldn't say so. I would have preferred to book passage on a liner and go to England in style, but I bought a Portuguese passport in Lisbon, which wasn't good enough to get me a visa. But it was good enough to get me on *The Miranda*'s crew.

We made port hauling our small catch. I was ordered to the bow as we entered the harbor. A river tug nudged *The Miranda* into her berth. I threw the bowline to the pier and watched to make sure it was tied down tight.

The captain told us we would get a good price for our catch, but because it was small, our share would be small. But that was before we experienced problems on the pier. Union workers were not unloading for foreign fisherman. We flew the Portuguese flag and they challenged our registry, and claimed they didn't know who would benefit from the sale of our catch.

Men were milling around on the piers. They were the same union workers who refused to unload foreign ships, as well as scab laborers hired by shippers to get their cargo moved. There were bloody fights on the piers. In the face of that, the captain still decided to use non-union labor. The captain made sure the first load was secure on the pulley, and then tried to disembark. He got as far as the end of the gangway, where the Royal Marines turned him back. The harbor was off limits to all foreign seamen, and there would be no shore leave for any of us. The British Marines were there to enforce the edict.

The captain was furious, but he let the catch be unloaded when he was told that buyers would come to bid on it. The captain didn't think he had a choice. If he didn't unload the fish, they would spoil before he could make any other port.

There was a lot of movement on the pier, but little was getting done. Men moved back and forth with no seeming purpose. The carts weren't filling up. *The Miranda's* crew was working quickly, but the thieves on the dock were working just as fast.

The captain stopped the unloading. He shouted at the men on the pier who were handling the cargo. They were standing by and watching as the fish were stolen. The striking longshoreman had put the boys up to it, and they were sharing in the take.

The captain tried to disembark again. It took four guards to subdue him. All he got for his trouble were two nasty lumps on the head. The first mate and several of the crew tried to help him, but they were turned back at gunpoint. The marine guards on the dock made it very dangerous for anyone to try and jump ship there. But I was going over the side. I would make my entrance to England through the river.

A constable watched the altercation at the ship, but he wasn't disposed to helping any foreign sailors. We stopped unloading, and the constable came on board to talk to the captain. He arranged for a fishmonger to meet the captain and buy what was left of his catch. The captain again had no other choice.

The constable came back with the union boss. They met at the end of the gangway. "You used scabs;" the union boss said, "we 'ave strict rules!"

"I had no choice," the captain said in his broken English.

"You could've arranged for a local buyer," he said, "then the buyer would've arranged with me to unload your cargo."

"I want a buyer," the captain was resigned to his loss.

The union boss turned to a henchman on the dock. "Go get the Jew at the fish market," he said. He looked at the captain, "The Jew will buy what's left."

It took only a few minutes for the stevedore to return with Sylvan Feldman, a fish market owner. "He'll buy your fish," the constable paused. "Get this over with so you can be on you way. I want you sailing with the tide."

Feldman bought the fish, and the captain used the money to pay a ship chandler to stock the ship. The Royal Marines were making us leave with the tide, or face confiscation of the ship and incarceration of the crew.

We were being watched closely by the Marines. When we were done loading the stores, we were ordered to pull the gangway. The captain had had his fill of English hospitality. He stood on the deck and shouted obscenities at the men on shore. He railed on for a while, but when he tired of it, he headed to his quarters. He went by me, and I heard him mumble, "Thieving bastards."

"Aye, sir," I said.

He looked at me and grunted. He turned back and shouted more obscenities at the men on the dock. The crew cheered and egged him on. I used the commotion to slip below decks unnoticed. I pried up a board under my bunk and took out the package containing cash vouchers and letters of credit I'd gotten from my dealings in Lisbon. I took a canteen from my duffle and rolled the papers up, one by one, and put them in it. I tied the canteen to my money belt and secured it around my waist under my shirt.

I went on deck and slipped back in with the crew, unnoticed. The captain had bad news. There would be no shares for anyone, and he told us what we already knew – there would be no shore leave. Some of the men wanted to sneak ashore, but they changed their minds when they were told the British Marines had orders to shoot on sight. But I was already resolved to going over the side.

The crew was taunting the Marines, and I used that diversion to walk around the deck and scout the harbor. The ship was set to sail with the tide, and that left me little time to jump. I wanted to wait until dark to make my move, but we were casting off. I went to the stern, climbed over the railing, and let myself down as far as I could. Then I let go of the railing and went feet first into the murky water. I fell straight down. It was getting dark and the dock was poorly lit. The force of my entry took me all the way to the bottom, and I felt my feet go into the silt. I bent my knees, kicked up and started to ascend. At the surface, I gasped for air as I bobbed in the water. The force of the current at high tide helped me drift toward shore. I heard the captain call to the crew to cast off the last line. A tug had maneuvered into place to guide *The Miranda* out to open water. I ducked under the surface and swam slowly underwater, moving with the current. The water was colder than I had expected; my body began to ache, and I had trouble breathing.

I was in Satan's domain again, but I was determined to cheat him one more time. I swam as hard as I could for the dock. I was splashing and cursing the cruel fates as I fought my way through the water, and I didn't care who might be watching.

A strong current pushed me clear of the main dock. I stopped swimming and a feeling of peace overcame me. Then like a message from beyond, I heard my mother's voice say, "Never be fooled by the demons of the deep." I was almost frozen stiff, but I made for the shore with all that was left in me.

I have since apologized to the fates; they were good to me in the end. I pulled ashore at a small, private marina. There were three small fishing scows tied to a dock. I broke into the biggest of them, and went below and found a stack of canvas sails. I took off my clothes and wrapped myself up in the sails. I fell asleep thinking of all the warm places I could have gone to, if James hadn't made me feel obligated to personally deliver him his share of the money.

The next morning, I went to a second-hand store in Portsmouth and bought clothes. I took a train to London, and then a cab to James' apartment. To my surprise, his flat was in a very elegant section of London. I took the lift to his third floor flat, and rang the bell – but there was no answer. I put my ear to the door, and heard James inside.

"Let me in, you limey son-of-a-bitch!" I shouted.

"One damn minute, you 'eathen," he said. His voice cracked, and he was coughing.

"What are you doing in there?" I asked. He fumbled with the catch on the chain and the door swung open. He looked like death warmed over. I asked what was wrong with him.

He spoke slowly. "They tell me it's the rum." He laughed and coughed, "Yeah, they say it's the rum."

He hadn't eaten in days. I'd seen men die from drink before, and he was a goner. He reached out and gave me a hug. "I'm glad to see you, Percy," he said. He closed the door behind me and motioned me in, and offered me a chair in his sitting room. "What's the matter, Kaffir? Cat got your tongue?"

"Don't call me that."

"Huh?" He feigned surprise. "Well, fuck you!"

"Fuck yourself, limey!" I shouted.

"Maybe you like 'nigger' better?"

"Suit yourself, Mr. Jefferson."

"Thank you, Mr. Hays, I will."

We both laughed. "What happens now?" I asked.

"I die," he said, matter-of-factly.

"Just like that?"

"No. I 'ave to do what I 'ave to do, and I've been planning it ever since I got the word from the doctors."

"What the hell are you talking about?"

"I'm going to plan my death." James looked me in the eye. He leaned over to me and whispered, "I'm going to do it with drink!"

"That's suicide!" I laughed. "It'll keep you out of heaven."

"Who are you kidding? Like I was going to get in there anyway!" He put his arm around my shoulder. "Percy, truth be known,

I never figured 'ow to get in there. I fucked that up a long time ago. I made my 'eaven here on Earth. I'm going in the fucking ground face-down so I can see where I'm going, and in time, so are you!"

"Yeah, but it looks like you're already pretty well along the way."

"I 'ope you're right," James said with a lilt in his voice.

"Why'd you need me here? I could have sent the money."

"To 'elp me die," he said. He tightened his grip on my shoulders.

"What am I supposed to do?"

"Get drinks in me."

"You want me to kill you?"

"No. Drink with me, and 'elp me do the job myself."

There were many quicker ways he could kill himself, but it was clear he had given it thought and made his choice. I said, "James, you know, it ain't all that bad a way to go. I'll drink with you 'til one of us drops."

"When I'm gone, I want you to 'ave all my stuff."

"Let's not talk about that."

"We 'ave to," he insisted. "I want to do it while I'm still clear-'eaded. Percy, it's important."

I nodded. He led me into his library. It was the largest room in the apartment. There were books from floor to ceiling, and the ceiling was fourteen feet high. He had a ladder on wheels to get to the high shelves. "I want you to 'ave all my books."

"James, that's real nice of you," I said, "but I don't have the time to read them."

"'ell boy, most the books ain't to be read. You'll ruin 'em if you read 'em."

"What do you mean?"

"This is my collection of first editions. It's where I put the money I made over the years."

I changed my tune. "That'll be just fine," I said. "Thank you very much, Mr. James Jefferson, for your kind consideration."

"Now, 'ow much money you got for me?"

"Ten thousand pounds."

"Damn you, Percy. You fucking gave away the store. You gave them fucking Kaffirs more guns, didn't you?"

"Yeah, I did!"

"Gave 'em your share, too, didn't you?"

"I did."

"Why in the fuck do you do that shit? It'll only get Matumbo in trouble. You've gotta know that."

"I don't know what to say to you."

"Oh 'ell, it's not important. Ten thousand pounds will buy enough liquor to kill an 'undred men. It's more than I need, and it'll pay for my burying too. After you put me in the ground, you can 'ave what's left of the money too." He laughed. "Let old Matumbo 'ave 'is guns. I'll even drink to it. What do you say to that?"

"Let's have at it!" He wasn't going to get an argument from me. I went to a neighborhood pub and bought up all the good stuff they had. I bought Cuban rum, Russian vodka, Scotch whiskey, and Cuban cigars. We had our little tontine, and the smart money was on me.

Near the end, he wanted a bottle of Mount Gay Rum. We had an endless supply of the best Cuban rum money could buy, but it wasn't good enough for James. He wanted Mount Gay Rum from Barbados. I shopped around, until I found it at a small liquor store in Southwark. James died clutching a half empty quart bottle of Mount Gay Rum.

Chapter 22

James was unconscious most of the time during his last days. I'm not sure how much he heard of what I said, but I was talking more for my benefit, then his. I spoke of the old days and the things we did. I talked about the people we had met together, and the women we had known. But the only women that meant anything in my life, he had never known; my mother, Thelma, and Regina. It made me feel lonely, and I knew his passing would take another toll on me. With all that had transpired between us, I still considered him my friend.

When he passed, I quickly turned my attention to the business of his estate. I had a solicitor sell his books and personal effects. I switched identification with him and had the death certificate issued in my name. He was laid to rest in a grave overlooking the Thames. The headstone read, "Jean Percival Hays has moved on to a better place."

I commissioned a large headstone with James' name on it before I left, and arranged for his monument to replace my grave marker on the third anniversary of his death. I honored his last wish: he was buried face down.

I was concerned that I was still wanted for piracy. The news of my death at the hands of the Basque terrorists in Madrid hadn't been acknowledged. The report of my untimely death in England didn't receive any public notice either. I forwarded an obituary notice to the *London Times*, and the British Admiralty. I hoped the notice of my burial in England would end any pursuit of me.

My plans were to go to Monterrey. Mexico was the easiest place to get into, and Thelma was hopefully still there. A matador I met in Spain had spent time in Monterrey, and he had met Thelma. She had never married, and ran a tourist shop not far from the bullring where I had worked. She sold a toy bank about the size of a cigar box. You put a coin in a toy bull's mouth and then pulled back a miniature man's arm that had a little sledgehammer, and then released it. The man hit the bull in the head with the hammer, and the bull's mouth opened and the coin went in it. She told everyone the story of Percy and his hammer.

I was waiting in James' apartment until it was time to sail, when I received a wire addressed to James from Pappy's grandson, Willie Jonson. He wanted James to get the message that Fritz had died to me, and I was needed in Baltimore. I changed my plans and headed to America.

I left England in early February 1940, on a cruise ship bound for New York; I traveled as James Jefferson. Two days before our scheduled arrival, the captain announced that we had to make an unscheduled stop in Norfolk, Virginia. He said the ship needed a rudder repair, and we would suffer only a short delay.

There was talk on the ship that the Americans were shipping arms to England on cruise ships. We were given the option of disembarking in Norfolk and taking a train to New York, or staying with the ship. I rushed to be the first one off the ship. I faked a British accent, and I slipped through customs on James Jefferson's British passport, without questions. I made the last train out of town that night. My ticket was through to New York, but I got off when the train made a stop in Baltimore.

Helga's house was in a block of clean row homes, in what had once been an all-white neighborhood. All the houses were the same, red brick with white marble steps. It was very late to be calling when I got there, but I couldn't wait until morning. I knocked gently on the door. No one answered, so I knocked harder. Lights went on in nearby houses.

I recognized Helga's voice, "Who's there?"

"It's Percy."

"Gott 'im, Himmel!" she shouted and opened the door. There were tears in her eyes. She had aged badly in the twenty years since I last saw her. She motioned me into the house. I put my bag down in the hall. We went into the kitchen and she gave me some cake and milk. She told me what life had been like for them, and she broke down when she told me of Fritz's death. And then she told me of my son Schätze's murder at the hands of his wife's brothers, and the threats being made against my granddaughter. I cautioned her never to mention our conversation to anyone, and not to worry about Pearl's safety anymore.

Helga took my hand and led me upstairs to Pearl's room. "Be quiet," she whispered, "I don't want to wake her." She opened the door and turned the light on. "Isn't she beautiful?"

I stepped past Helga to get a better look at Pearl. The light woke her, and I saw her green eyes. *She's wonderful*, I thought. She had me to protect her now.

I told Helga I had some bad thoughts when Schätze was born, given that he looked as he did. She looked at me knowingly. "What thoughts, Percy?"

"I had questions, but I never asked them. I was afraid of the answers."

"Fritz is gone now, so you can ask me anything you want." She began to cry again.

"There's no need to ask now."

"Yes, there is," she said through her tears, "Regina was Fritz's daughter. I couldn't say anything." Tears filled her eyes. "Fritz swore me to secrecy." She paused and wiped her eyes. "I asked him to tell you, but he wouldn't. He made me promise never to tell anyone. I can't keep the promise anymore. Pearl is in danger, and you need to know everything."

That answered a lot of questions, but I wanted to know more. "Schätze looked a lot like him," I said, "so I thought...."

She interrupted. "Fritz and I raised Regina. Her mother died of the plague in Africa. At the time, he told everyone that both her parents were dead. He feared he would lose his place in the church if anyone found out the truth about who Regina's real father was. He wanted to leave her in Africa when we left, but I couldn't do it. Fritz was a man who kept a lot of secrets. He always worried about people finding out things about him."

"Did Regina ever know he was her father?"

"All she knew was that she was our special gift from God."

Her words were painful. Schätze needed me, and I hadn't been there. I wondered why Fritz didn't trust me enough to tell me about Regina. That would have been all I needed to know. My whole life swung on the decision to send Schätze away. Helga didn't understand what their silence had done to my life. She only told me now to motivate me to protect Pearl. First, I felt a deep sorrow, and then an uncontrollable rage build inside me over my son's death.

Baltimore was as much a part of the old South as New Orleans. They were still fighting the Civil War in some parts of the city, when I got there in 1939. People commonly flew the Stars and Bars from their homes and businesses, and the Ku Klux Klan was active in the area. Schätze could pass for white, but that was complicated by the fact that if you had reason to suspect he wasn't white, you could make a case for him being colored. The Muelly brothers had found out Pearl was colored, and figured the father had to be colored too. Anything else would have been unthinkable for them.

Several days after Pearl's birth, while Schätze was at work, they forced his wife to leave Pearl and go with them. On his way to get his wife back that night, Schätze was killed in an ambush. No one was ever arrested. The police said they didn't have enough evidence to tie the Muelly brothers to the murder, and they wouldn't arrest them. Schätze's wife suffered from depression because of her forced estrangement from her daughter and the death of her husband, and she committed suicide.

Her brothers, Thomas and Jack Muelly, owned a neighborhood bar in east Baltimore. I went to pay them a visit. I intended to size them up, and nothing more. I walked into Muelly's bar early one afternoon. There were no patrons at the time, but there were two men standing behind the bar arguing over some money. The smaller of the two, Jack Muelly, called out, "What do you want?"

I did my best to sound like a poor colored man, and said, "I be lookin' fo' a job, sir." I stood a few feet inside the door with my head bowed.

"Get outta here, nigger!" he said.

At that time, on that day, I knew in my heart of hearts that those boys were a real danger to my granddaughter. I say that I had only intended to size the brothers up that day, but that's not to say I wasn't prepared if there was trouble. I had a matched pair of African throwing-daggers in my pockets. My son had been stabbed to death, and I planned to take my revenge with a knife. For that reason, I had left my pistol at home.

Jack Muelly spoke up again. "I ain't gonna say it again. Outta here, nigger!"

I took a step forward and said, "I be looking for work, sir."

"We don't need no help from the likes of you! Get the fuck out of here!" Jack Muelly looked to his brother and laughed.

I took a firm grip on the daggers in my pocket, and I started walking slowly toward the bar. The room was dimly lit. Light came from a room in the back, and I heard someone rustling around in there. I stopped short of the bar, and said, "I do good cleaning, sir."

"Best be on your way, boy," Thomas said.

"But, sir...."

"Don't be *sirin'* him, nigger!" Jack said.

I kept moving toward the bar where they were standing. "I'm telling you for the last time!" Jack stepped back. I moved closer. He shouted, "Frank!"

A uniformed policeman came out of the backroom. He came right at me. He unsnapped his holster and pulled out his revolver. "Out the door, boy," he said.

I turned to go. The Muelly brothers were laughing. I turned to face Jack. "What's your fucking problem, boy?" I said.

"Who the fuck are you calling 'boy,' nigger?" He shook his fist. "Frank, get this turd out of my sight!"

"No problem, Jack," Frank said.

Frank called him by name, and that was all the confirmation I needed. Frank grabbed my right arm, and lowered his gun as he held me. I took a dagger out of my pocket with my free hand and stabbed him in the heart. Before he fell, I wrestled the gun from his hand. He hit the floor with a loud thud.

"Holy shit!" Thomas Muelly shouted.

"Don't even think about moving," I said. I pointed the policeman's gun at the men.

"Here, take the money," Jack said nervously. He held out his hand with the money he was counting.

"Not so fast, gentlemen!"

"Take the money and get outta here," Thomas said.

"You boys think this is a robbery?"

They looked at each other. They had no idea what was happening. "I asked you if you think I came in here to rob you."

"Yeah!" Jack said.

"But suppose I came for a job, like I said."

"Well, then, we could use someone to sweep up and all. Couldn't we, Tom?"

"Yeah, Jack, we could use someone like that."

"I guess you could, but what about the boy lying there?" I asked.

Jack jumped in. "It was self-defense. He was going for his gun."

"Yeah, I saw the whole thing," Thomas said.

I nodded. "You're right. He was going for a gun, wasn't he?"

"Yes he was," Thomas said.

"Cut the shit, boys! I came in here to meet *you*. I'm Schätze's father."

"Motherfucker! He's his father?" Jack said, incredulously.

I cocked the hammer on the revolver and pointed it at Jack.

"Oh shit! I didn't do anything!" Thomas hung his head.

"Shut up, you dumb fuck!" Jack grabbed Thomas' arm.

Thomas was shaken. "It wasn't me. I tried to stop him."

"Stop who?" I said.

"Shut the fuck up, Tom."

"Jack! It was Jack!" Thomas shouted, pointing at his brother.

"No good! Should've stopped him," I said. There was silence.

Jack let his brother go, and they backed up from the bar. "Put your hands on the bar where I can see them."

"Please!" Jack sobbed.

"Put your hands on the bar!" I shouted.

They leaned forward and put their hands on the bar. "I think you boys know why I'm here, don't you?"

They looked at each other, but didn't answer.

"I asked you a question!"

"You're the man the old lady said would get us," Thomas said.

"She did, did she?"

"Yeah," Jack said.

"Good. Then you were expecting me."

"We didn't mean to kill no one. It was an accident," Jack said.

"An accident!"

"Honest to Christ, it was an accident. We just wanted to scare him."

I took a step toward them. "You scared him, all right!"

"I'm telling you, he fought with us. He was struggling and...."

"Shut up, Tom. You dumb shit." Jack glared at me. "You shoot us, and you'll get caught! There's people on the street out there."

"I'll take my chances." I kept the gun pointed at Jack.

"You fucking nigger shit-hole bastard!" Jack shouted. He grabbed for a shotgun behind the bar. He turned toward me with the gun in his hands.

I fired and the bullet hit him in the chest. He staggered backward against the back liquor cabinet. The shotgun fell to the floor. Thomas dove under the bar. I shot three times at the spot where I thought he had landed. I heard him moan. I went quickly to the bar and looked over and saw Tom wounded and squirming on the floor. He looked up at me. "I didn't even know his name," he whined.

"He was Percy Jefferson," I said angrily, and fired a shot into his forehead.

Jack was still slumped against the counter. I wasn't sure he was alive. I shot him in the head for good measure. He straightened up for a second and then slithered down the liquor cabinet to the floor.

I took the second dagger out of my pocket. I held it by the leather grip and wiped the blade clean of fingerprints on my sleeve. Then I reached over the bar and put it on the shelf under it. I wiped the gun clean and put it in the dead policeman's hand, and then I wiped the grip of the dagger that I had left in the policeman's chest.

I walked slowly out of the bar with my eyes cast down. I would have also preferred killing the Muelly brothers with a knife; but dead is dead and they would never bother anyone again. But the shots were heard, and three men were running toward me. I turned and started up the street away from them. A police car pulled to the curb in front of me. A cobbler came running out of his shop, yelling that he had heard shots. He waved at the police car and pointed in my direction.

I followed his lead and started waving my hands and shouting. I pointed toward the bar. I called to a policeman getting out of his car. "There's been a shooting in the bar over here."

The policeman pulled his gun and told me to get against the wall. Another policeman went into the bar. "Oh shit! Come in here!" he yelled.

The first officer went into Muelly's. "Holy mother of God!" He shouted.

I inched away from the wall when the policeman left me and looked in the bar. Before I got to the corner, he saw me. "Hey, where do you think you're going?" he said.

Before I could answer, the other officer came out of the bar. He pointed at me and asked if I was a witness. The policeman guarding me said I was. He asked what happened in the bar. He was told that Patrolman Frank and the Muelly brothers were dead.

They held me there until a detective came to the scene. "Something's up with this one," the officer detaining me said, pointing at me.

"Watch him. I want to talk to him," the detective said. "I'm going to take a look in the bar myself." When he came out of the bar he asked, "What happened in there, boy?"

"There was an argument, and the boys got into it."

"What were you doing in there?"

"Looking for work, sir."

"Yeah, well, what did you see?"

"One of the men was arguing about money with a cop. The other boy threw a knife at the cop. Then the cop pulled his gun and unloaded it on the boys."

"You saw that, did you?"

"Yes, sir."

"You're sure about that?"

"Yes sir!"

The detective took the policemen off to the side. They kept their eyes on me as they talked. "We're going to have to take him to Central now. If homicide wants him, they'll keep him. Cuff him."

The detective asked, "You got anything to say, boy?"

"Them boys was mad at each other, is all."

"You can avoid yourself a lot of trouble by telling me what really happened in there, boy," he said.

"I told you everything."

"Who else was in there?"

"No one, sir," I said. "Honest! It was just them boys in there."

"You're in some big trouble, boy. You'd best think about coming forward with the truth," the policeman said. "Put your hands on the wall!"

They handcuffed me and held me there until the homicide unit arrived. Another detective questioned me. I stuck to my story. There was blood everywhere and three dead white men on the floor. I had blood on my shirtsleeve and told them that I had checked to see if the boys were alive. But the blood was enough for them to arrest me.

I was taken to the Baltimore City lockup. I was questioned for hours, but I told them the same story over and over again. They didn't find any weapons on me, and my prints weren't on any of the weapons in the bar. They found the second knife right where I put it on the shelf under the bar. They assumed that the knives belonged to the Muelly brothers. The police revolver was in the dead policeman's hand, and the shotgun lay at Jack Muelly's feet. They had nothing on me, but they held me as a material witness.

I was able to call Willie Jonson. He called Helga so she wouldn't worry. I offered to pay Willie whatever it took to get me out. He was a small man like his grandfather, and that's how he got his nickname, Little Willie. But nothing moved in Baltimore that Willie didn't know about. He said he would take care of the situation.

Little Willie knew about me from his grandfather. He had a lot of markers out around town, and he was prepared to use them to get me out. Even though he was very young, he had been Pappy's right-hand man right up until he died in 1934. Willie had a lot of money and power. He inherited Pappy's businesses, and Fritz also turned his business interests over to Willie when his health began failing in 1937. The man closest to Fritz when he died in the winter of 1940 was Little Willie Jonson.

Little Willie always tried to make the system work for him. The system in Baltimore was a big political machine that ran smoothly when it was well greased. He wasn't at all above getting a little dirty making sure it had just the right amount of lubricant. Willie never asked anyone for a favor or a meeting, unless he could afford it.

Willie went right to the mayor of Baltimore City. The mayor sent Willie to a connected attorney named Santini. The mayor told Willie I needed representation close to the administration, and though Santini was expensive, he was the one.

Willie and Santini agreed on the fee, and I was released the same day. There were police who questioned my release, but they saw me as an old man. I showed them what they wanted to see: a foot-dragging, old colored man not capable of killing three strong white men. At the same time, the Baltimore papers covered the story; their articles mentioned an elderly colored witness who was released, but my name was not given.

Chapter 23

The events at Muelly's bar had drawn me unwanted attention. The authorities were asking questions, but they couldn't prove anything. Santini saw to it that no indictment ever came down against me. He said that I was lucky the killings hadn't happened a few years earlier, because back then, a lynch mob would have shown up at my door. He cautioned me to be careful what I did, and where I went.

I tried to keep a low profile, for everybody's benefit. But I found it hard because of a persistent reporter from the *Baltimore News American* named Herman Garonski. He came by Helga's house frequently to check on me. Willie said that he was a friend of his, and that he wasn't a problem. He told me that Garonski planned to write a book about coloreds who had contributed to the City of Baltimore. He was also chronicling Baltimore's prominent colored families, and was going to write a book about the problems faced by interracial couples. Garonski was married to a colored woman.

Garonski knew that Schätze was my son, and assured me that he would never use the information. I was worried that Willie could have been wrong about Garonski; I had him tell Garonski to stay away from me and my family, or there would be trouble. After that, I never heard from Garonski again.

I wanted to go to Monterrey, but Helga insisted I stay in Baltimore for Pearl's sake. Her being under my protection added a sense of purpose to my life. I suppressed my desire to be with Thelma. After a lot of soul searching, I sat down and wrote her a letter. Several weeks later, I received a reply from her. We corresponded on a regular basis for a while, and I wrote of my desire for us to be together again. But neither one of us was ready to give up our lives and go to be with the other one. After a time, my desire to be with Thelma faded, and as it did, I realized how much I had loved Regina. I had kept the memory of what we meant to each other stored away, and never dealt with the reality of her passing. I felt a great deal of pain as I started the too long-delayed mourning of her loss, and that of my son. I dealt with it as best I could, and I devoted myself to Pearl.

I was happy, and despite the war raging in Europe, I was making money in the summer of 1940. Wealthy European refugees needed gemstones to bribe their way out of occupied countries. They didn't trust paper money, and wanted diamonds they could easily hide on their person. Those who made it to the United States wanted to convert their gems into gold – which was perfect for me, because Americans couldn't own gold bullion at the time, and I could get access to South African gold coins. It was time for me to get back into the diamond business.

I contacted Matumbo. He had ascended to great power in the Natal, and was serving right under the Zulu king as head of the Council of Chiefs. The tribes had accumulated a large stash of gold and diamonds, which Matumbo was commissioned to trade for weapons. He was having problems with my Swiss friends, because they wouldn't deal with him directly. The Germans had put themselves in as middlemen, and were taking the lion's share of the profit. I planned to rework the deal through myself, and to get a better deal for the Zulu.

First, I had to get away from the house to conduct my business. I took a streetcar from Helga's to check out the businesses along its route. I found a *Help Wanted* sign in a drugstore window, in a quiet suburban neighborhood several miles from the house. I stepped off the streetcar and began a new life in America.

I went into the drugstore with my head deferentially lowered. I asked a cashier who I should see about the job. She pointed to the back of the store. "Go see Doc Allen," she said.

He was busy talking to an elderly woman. I stood off to the side by a cosmetics case. There was the scent of lilies of the valley, and it reminded me of Neddi and Paris. I missed her. I felt a rush. She had set me up in the drug deal. That should have been enough to make me hate her. *What the fuck is wrong with me,* I thought. Doc Allen startled me when he raised his voice to communicate with the old woman. She didn't understand his English, and he couldn't understand her German.

I listened for a minute, and then interceded on her behalf. "She's asking you for a stomach remedy for her father," I told him.

Doc stuttered, "Wha...What's bothering him?"

"Her father has a pain in the back of his neck, and shooting pains in his left arm."

Doc called the fire department for an ambulance while I spoke to the woman. He told me to tell her to go home and meet the ambulance there. I volunteered to go with her.

I waited with her at her house until the ambulance left for the hospital, and then went back to the drugstore. Doc saw me and called me to the prescription counter. He thanked me for my help. I wasted no time in asking him for the job. After an awkward silence, he nodded *yes*. He explained that it was a custodial job, and he hadn't had any other applicants.

Willie was upset when I told him about the job. He said I could have any job I wanted in his organization. He urged me to join him. He said Pappy would have wanted it that way. I was once again impressed with the boy, and I knew what he was getting at, but he didn't know what I had in mind. I needed to do my own thing without any interference from anyone – not even him.

I assumed as much responsibility as I could. I was the first one at the store every day, and I stayed until all the mail came. I was careful about what I said and how I acted around Doc Allen. If I lost the job, I wouldn't be able to get my packages containing the contraband.

I made friends with some of the merchants in the neighborhood. My two best friends were the owners of the hand laundry next door to the pharmacy: Benny Chu, and the barber in a shop two more doors down, Vicente Ramos. I met Vicente when he hurt his leg, and Doc Allen asked me to give him a hand cleaning his shop in the evenings before I went home. He was from South America and had a penchant for cigars and rum. Of course, we hit it off right away. I spent a little time everyday with Benny, speaking French. I was one of the few people he could speak to, as he knew no English and was adamant about never, ever trying to learn it. His family had left China when he was an infant, and he was raised in Indochina. He said I should go there with him and his family after the war, because neither one of us was white enough to get ahead in the United States.

But he was wrong; I *was* getting ahead, and I wasn't going any-where. And even if I weren't, I wouldn't go and miss spending time with Pearl. On Sundays, when the weather was good, we would go lots of places together. I took her on streetcar rides all over the city. She liked the harbor and the zoo the most, and we went there fre-quently. A lot of those times we would take our lunch in the restau-rants that would seat us. I never chanced going in a place that would

196

have questioned her about being colored – but truth be known, I wouldn't have frequented those establishments anyway.

I had a wonderful life. I was making considerable money, and things were pretty much under control, until one day in February 1942. Doc Allen was twenty minutes late, and he seemed preoccupied when he finally got there. He fumbled with the keys and then dropped them. I picked them up and opened the back door for him.

He was nervous. I figured he'd had a falling out with his father or his brothers. I thought it was going to be one of those mornings for Doc, the kind that occurred from time to time when he had a fight with his family. They were his partners in the business, and they had a love-hate relationship and fought among themselves a lot.

I went to the front door and unlocked it. Geraldine, the fountain lady who was a woman in her early fifties, was waiting to get in. She had once asked me if I was really colored. I told her that God made some folks dark on the outside and light on the inside, and for others, He just reversed it. I was darker on the inside. I don't think she had a clue what I meant.

She took her place behind the soda fountain and busied herself, getting ready to open. Doc sat down on a stool behind the prescription counter. I got my wash bucket and filled it with water and a splash of ammonia. I started the day as I always did, by mopping the floor.

I looked up to see two men in dark suits enter the store. They were walking stiffly, and I sensed trouble. They went to the back and spoke to Doc. I watched them out of the corner of my eye while I mopped. They left the prescription counter and walked toward me. I turned and started for the front door. They grabbed me from behind and pushed me up against the wall with their guns drawn.

"FBI!" John Morgan, the larger of the two agents, shouted. "Hands behind your back!"

I didn't resist, and they handcuffed me. Morgan searched me and found my pistol. He handed it to William Hansen, the other agent. He held my pistol up. He looked at it and laughed. "Old man, tell me, what's this for?"

I straightened up. "Sir," I said, "that there is an heirloom."

"Yeah, but what's it for?" Hansen asked again.

"For keeping," I said. "It's a family treasure my father gave me."

"Don't try my patience, boy," Hansen said. "If we're going to get along, you're going to have to pay more attention. Now, why are you carrying the gun?"

"No particular reason, sir."

"And you expect me to accept that?" Morgan asked.

"I do," I said. "You see, sir, I was going through some of my stuff this morning, and I found it. I forgot I even had the old thing. With my granddaughter at home and having her friends over, and all, I didn't want to leave it lying around the house. You know how dangerous guns can be in the hands of children, sir."

"You've got a gun! We're taking you in," Morgan said.

"It don't even work anymore," I said in a low voice.

"Tell me, boy!" Hansen said. He took the Derringer, pointed it at me, and said, "You willing to bet your life on it?"

I didn't answer.

"I'm willing to bet *your* life, boy."

I didn't flinch. I wasn't going to give the bastard the satisfaction. Hansen pulled the hammer back and aimed the pistol at my head. *What a fucking way to die*, I thought. As he squeezed the trigger, he raised the barrel. There was a flash and the sound of a bullet hitting plaster. I flinched. The powder burned my forehead. If a New Orleans policeman had done the shooting, I would have been dead.

Doc Allen looked up when he heard the shot. In the front of the store, Geraldine fainted behind the soda fountain. A woman came into the drugstore just after the agent fired. She grabbed her chest and leaned against the doorframe. She steadied herself and turned to leave.

Doc called to her. "Ma...Mrs. Ga...Goldberg, it's o...okay. Ca...come on ba...back here."

She scurried to the back of the store, keeping her eye on us all the while.

The whole time I worked for Doc Allen, I had done everything he asked without complaint and I had never asked for a raise. I felt sure he was happy with me in his employ, but I did notice a few changes after the Japanese attacked Pearl Harbor. There was a lot of talk around the store about "the enemy within." Doc Allen viewed himself as a patriot, even though he stayed out of the military by getting a draft board exemption. He convinced the board that he was necessary to the community. He signed up and did some service in the WPA. He told everyone who would listen of his exploits in the program. He said he was a driver for a big-shot general on weekends, but had had to do it part-time because of his service to the community in the pharmacy.

I believe Doc wanted to do his part for the war effort – that is, as long he wasn't exposed to any personal risk. I should have picked up on things when he began watching everybody. He asked me some questions about how I knew German, and I told him I spoke other languages too. That was a mistake. And he even asked me once if I had any oriental blood. I told him no and assumed the matter was resolved.

And then, I underestimated Doc again, when a change of address form from my Swiss bank got into Doc's mail. He started watching me when the mailman or the parcel post driver came to the store. He saw I was getting packages from Rhodesia, South Africa, and Switzerland. I told him, when he asked, that I was getting candy from some friends and showed him the chocolate. I gave him some, and he liked it. I made hot cocoa for him. He loved that too. I didn't think he had a clue that I was smuggling diamonds in the candy.

Hansen put my pistol in his pocket and said under his breath, "You got yourself some big trouble, boy!" He grabbed my right arm and held me.

I turned to Doc and shouted, "Please get a message to my granddaughter, Doc. Tell her I'm okay."

"I wa...will. I'll ta...take her the ma...message myself." His head was down. He walked to the prescription counter. Mrs. Goldberg joined him there.

"Can I use a phone?" Morgan asked.

"Yeah, the wa...one behind the counter in the fa...front."

"What's that all about, Doc?" Mrs. Goldberg asked.

"Na...nothing."

"That was nothing?"

"A ma...misunderstanding, na...nothing more. It'll ba...be okay. Ha...how can I ha...help you?"

"Who's going to deliver now, if I have an emergency?"

"Da...don't worry, Ma...Mrs. Goldberg."

"I have to worry. I'm a sick woman. Who's going to deliver with Percy gone?"

"If I ha...have to, I will!"

Agent Morgan told headquarters that he was bringing in a real winner – an old High Yubbie. I needed Santini.

Chapter 29

I was taken directly to the FBI building in Washington, DC. The interrogators there conducted a series of half-hearted interviews. They asked me a few questions about the packages I was sending and receiving. They were naïve and believed me when I told them I was a candy connoisseur, and ordered chocolate from vendors in Africa and Europe. I told them how I loved chocolate. All they saw was an old man of the colored race.

The agents contacted the investigators from the postmaster's office who had checked my shipments. They gave the FBI the file from their six-month investigation, including the interviews with Doc Allen and his neighbors. They made the determination that I was not a security threat. Fortunately for me, they had concentrated only on the large shipments. The diamonds were hidden in the smaller packages of chocolate. But even if they had checked all the shipments, they wouldn't have spotted uncut diamonds in among the lumps of cocoa, unless they knew what they were looking for. The only way to find the diamonds was to melt the chocolate and strain it.

I told the FBI that I was shanghaied in Galveston, and ended up re-entering the United States on James Jefferson's papers. I gave them my real name and told them where I was born. I expected the worst, but Santini filed a writ of *habeas corpus*, and they were going to let me go.

On my way out of the FBI building, I was taken into custody by Army MPs. They came for me because an overzealous FBI agent, Roger Broussard, had contacted the War Department. He didn't want me to be released. He told them to hold me as an enemy combatant. I was taken to the Pentagon and quizzed by a team of Army interrogators about my friends and my travels.

I didn't cooperate. I didn't know what they knew, or what they thought they knew. I wasn't going to help them build a case against me. I figured they would let me go if I kept my mouth shut. But the army showed some interest in my overseas contacts, and wanted to know who and where they were. Broussard involved himself in the questioning. I asked him to see my attorney, but he said that he wanted to talk to me man to man. I was leery; I decided to take my chances with the army interrogators instead.

They transferred me to a detention center in Alexandria, Virginia, and questioned me day and night, for four days. I told them nothing, but I learned from their questions that they were way behind the British in recruiting agents. I couldn't believe that they really wanted someone like me. They needed someone who had contacts in Europe and Africa, who understood the cultures there.

They could hold me indefinitely, and they saw I wasn't going to help them that way. I think they were sorry they ever started up with me – that is, all but Broussard. He wasn't buying my story at all. He was a hardheaded Cajun from the Louisiana bayou country who never gave up easily on anything. He'd heard enough of my accent to know I really was from New Orleans. He told me that he had dealt with boys like me before, and that he knew where I was coming from. He maneuvered things and got assigned to work with Army Intelligence.

Broussard was determined to get me to work with him. He wanted me to tell him everything I knew. I told him that if he told me what he thought I knew, I would confirm or deny it.

He sent me back to the army interrogators. After three more days of questioning, they weren't sure whether I was senile or retarded. They were ready to throw in the towel, but Broussard interceded again. He was persistent, and he persuaded the army to offer me immunity. I understood what that meant, and I wanted it in writing and on file with my attorney. Santini read the document, and he assured me that the immunity they offered was complete. I was ready to tell them whatever they wanted to know.

The government allotted resources to build a network of foreign agents, and needed a way to save face. All I had to do was tell them what they wanted to hear, and I would be down the road. They wouldn't pay for my attorney, and I didn't want theirs. Santini offered to represent me *gratis*, but I thought it best to go it alone, because having him could further complicate matters by having to confide in him.

When Broussard heard I'd turned down counsel, he came to my cell and told me only a sociopath would turn down an attorney. He was probably right, but I thought I would be more believable if I faced them alone. I told him that I had nothing to hide. He left as fast as he came.

The next day, I was taken to a small room in the Pentagon conference center for the interrogation. The room held an oblong table and eight chairs spaced around it. They seated me with my back to the door. I could see the Potomac River though the window, and in the reflection in the window, I saw the two military guards standing behind me. I watched though the reflection as a stenographer came in and sat on my left, and then two uniformed intelligence officers who sat next to her. The last to come in were a young army lawyer, a major, and Roger Broussard.

The lawyer spoke for the record. He told me I had the right to have a lawyer present. I told him I didn't need one. He said he would get me one that I could trust. He would be an officer, and he would keep everything I told him confidential. I told him again I didn't want one. Broussard shook his head; I knew he thought I was crazy.

The lawyer asked my name, my address and where I was born. I answered him with an exaggerated drawl. He took my pistol from a bag and put it on the table. "First, I want you to tell me about this gun."

I looked at the pistol and said, "It's mine. My father gave it to me."

"Why did you have it on you when you were picked up?"

"Because I didn't know I was going to be picked up."

"You're telling me you wouldn't have had it on your person if you knew you were going to be picked up?"

"That's right, sir. Well, actually, I wouldn't have gone in to work that day if I knew I was going to be picked up."

Broussard laughed.

The lawyer didn't see the humor. "I want to know why you were carrying a weapon," he said.

"I feel more secure when I have it with me than when I don't."

"Do you think someone is after you?"

"No."

"Then make me understand why you were carrying a loaded weapon to work."

"It's just something I've always done, and it's gotten me out of trouble a couple of times."

"From the way it looks to me, it got you in more trouble now than it ever could have gotten you out of." He looked at me for a moment. He shook his head. "It's a small caliber, and that makes it an unreliable weapon at best."

I didn't expect them to understand my affection for the Derringer, but I wanted them to understand that I was not the kind of man people should mess with. "If you want, I'll show you something with my gun, sir."

"That won't be necessary," he said, "I know about these pistols."

"Do you?"

"It's a woman's gun," he said, trying to be funny.

"Give him the gun," Broussard interrupted.

The lawyer showed displeasure with Broussard's interference. He looked at the major, and the major nodded his head in the affirmative. The lawyer checked to make sure it wasn't loaded and then slid it across the table to me.

I thanked him, and picked up the gun. I looked it over for a moment, and then I moved my hand with the pistol in it, slowly toward the lawyer. He thought I was going to hand the gun back to him. When he reached for it, I made it disappear. I held up both my hands to show them that it was gone.

Broussard clapped his hands and applauded. "Well done, Mr. Hays!"

The lawyer jumped in. "Where's the damn gun?"

"Where do you think it is, son?" I said.

"Give me the gun, Mr. Hays," he demanded.

I made the gun reappear in my hand, seemingly out of thin air. Again, I reached across the table to give the attorney the gun, and again I made it disappear.

"This is not funny. Give me the damn gun," the attorney said angrily.

"I would if I could, but Broussard has it." I stood up and reached over the table to Broussard and produced the gun from behind his shoulder.

"Amazing!" Broussard said. "Simply amazing!"

"I've had enough! Give me the gun!" the lawyer demanded.

Broussard said, "Sit down, Murray. This is fun."

Holding the gun in my right hand, I said, "Let me tell you something about this gun." I looked at Broussard.

"I'm listening," he said.

"This weapon has been with me since I was a boy, and I guarantee you" – I took a deep breath – "I wouldn't be here if it wasn't for this gun."

Murray interrupted. "I don't think you understand me. They would have picked you up even if you didn't have the gun. They had orders to bring you in. Why don't you understand that?"

"That's an actual fact. But what I meant for you to know is that this pistol saved my life several times."

There was laughter.

"Mr. Hays...," Murray raised his voice.

"Hold on there, Murray," Broussard interrupted. In his heavy Louisiana accent he said sarcastically, "Will you please stop being a lawyer for one damn minute? I'd like to hear about the times that this little pistol saved Mr. Hays."

Murray grudgingly agreed. "Go ahead, Mr. Hays."

I sat down. "The first time I used the pistol was...."

The major interrupted me. "Before we get to all that, I would like you to tell us how you came to be in Baltimore. Can we start with that, Mr. Hays?"

I looked at Broussard. He had taken the lead. He nodded his approval. I started to tell my whole life story. I was going on for the best part of an hour, when the major jumped in. "Let's do this a little differently, Murray." He turned to face me. "Tell us about it your own way?" He turned back to face Murray, adding, "But make it short, Mr. Hays."

206

I got the message. I figured I could relate to two of the men in the room, the major and Broussard. I tested that theory when I asked, "Could I have a drink, please?"

The major told a military policeman to get me a glass of water. I looked at it and pushed it away with disdain. "Thanks," I said, "but I thought maybe I could have a real drink. Like a tall glass of rum and Coca-Cola."

"This is not a bar, Mr. Hays," Murray said.

Broussard stared Murray down and nodded to the major. The major told one of the MPs to get me some rum.

"Thank you, sir. Oh! Could you make that on the rocks, sir?"

"Bring some ice too," the major called to the MP.

I looked at the men sitting around the table. They each saw me differently. "I want to make sure I understand," I said. "If I tell you everything you want to know, you're going to let me walk out of here and go on about my business."

The major said, "That's correct."

"No matter what I've done?"

Broussard nodded. "That's right."

"Just like that? Walk right on out of here and go on about my business?"

"Yes, you have my word on that," the major said.

"How about my pistol?"

"Don't push your luck, Mr. Hays," Broussard said.

"But I want my pistol."

"We'll see about that," the major said.

I drank their rum, and I told them a story of my life that I fabricated as I went along. I figured I was doing a pretty good job too, because they just let me talk. Late in the afternoon Broussard interrupted me. "You're an American, Percy. Don't you care about your country?"

"Sure, I do, Mr. Broussard. I'm an American through and through. But through no fault of my own, I had to sneak back into the country after years of living abroad."

"Do you see yourself as a victim?" Broussard asked.

"A victim?" I laughed. "No, sir. I was never a victim."

"So then you don't think the government kept you out of the country?"

"No, no."

"I see." He paused and looked at the ceiling and then back at me. "Let's start over. You chose to live outside the country, right?"

"If you put it like that, then the answer would have to be yes."

"You made contacts and did business with men around the world?"

"Yes." I didn't know where he was going.

"I need to know about your contacts in Europe and Africa. It's a matter of our survival as a nation. Do you understand that?"

"I understand it. Yes, sir. But they're just regular people."

"We are at war. We need your contacts," the major added.

"If I tell you, you might steal my business."

"Your business! For Christ's sake, I don't give a rat's ass about your business. All I need to know is if your people are of any use to us. That's all I want," the major said.

"I'm a chocolate merchant! I deal in confections! They're my suppliers, sir."

"You're pushing it! Don't push!" the major said.

"Mr. Hays, listen to me," Broussard said.

"I prefer you call me Percy!"

"Okay, but you have to talk to us, Percy. You have to tell us everything. If you come clean and tell us what you're dealing, you'll have complete immunity. I hope you understand what a blessing that can be for you and your family. You'll be starting over with a

208

clean slate," Broussard said.

They suspected something was going on, but I didn't know how much they knew. I had to go slow. "I deal mostly in chocolate, you know."

"We'll see about that, Mr. Percy Hays, from New Orleans, Louisiana," Broussard said abruptly. "Now let's get to it!"

The attorney leaned forward and said, "If you don't tell us...."

"Murray," Broussard said, "will you shut up?" He looked around the room and said, "Okay, guys, give me a few minutes alone with Mr. Hays."

Murray looked around; he was upset. He went to the major and started talking to him. Broussard motioned to the stenographer, and she got up and left. The major also left, and everyone else followed.

Broussard waited for the door to close and then started talking to me quietly. "Now, we are going to have to come to an understanding, boy."

My jaw clenched, and I peered at Broussard. "I don't like being called boy!" I said.

Broussard smiled. "If looks could kill." He stood up, walked to the end of the table, and leaned on his hands, staring at me. "Now, you listen to me, and listen to me good. We may both be from Louisiana, but that's not going to help you here. This meeting is about you, not me. Not me *and* you. Just you. Know what I'm saying?"

"I'm an old man, and there was a day when your kind would be sorry for talking to me the way you are."

"Let me tell you how it's going to be, Percy. I am an FBI agent on assignment to Army Intelligence. You, on the other hand, are a colored man without a country, facing deportation – to where, I have no idea. It seems that nobody wants you. I believe you when you say you're an American from my home state, but there's no proof you really are Jean Percival Hays. And if you really are this Mr. Hays, how do you explain this?"

He slid a wire from the British Admiralty across the table. It said that Captain Jean Percival Hays, wanted for piracy on the high seas, died in London of natural causes on 20 January 1940.

"Now, whoever you are, let me tell you this!" Broussard said. "The only thing in your favor is that you have some contacts around the world, so if you're going to share them with us, then we can talk. If not, I'm content to see you rot in prison until some country claims you. It's up to you, Percy, or whoever you really are!"

"You know I'm Percy Hays! Now, what do you really want to know?"

"Everything. I want you to start at the beginning."

"Okay. As you know, I was born in New Orleans, Louisiana, sometime in the month of May." It was May, I thought. "I'm pretty sure it was in May, either 1874 or 1875. I got to tell you that I'm not sure when I was born. I'm confused about that, but I am every bit as American as you are."

"Don't you want to avoid trouble?"

"You promise me immunity and then you threaten me? Why do you have to be messing with an old man like me? How do you expect a man who doesn't even know for sure when he was born to handle sophisticated foreign agents?"

"Let's say you are who you say you are. According to the British, that person was born on May 15, 1874, in New Orleans, Louisiana, and died January 20, 1940, in London."

"I faked my death."

"I suppose you could have arranged it, but how do explain this?"

He handed me another newspaper clipping, this one from a Madrid newspaper dated July 1, 1938; it was a the story of how I was killed by a Basque terrorist. After I read the article, I looked up at Broussard and smiled. "You can read Spanish – I am impressed!"

"Cut the shit. What have you got to say for yourself?"

"Nothing."

"Whether they claim you died in Madrid in 1938, or in London in 1940, doesn't mean a damn thing to me. I believe you arranged all that shit. Now, you listen to me, boy, and you listen to me real good. If you want out of here, you'd best give me a reason to let you out. Who in the hell do you think you're playing with? Talk about immunity – immunity from what? Because you didn't pay tariff on some chocolate? Give me a break! For God's sake, give me a break!" Broussard shook his head in frustration. "You don't know when you were born? Am I wasting my time with you?"

"You might be. That depends on what you want from me."

"I want your contacts. They may be hustlers and cutthroats, but they'd be more than we have now."

"You keep saying I have contacts. I say I have some friends with whom I deal in some chocolate from time to time. They know I like chocolate, and so they send me some candy. What do you think my friends can do for you?"

"They can keep their eyes open. They can verify things. They can report things we would be interested in, and we'll pay them for the information."

"Why didn't you say that before? We're talking business. Now, if I give you the contacts, what do I get?"

"What do you want?"

I thought for a second. I began speaking very carefully, weighing each word. "I would like – no, I *demand* – my life back. You can have my contacts for all the good they'll do you. But I want my life back."

"Are you ready to buy your life back, boy?"

My face got taut, and I held my breath.

"What's wrong, Percy?"

"I don't think it would be a good idea for you ever to call me boy again."

"Hey! I didn't mean anything by it. It won't happen again. Some habits die hard, Percy."

I shook my head. I let it pass. I looked out the window and thought about what was ahead for me. I knew what my decision was before I entered the room. My life was about my business, and my goal was no different now from what it had been all along. I wasn't sure what it would cost me, but I needed protection and this was a good way to get it. The economics were simple: get the money, hard currency. "What if my guys won't cooperate?"

"Don't think too much, Percy. It'll work out. We both have a common purpose and if we go slow...no, if we bide our time, everything will work out just fine." He paused before saying, "We have to give them army boys something to hang their hats on."

I smiled at him. Broussard was going to be easier to deal with than I'd thought. I lowered my head a bit, as a man like Broussard would expect me to do, and said slowly, "I understand."

"Good then, Percy. You have a deal." He offered his hand.

I stood and started to take Broussard's hand, but I stopped and said, "There are some things we need to take care of, my new friend."

"Of course there are." He thought for a moment. "But men with a common purpose like us can work out the details."

"My freedom is more than a detail." I was still standing with my hand partially extended.

Broussard reached over, clasped my hand, and said, "I'll drive you to Baltimore myself, Percy."

I took his hand and held it firmly, not letting him shake it. I let him feel the strength in my hands. "What about my pistol?"

"No problem, Percy. After all, both you and the gun are both classified as antiques."

We drove back to the drugstore together, so Broussard could arrange for me to return to work. I took Broussard into the store through the back door. He had met Doc before. He asked, "Is there a place where we can talk?"

"Ca...come with me." Doc motioned with his hand.

We followed Doc behind the prescription counter, but that wasn't private enough for Broussard. He wanted a more private place. Doc led us down to the cellar. Piled in the middle of the basement were bags of my contraband sugar. There was a gas stove against the far wall and next to it were dozens of empty glass gallon jugs I used to make syrup.

Broussard sat down on the sugar. He patted the sacks under him, and winked at me. "If you're right about things, Percy, I'm sitting on a small fortune." He laughed.

"Wa...hat?" Doc asked.

"An inside joke," Broussard laughed

"O...okay."

"Now let's get down to business, Doc. I can't thank you enough for helping us find Percy."

"Wha...what's going on here, an...anyway?"

"Don't get your bowels in an uproar," Broussard paused. "Everything's fine! Percy here has been a huge help already. I think that with your help, he can be even more useful in the future."

"How ca...can I help?"

"Information! Communications! We have a big opportunity here, Doc." Broussard stood. "Doc, this is *big* – bigger than we expected when you called us. We need you to run interference for Percy now."

Doc cleared his throat. "In...interference?"

Broussard stood and walked right up to Doc. "Yes. So no one else gets suspicious and calls the authorities."

"I...I see." Doc stiffened.

"Relax, Doc. The same reason you turned him in is the reason you have to run interference for him now. He has contacts all over the world. He could be.... Hell! He's already an asset to us. Now, if you were suspicious, what do you think other people will think? It's up to us to keep prying eyes away from Percy. Doc, we need your help."

"I...I...I'll ha...help." Doc was perspiring.

"I knew you would," Broussard said. He turned to me. "Look at us, Percy! The three of us, down here in this cellar, down here as cold as it is. You would've thought one of us would have the good sense to move closer to the furnace. We don't know enough to get out of the cold, and yet here we are, thinking we're one step closer to solving all the world's problems." He laughed.

"Wha...what sha...should I do?" Doc called after Broussard, as he started up the stairs.

"I'll give you my number. If anyone gets too nosy, warn Percy, and then give me a call," he said without breaking stride. "Oh, and make sure Percy gets all his packages. That's important too."

"Ya...yes, sir!"

I climbed the stairs behind Broussard. I had no desire to save the world, you understand. The way I saw it, it didn't deserve saving anyway. Maybe the war would change things. And maybe it was someone else's turn to be in charge. But I saw a benefit in me letting them believe I was going forward with the plan.

Broussard offered to drive me home. We went down Liberty Heights Avenue to Druid Hill Park, then part way around the reservoir to Auchentrolly Terrace. He asked, "We're not far from where Mrs. Wallace Simpson used to live, are we?"

"I heard she grew up around here somewhere," I said.

"King Edward gave up the throne of England for her. Isn't that something?" Broussard was impressed that a man would give up everything for the love of a woman.

"I saw her in Paris after the war and, you know something? She really wasn't so much. It seems to me the King was just tired of being king."

"Yeah, you're probably right."

"I am right! 'Cause when you really want to be king, there ain't nothing in the world more important; nothing else matters."

"I never gave it any thought before," he said.

Chapter 25

A young colored boy was hired to do the cleaning and delivering at the drugstore. Doc said it was to help me, but it wasn't. He had become uneasy about my presence and wanted me to retire. To avoid his scrutiny, I spent most of my time visiting my friends in the neighborhood, and in the basement reading. I stayed close to the store waiting for my shipments – shipments that stopped coming because of the war in Africa. Matumbo tried to keep me posted, but the communications dwindled down to some random coded letters that found their way to me at the store.

I didn't trust Broussard, and worried what might be going on with him. After a year of weekly contacts, I hadn't heard from him in two months. In early January 1943, he came to the drugstore to see me. I was in the basement reading a newspaper when I heard him greet Doc upstairs. A vent in the prescription counter went to the basement, and I could hear everything said in the back of the store. Doc told him I was in the cellar.

Broussard came down the stairs. I backed away from the staircase and watched him. "To what do I owe the pleasure?"

"We have to talk, Percy."

I was prepared for what I thought would be bad news. What was important to me was my survival – not the FBI, not Army

Intelligence, not anyone else was going to take me into custody ever again.

I moved to the back of the cellar and stood in the shadows.

"We have to talk," Broussard said.

I had a stiletto in one pocket and the Derringer in the other.

"Come over here and talk to me," he smiled.

I moved out of the shadows. "About what?"

"Just, talk." He paused, and sat down on the sacks of sugar. "Come on over here, Percy."

I sat on a chair across from him. I never took my eyes off him.

"Percy, we're not getting very far with your network."

"That doesn't surprise me."

"It does me. I thought it would work. I really did. Maybe not spin the world on its ass, you know, but help a little bit."

"It didn't make any sense to me from the start."

"Do you think your boys are involved in some shenanigans over there?" Broussard looked me in the eye. The British had contacted the army. They were concerned about shipments of gold and industrial diamonds finding their way from Africa to Germany. They wanted to know how the assets were getting to Germany. They suspected that some of the money was ending up in Switzerland, and that Swiss bank credits were paying for some of the gold. But they couldn't be sure. Broussard had come to find out if I, or any of my African contacts, knew anything about it.

"My friends involved in shenanigans like that? Hell, I'm all but out of business over there. This has been a disaster for me."

It wasn't what he wanted to hear. "We have a deal, Percy. I expect you to live up to your end."

"Listen, my boys are really hurting over there."

"Yeah, right. They're hurting." He paused. "There's gold moving in South Africa, and you know about it?"

"Why would you think that?"

"You're the man, Percy, and you know that!"

"I don't know anything of the kind!"

"Yeah, you do! I haven't figured out why you live like you do, or for that matter, why you do some of the things you do."

"Don't that beat all! I can't imagine anyone would be thinking old Percy was somehow involved with the movement of gold in Africa."

"Don't try to shit me, Percy!"

"I gave you the names and made the contacts for you!"

"I need you to do more." He was pleading.

The change of tone confused me. "How's that?"

"We need to build a relationship with British Intelligence."

"What's that got to do with me?"

"We have to give them something. Your friends are all we have."

"The British! You're crazy! My so-called 'boys' don't like the British, and I don't like them either. If you know anything about me, then you must know that."

"Doesn't matter what you like."

"Oh. It matters. Be sure of that."

"There's a war on, and the English are our allies."

"There's nothing I can do."

Broussard smiled and stood up. "I've been told about your contacts in Africa."

He knew I was still working with Matumbo. His people's lives depended on it. The gold was the tribute the Germans demanded to leave the Zulu alone with the diamond trade. Everything had started with the deal I set in motion in Portugal. Things were working, but not smoothly, and I hadn't gotten paid. Still, I continued to fund the sales through my Swiss bank. I owed that to Matumbo and my Zulu brothers.

I told him that I couldn't help him, but he still insisted on knowing more about my contacts. He hadn't come to the store to finesse me. "What can an old colored man do to save the world from the Nazis?" I said.

"Your part!"

"I've done my part!"

"You ain't done shit!"

"I must say, Mr. Broussard, a man like me, given the circumstances, couldn't have..."

"Cut the shit!"

"Well, you get the idea," I laughed, "and what do you think I can do?"

"Stop gold from getting to Germany from Africa."

"It's good that you don't want much from me!"

"I want your friends, the Zulu, on our side. We need their help."

"I'll send a wire to Matumbo, and I'll tell him if he's dealing with the Germans to stop doing it."

"No! I want you to do more!"

"And what does 'more' mean?"

"More means just that – *more*. I went out on a limb on this thing. I told them you would go with me to South Africa and tell Matumbo yourself."

"You must be out of your fucking mind!"

"Eh...everything okay dow...down there?" Doc called down.

"Everything's fine," Broussard called up. He looked at me and gave me a sneaky smile. "Are you in?"

"You want me to go with you to South Africa and tell Matumbo to stop dealing with the Germans in person?"

"Right!"

"You are fucked up, Mr. Broussard."

"It's Roger, Percy. And maybe I am fucked up, but that's what I want you to do!"

"Alright, Roger, let's say I ask him to do what you want, and he does it. Where will he get arms, then?"

"The British will help with that part. The army will set it up. They want to stop the trade with Germany."

"I told you, Roger, I don't like the British, and now I'm telling you Matumbo will never agree to work with the British. The fucking limeys are his enemy! Mine too!"

"We can work it out. The British need our help, and we need theirs."

"The Zulu have no use for them. I'm telling you, it won't work." I knew what Broussard wanted, but he had no idea how to do it. It could cost me a lot of money, but then I thought, *I could turn the African deal around and make some serious money.* But there was a downside. I could get my friend in real trouble, and there's no guarantee his people would survive.

"How much do you know about all this?"

"If I stop the payments to the Nazis, and sell to the Allies, the Germans will attack Johannesburg."

"That's crazy. The Germans are tied up in North Africa. They're not going into the South."

"I say we could bring the war to South Africa."

"The Germans can't spread themselves that thin. They're not interested in South Africa."

"Not interested in gold and diamonds?"

"It would be a stretch for them to go there."

"You have to understand: the smart money says the only reason the Germans haven't attacked South Africa is that they're doing business there."

"Here's what I understand. You have contacts in South Africa, and we're going to use them."

"That may not be the best solution to the problem, especially if we bring the war to South Africa," I said.

"We'll have to leave all that shit to Roosevelt and the general staff. Percy, we're going to Africa."

"Do I have a choice?"

"Not if you're the man I think you are."

"I'll tell you something, Roger. Today's your lucky day."

"Why's that?"

"I need a vacation."

Chapter 26

I met Broussard at the Baltimore Harbor Airport at 6:00 PM. I dressed in my very best attire. I wore my double-breasted, blue pinstripe suit, white linen shirt, and red striped tie. I slicked back my hair with Madame C.J. Walker's Pomade, and used Burma Shave with a razor for the first time in years. I was carrying Pappy's ivory-handled umbrella with a concealed blade that was given to me by Little Willie. I felt good about the trip, and I was ready for action.

We walked to the end of the pier and boarded the plane. The pilot made his taxi run through the harbor, and out to Chesapeake Bay. The plane picked up speed as the pilot cleared the shipping channel and then surged forward, bouncing off the water several times before climbing into the sky. I looked out the window. It was dusk, and I saw a sunlit western sky.

"God, how I love the sunset!" I shouted over the drone of the engines.

Broussard leaned across the aisle, "Yeah, I love the sunset too. It's something to see from a plane." He got up and pushed his way past me to the cockpit.

The trip took us to a seaport off the Maine coast. From there, we boarded a larger plane and flew to Ireland, then took a scheduled flight to Lisbon.

In Lisbon, I met with my Swiss bankers, and I authorized them to accept letters of credit for shipments of gold from South Africa. I assigned the letters of credit to the benefit of my agents. Then I gave Broussard access to my entire network of precious metal and diamond dealers, which he'd been asking for. I pledged my entire fortune to cover the credit the Swiss extended on the gold shipments. I made Broussard understand the full gravity of this, and what it all meant for me.

I took leave of Broussard and went to see Paulo Méndez. I found him doing well. He had fixed up the bar and was catering to an exclusively German clientele. Pepe, the bouncer, remembered me. He backed away from the door when I walked into the cantina.

"Hello, Pepe," I said.

He kept his distance.

I saw Méndez at the bar. He waved me over to join him. The bar was crawling with Germans. Some were in SS uniforms. "What brings you here?" he asked.

"I just happened to be in town."

He was suspicious. "Not here on business?"

"No! But you might think about your choice of friends!"

"I like my friends."

"Suit yourself!"

"In these times, you don't get to choose. But enough about those guys. Where are you staying while you're here?"

I gave him a phony address, and I made sure I wasn't followed when I left. I suspected the Bosch would be looking for me. Méndez had rolled over to the Nazis. The visit was worthwhile. I warned Broussard about Méndez, and he alerted the British.

On our last day in Lisbon, I took Broussard to the bullring. He found the Portuguese style of bullfighting disappointing. He expected to see the carnage he had associated with bullfighting in Spain. He told me he wanted to see the bulls die. I told him that I liked the Portuguese fights, and the fortitude of the men who fought in the ring. He spent that afternoon complaining; but after all, he was just a Cajun boy from the bayou. And I didn't want to be too critical of him, because there was always a chance that we were cousins, however distant.

We received travel credentials from the British Embassy on the day of our departure. We made our way to Morocco on a Portuguese trawler. From Casablanca, we flew in small planes that hopped and skipped across the African continent, ending up in Johannesburg.

Broussard wanted me to go with him to a meeting with the leader of the Afrikaner home guard in Johannesburg, but I wouldn't go. I was concerned that he would recognize me. When Broussard came back from the meeting, he told me that either they didn't have a clue who I was, or they didn't give a damn about me anymore. He got travel passes for both of us through all the areas controlled by the Boer militia.

In Pretoria, he got the British to grant us safe passage through the colored townships with the approval of the local South African officials. The passes were also valid for the Zulu, Xhosa, and Bantu tribal lands.

Broussard was called to a meeting at the U.S. Embassy. I was leery and prepared to disappear at the first hint of trouble. I made sure Broussard was alone when he came back from the meeting. He said everything went well. I nodded as he'd expected me to do; he would soon enough see another side of me. I was on the Dark Continent with a serious purpose.

Broussard admitted that the British knew who I was, but he said that I didn't have to worry, because the United States government had taken care of everything. We got a lorry, all the supplies we needed, and a guide to take us to the interior. That eased my mind some, but still I had reservations.

Broussard was as eager as I was to get started, and he pushed everyone hard for an early departure. Our British liaison took us to a compound where they had everything waiting, and they introduced us to our guide. He followed the directions given him by the British. They modeled their plan on the bogus agenda I had given Broussard. We left Pretoria, and headed toward the Bantu homeland in the south. I was the only one who really knew where we were going.

I had the driver stop and get out of the lorry when we reached the end of the paved road outside of Pretoria. I had no use for him, and I dismissed him. He protested loudly; I thought about the driver my father chased away when I was a boy, and went for my pistol. But Broussard interceded and gave him money for his trouble, and the driver quieted down and walked away. I wouldn't have given anything; he was a lackey for the British.

Broussard got back in the lorry and drove. What I had done with the driver bothered him, and I wasn't doing anything to make him feel easier. I had taken over the operation, and I wanted him to get a taste of what the journey would be like for him. Then if he wanted, he could get out early. He knew he was a white man traveling alone with me on an unpaved road in the bowels of a racially torn country.

When we were clear of all civilization, I stripped down to a loincloth in the lorry while Broussard drove. I stared at him until he looked over at me, and when he did, I said, "What's the matter, boy? Never seen a white nigger before?"

"Christ almighty, those scars! What the hell happened to you?"

"I'm accident prone," I laughed.

"And you're whiter than I am!"

"Ain't that a bitch!"

Broussard smiled and then laughed.

"What's so funny?"

"All you have to do is show up looking like that, and you'll scare people to death."

"If that were true, I wouldn't have all these damn scars."

"I was kidding. I meant...."

"I've had to engage some enemies at close range. Let's leave it at that." All I wanted him to know was that we were going to meet Matumbo.

We were on a rough dirt road that deteriorated more and more, the farther we got from the city. It wasn't long before there was no road at all. We were near the border; I was concerned that we might accidentally cross into Rhodesia, where we didn't have safe passage and would be at risk if we had to get petrol. We couldn't afford any detours; we had just enough petrol to reach the Zulu stronghold north of the Natal.

We stopped to refill the tank from our reserve. While we were stopped, I took a throwing dagger, my Derringer, and a revolver out of my briefcase. I laid them between the seats. I held the Derringer up for Broussard to see. Then I made it disappear.

He laughed. "Where do you put that thing?"

"That's for me to know and for you to find out!" If he had searched me, he wouldn't have found it: I had perfected the art of holding it in my ass cheeks. I reached into the back of the truck and got the umbrella. I twisted the handle and separated the shaft from the canopy, exposing the scabbard containing an eighteen-inch blade. I tied a cord on both ends of the scabbard and put it over my head. The sword hung at my side. Then I got my talisman out and tied it around my neck with a leather strap. I let out a loud, shrill, melodious scream that caused Broussard to almost jump out of his skin. "I'm ready now," I said.

"Holy shit, Percy. What the fuck are you trying to do, scare me to death?"

"Just wanted to let you know I'm ready."

"I'm ready too!" He pulled a twenty-five-caliber automatic pistol out of his pocket.

I laughed when I saw it. "You can't hit anything with that. I'll have to do all killing myself."

"Don't be so sure of yourself." He pulled up his pant leg, exposing a thirty-eight-caliber revolver in an ankle holster.

Chapter 29

I told Broussard to stop. I got out of the truck and I checked a compass to get our bearings. I climbed back in the lorry. We were close. I told Broussard that I was taking charge, and he had to do what I said without question or delay. He wanted to know what was going on. I said, "You're entering a different world now. It's a world where if there's one mistake, one wrong word from you, we could both be killed."

It was enough said. He drove slowly, heading north. We crossed miles of open grassland, and came to a cluster of trees on the edge of some high brush. A few hundred yards into the brush, the road turned sharply to the right. Around the turn, we came to a roadblock. Zulu warriors with shields and stabbing spears appeared from the brush on both sides of the truck. Four Zulu riflemen moved into position in front of the truck and motioned us out of the vehicle.

Broussard reached for his gun. I grabbed his wrist. He tried to pull his arm away. I held on. "Remember what I told you!"

Broussard released the gun. I got out of the truck, holding my hands in front of me. I recognized the men. We greeted each other. I watched Broussard out of the corner of my eye. "Come over here," I called to him. "Meet my brothers."

He came over and offered his hand. They just looked at him. I introduced everyone. I had four of the men remove the roadblock. I walked toward the village with the riflemen. Broussard followed us in the truck until we were a short distance to the village. He joined us and we walked single-file on a path through the brush. We were greeted by shouting and cheering villagers at the edge of the village. We met Matumbo, who was waiting for us in the center of the village. He smiled and opened his arms to me. "Welcome, my brother." We embraced.

I turned to Broussard and motioned him over to us. "Roger, this is my brother, Matumbo, Headman of the Natal Zulu."

"A pleasure, sir." Broussard bowed clumsily.

"It is good to meet a man who has traveled far with my brother *Balaa Dekua Baa.*"

Broussard looked at me.

"It's what the Zulu call me."

"Roger, you have traveled far with *The Man Who Brings Death to His Enemies,*" Matumbo said, "and you do my village an honor coming here to help."

I hadn't told Broussard of my plan. All I wanted him to know was that we going to stop the Nazi gold trade. The *how* it was to be done was up to Matumbo and me.

Broussard and I sat down with Matumbo in his elevated thatch house. I got right to the point. I said, "We must change our business plan."

"Why, my brother? Everything's working well for us. We have many guns now."

"That's good for today, but things won't go well for the Germans. They'll lose the battle in Africa. You'll suffer more greatly from the British if you help the Germans, my brother."

"The British are our enemy."

Broussard started to speak. I motioned him to be quiet. I said, "America has joined the war as an ally of the British. They are fighting together, and they will win. You must make peace with the British. Right now, they're willing to make a deal with the Zulu."

"Is it your wish that we make a deal, my brother?" Matumbo was noticeably uneasy with the idea.

"I wish only that you would consider such a deal. If it is good for the Zulu, then I want you to make a deal."

"With the British?" He shook his head no.

"Yes. And with the Boers too."

Broussard couldn't contain himself. "We'll guarantee the deal," he blurted out.

I glared at him, "I will guarantee the deal!" In Swahili I told Matumbo that the Allies were winning and that Rommel was being driven out of Tunis. Soon the Allies would run the Nazis completely out of North Africa. I said there was no time for delay; he had to make the deal right away.

I said to Broussard, "The British will have to supply weapons for the tribe. We can't let them be exposed. That's the deal."

"The British garrison in South Africa and Rhodesia will give the Zulu tribes all the protection they need," he said.

"No!" Matumbo jumped up. "We don't need their protection. We want their guns. Lots of guns and full amnesty for all the Zulu."

"The guns and the amnesty are a given, but they're offering protection too," Broussard said firmly. "Why not take it?"

Matumbo laughed. "Young man, you'll understand someday."

"Don't worry," I said, "the deal is done." The weapons were the centerpiece of the deal for the Zulu, but for everyone else it was based on gold and diamonds. Matumbo had what the Allies wanted, and the Allies had the guns and ammunition he wanted. I told Broussard either the Zulu got the guns they needed, or the deal would fall through.

Broussard was stubborn. "The Germans aren't going to attack in South Africa," he said.

"Are we back to that?" I said. "You think they won't attack down here, but you don't know shit!" I spoke aggressively, mostly for Matumbo's benefit.

"What will happen to the deal if they do?"

Matumbo laughed at him.

"No one here is afraid of the Germans," I said. I gave Broussard a look.

"I'm going to be looking to you after the war!" Matumbo said. He touched Broussard with the point of a stabbing spear.

Broussard took a step back. "The British have promised the Zulu land – their own country," Broussard said nervously. He looked to me for approval.

"We just have to be sure everyone keeps their end of the deal."

"It's going to work!" Broussard said.

"They need guns *now*, Roger. They have to defend their families. Do you understand that? They need the guns! Remember? No fucking guns, no fucking deal."

He nudged me and whispered, "Whose side are you on?"

He should have left things alone. Matumbo picked up on it, and jumped in. "Roger, if not for the guns, why would I deal with you?"

I interrupted, "In times like these, a man of honor makes a deal or walks away from it. If we don't have a meeting of the minds, then there is precious little for us to do here." I put my hands on Matumbo's shoulders. "I apologize. My associate knows nothing of the ways of this land. He thinks he understands the politics of your enemies, but he doesn't. Perhaps one day he will understand, my brother."

Matumbo asked Broussard, "Do you speak for the English or the Americans?"

"The United States government," Broussard said with pride.

Matumbo laughed. "Good answer. But will the United States government guarantee the money for the guns?"

I motioned Broussard with my hand not to answer.

Matumbo turned to me. "What do you think, my brother?"

"If you have the money, guns are always available," I said. "Roger, tell him the deal."

"I can get you paid, but I can't deliver guns," Broussard said.

"U.S. dollars?" Matumbo asked.

"Yes," Broussard said. "I can buy your gold and diamonds at a better price than you're getting now, and I'll get you paid in dollars. Do we have a deal?"

"You get me the dollars, and I'll buy my own guns."

Broussard followed me out of the hut; when we were out of earshot, he said, "I just made a deal I can't guarantee. What do I do now?"

"Nothing! You should have kept quiet and paid better attention. I said I would guarantee it. All you have to do is cover me with the army. The money's no problem. There's plenty of profit in it for me, if I have backing from the Allies."

"You're talking millions of dollars, Percy."

"The Germans will be out. That's what you wanted, right?"

"Yes. But what was all that talking you were doing with Matumbo, what was that all about?"

"I was just reassuring him you weren't a British agent. Limeys aren't well liked around here. All you have to do is get the British to part with some weapons."

233

"I have no say in that!"

"Well, if they don't sell us the guns, then I'll take the guns from them and pocket the gold myself."

"Watch yourself! You're talking treason!"

"I'm doing this for the Zulu!"

"And you have enough money to fund this deal?"

"Yes!"

"If the money is there, I think I can get weapons from the Boers. I'll talk to them when I get back to Pretoria."

"Okay, but don't tell them you have an alternative source for money. Just make the first buy as fast as they can deliver," I said.

"I'll ask for guarantees for Zulu freedom," Broussard said.

"Suit yourself. It doesn't matter. I don't trust the bastards anyway, and neither does Matumbo."

"But Matumbo is exposed, and he needs the help. I'll get the British to go along with the deal."

"Keep it simple. No matter what you think, the British can't be trusted. There's a history there. The Zulu are just looking for weapons to defend themselves. Don't give up too much in Pretoria."

Chapter 28

Broussard returned to the village from Pretoria with a promise that the Zulu would be given arms and ammunition. To my surprise, the British and the Zulu were now allies, and the flow of diamonds and gold to Germany was stopped. Matumbo was promised a homeland for his people. Matumbo and I agreed from the start that the purpose of our exercise with the Allies was to arm the Zulu nation with modern guns. Once that was accomplished, he was to take his chances on fighting to win his people's independence after the war was over, in the event the British reneged on their deal.

Before I left to return to America, Matumbo planned to attack a group of Afrikaners camped near his village, and he insisted that I join him. They were outlaws who waylaid foreign miners and prospectors in the border country. He also suspected they had raided a Zulu village and killed women and children.

He arranged festivities to divert Broussard's attention, so we could sneak away with a raiding party. Broussard watched Zulu warriors dance. The dancers were not in our raiding force; they were young warriors, armed with ceremonial shields and stabbing spears.

Matumbo and I slipped away unnoticed. We had to catch the Afrikaners in the Transvaal before they crossed into Rhodesia. If they got across the border, it could break the fragile truce that existed between the Rhodesians and the Zulu. But Matumbo took the chance, and was out for revenge – and when it was about revenge, he would go wherever he had to. He planned to punish them. I planned to take any diamonds and gold they had. I expanded on Matumbo's plan, by including a raid on a De Beers trading compound near the Afrikaner's camp.

De Beers bought diamonds with no questions asked from anyone, but they were treacherous in their dealings. Many of their agents bought diamonds and then killed the seller. My plan relied on their greed. We would take the diamonds from the De Beers outposts, and then sell them right back to them in Johannesburg.

De Beers' security agents were in cahoots with the Afrikaner raiders, the British, and any other scoundrels who dealt in diamonds. They had taken complete control of the diamond business. But there was one thing De Beers' men feared, and that was *The Man Who Brings Death to His Enemies*. It had been years since I had left, and yet many of them were still unable to sleep on bivouac, because they feared I would return.

When we got to where we thought the Afrikaners' camp was, they were gone. So, what had been an afterthought when we planned our attack became the main objective of our foray. A scout reported back that the Afrikaners were at the De Beers compound.

When we arrived at the compound, it was still. A lone sentry was at his post. I approached the sentry from behind with two warriors. He was sound asleep on a chair, with a rifle lying across his lap. I clamped my hand over his mouth and pulled him to the ground. The warriors jumped in. One slit his throat, and the other ran him through with his stabbing spear.

I sent one man to cut the telegraph line and another to scale the wall. He opened the gate from the inside. The rest of the raiding party entered the compound. I stationed two riflemen at the door of each of the eight barracks, and four others at the main hut.

The barracks were small thatched huts with two men in each one. The manager's residence housed a lone occupant. There were seven De Beers men and five Afrikaners in the compound. I had a force of seventeen warriors. Matumbo brought a boy along with him, and they stayed out of harm's way, outside the compound.

Matumbo agreed that we were to use minimal force. We were there to get prisoners. When my men were in place, I walked to the middle of the compound and gave the order to knock down all the doors. The De Beers men and the Afrikaners surrendered without a fight.

I had a man outside the door of the manager's hut and another man placed out of sight by the window. I fired a shot into the hut, above head level. I heard movement inside, and then the manager came running out with a pistol in his hand. He yelled, "Who the fuck shot at me?"

The warriors grabbed him from behind and disarmed him. He was put with the other captured men, in the center of the compound. Torches were lit, and in the light, I saw a man I thought I had killed in Léopoldville twenty years before – Hans Vanderlip. He recognized me and let out a scream, then lunged at me. Two of my men restrained him.

"Don't hurt him." I looked at him and smiled. "Yet."

"You fucking Kaffir!"

"Bring him here!" I ordered.

My men bound him hand and foot. He stood in front of me. "I heard you were dead and buried in England," he said, glaring at me. His chest was heaving up and down.

"And I thought I killed *you*! Hell, I knew I did! I saw you go down with a knife in your chest. I've got it – you're a zombie! You're a fucking zombie! Juju magic, that's it. Yeah! No! I've got it! You're a ghost. You're a fucking ghost." I laughed, and my men laughed too.

"It takes more than a stinking Kaffir's knife to kill me."

"I'll correct that soon enough. There has to be a reason you're here. God must be watching over me."

He struggled to free his hands. "If I had known you were alive, I would've come after you, you fucking Kaffir."

"You're a lucky man. You got a reprieve once," I said. "You know, Hans, when I killed your father, I knew I had to kill you too. I knew you would've come after me, just like I would've come after you. But you'll never know the joy of watching me die or the thrill that you get only from taking revenge. I am reserving that pleasure for myself."

Vanderlip let out a bloodcurdling scream. One of the men guarding him pushed him to his knees. He fell over. "I'll see you in hell, Kaffir." He was crying.

"Maybe, but you'll talk first."

Matumbo came forward. He asked Vanderlip, "Are those tears for the women and children you have killed?"

Vanderlip looked at me. "I was a soldier following orders. You should understand." He was fighting for his life. I could see the fear in his eyes.

The Zulu were growing impatient. Several of them got wood from a woodpile and began to build a fire in the center of the compound. I had all the prisoners bound, hand and foot, and placed with their backs to the fire. I watched Vanderlip when I spoke to his men. "It's not that you die. It's *how* you die."

Matumbo broke his silence. "Too much talk. Get on with it!" He motioned a boy to look over the men. The boy studied the prisoners, and pointed at two of them. Matumbo had the men brought to him. He asked the boy in Swahili, "Why did you choose those two men?"

"They were at my village."

"Why did they come to your village?" Matumbo asked.

"They were looking for diamonds."

"Are you sure these are the men that came to your village?"

The boy nodded. "They killed my family and burned our hut."

"Do you recognize any others?"

"No."

Matumbo looked at the men and spoke to them in Afrikaans, "The boy tells me you came to his village."

Both men talked at once, each accusing the other and swearing the boy was mistaken. One cried, "No, not me! I'm not guilty. Not me, not me!" The other man shouted incoherently, making no sense at all. I walked over to him, and hit him in the back of the head with the butt of my sword. He fell face first into the dirt. I looked to Matumbo. He threw his stabbing spear into the ground to signify death.

The Zulu cheered while they loaded wood on the fire, until it was piled six feet high at the center. Two warriors walked past the incoherent Afrikaner to the other man who was singled out by the boy. One grabbed his hair and dragged him toward the fire. He turned the man's head toward me. I asked him if he had the diamonds that he had taken from the boy's village.

He said that I had the wrong man and that he knew nothing about any diamonds. He looked at Vanderlip. Vanderlip nodded his head in approval. The man looked at me, and pursed his lips. That was enough of an answer for me. I nodded to the warriors, and they lifted the man off the ground and fed him slowly into the fire, feet first. He struggled and screamed. He pled for his life, but

Matumbo had pronounced a death sentence. We were honor-bound to carry it out. I planned to use the executions as an aid in the interrogations that were to follow. The Zulu were interested in revenge; I was interested in the diamonds.

The other man was lifted up so he could watch the other man burn alive. The burning man let out bloodcurdling screams. The Zulu chanted and celebrated, poking the other captives with their stabbing spears and gun butts as the flames consumed the man.

I asked the man, who had appeared incoherent, where the diamonds were. He asked what would happen to him if he told me. Before I could answer, Vanderlip shouted, "You'll wish they'd burned you if you say anything." A guard hit Vanderlip in the head and knocked him to the ground.

I asked Matumbo if I could spare the man to get information I wanted. He shook his head no. I had my orders. I went to the man and told him if he told me where the diamonds were, I would shoot him before they threw him into the fire.

He said, "That's no deal!" He spat.

He was thrown into the fire. Matumbo watched with the boy at his side until the man was dead. "Finish up here," he said. He took the boy and three of his men, and left the compound.

Chapter 29

There was a stench of burning flesh permeating the air in the compound. I didn't want to be there, but I had no choice. I looked at Vanderlip, who was on the ground looking right back at me. His hands were bound tightly behind his back. The other captives were lined up and seated with their backs to the fire. I told them all that they had a choice: they could live or die.

The Zulu piled more wood on the fire. I walked in front of the captives. "You know someone will talk," I said. I paced slowly back and forth. One man seemed especially nervous. I pointed at him, and two Zulu brought him to me. I grabbed him by the hair and asked him where the diamonds where. He said he didn't know. I pushed him away. He fell on his side to the ground and didn't try to move. I put my foot on his throat and shouted, "Where are the fucking diamonds?"

He sobbed, "They're here."

"Shut up Dehaan, you fucking fool!" Vanderlip shouted.

Two Zulu rushed to Vanderlip. One grabbed him by the shoulders, and the other put a dagger to his throat. "Hold it!" I shouted.

"He should die," a warrior shouted in Swahili.

"It's not time!" I shouted.

"I understand that, Kaffir!" Vanderlip said.

I walked in front of Vanderlip. "You could save us all a lot of trouble by telling me where everything is."

"You'll never find it!"

"We'll see," I said. I had the Zulu gag him.

I turned my attention to Dehaan, the man on the ground. I told him that if he wanted to live, he had to tell me where the goods were. He said they were in the big hut. But I had already had the Zulu go through the hut and they had found nothing, so I had them level the place. I watched Vanderlip closely as the men dug through the wreckage. He didn't react to anything that was happening; I knew there was nothing in the hut.

I went back to Dehaan and asked him again where the diamonds were. He said he'd already told all that he knew. I motioned for my men to put him in the fire. Two Zulu came and picked him up. He started to pray. "Hold up! I think he's told us everything he knows," I said.

I stopped the men who were digging under the hut. We had only a couple of hours until the Afrikaner raiding parties would return. I asked Dehaan where the men who met with Vanderlip in the hut went.

"They buried them outside the fence, near the river," he whispered. Vanderlip flew into a rage and struggled with his ropes. I was on the right track.

I cut the ropes on Dehaan's feet and helped him up. I asked him to show me where the men were buried. He didn't answer. I asked him again, and pushed him toward the gate. "I don't know." He said, and he broke down. "I saw them carried out of the compound."

"Who carried them out?"

"The burial detail."

242

I had him point out who was on the detail. He nodded at several of the men. I asked the men he identified who wanted to be a volunteer. No one answered. I pointed at the man who cooperated and said, "He told us what he knew." I paused and looked around at the men. "He will live." I pointed to the fire. The Zulu piled on more wood.

I had one of the men from the burial detail brought to me. I asked him where the diamonds were. He was defiant, and said he didn't know. I asked him where the men were buried. He said nothing. The Zulu were impatient, and before I could ask the man anything else, they grabbed him and threw him in the fire.

I had another man brought to me. I told my men to give him a chance to answer before they threw him in the fire. I asked him, "Where are the men buried?"

"In a clearing near the river," he said matter-of-factly. I'll show you if you let me go."

"What makes you think I'll let you go, even if I say I will?"

"I heard the white savage always leaves someone to tell his tale."

I unsheathed my sword and cut the bindings on the man's legs. A warrior helped him to his feet. Several Zulu took shovels from beside the communications hut, and we followed him on the trail to a clearing. He pointed to a spot about fifty yards from the compound. "We buried them right there," He said.

The soft soil was easy to move, and my men turned up bones a foot beneath the surface. There was nothing buried there with the bodies. I walked to the river, and turned back and looked at the camp. I wondered what a man who trusted no one would do with valuables. I saw from where the sentry was located outside the encampment that Vanderlip wanted to make sure that he could stop anyone from finding out that nothing was buried there. He had stashed it elsewhere.

I wasn't going to waste any more time on Vanderlip. Matumbo would have to make him talk when he got him back to the village. But I needed to do something to make the night's foray pay off for us. I planned to waylay the Afrikaners, whom I expected to come in the morning.

I kept the ten riflemen with me. Matumbo and three warriors took Vanderlip and the other captives to the village. Two injured prisoners and the man who volunteered the location of the graves were gagged, and tied to stakes in the compound. Vanderlip was bound hand and foot, gagged, and tied on a litter. Four of the prisoners carried him. The rest of the prisoners were led off, with hands tied behind their backs and a rope around their necks.

We put the sentry's corpse and more wood on the fire. The stench of burnt human flesh drifted downwind to the east, across the river. Anyone approaching from that direction would know something was wrong, long before they got close to the compound. But the river was deep and the only crossing was miles to the north; the main trail to the compound came in from the west. I felt it was worth the risk. I had the gates closed and four men hid inside the compound. I waited with the rest of my riflemen on the main trail, hunkered down in the brush.

We didn't have to wait long for the first of the traders to show up on the main trail. There were four men, and they seemed oblivious to what was going on in the compound. They came up to the gate and banged on it. The gate opened part way, and two men got in before the door was closed. The Zulu rushed the two men left outside, and killed them before I could stop them.

The dead men were dragged into the compound and put in the fire. The other Afrikaners had already been put in the fire. We took their diamonds. It was a small cache, but I didn't want to take any more risks.

I went to one of the wounded men and called a Zulu to help me untie him. Before I could let him go free, he screamed, "Don't kill me! Don't kill me! I know where the diamonds are!"

Michael Shure

Chapter 30

There was still daylight left when I got back to the village with my contingent. Everything there was quiet after a day of celebration. I went to the main hut and found Matumbo and Broussard sharing dinner. "Join us," Matumbo said.

"No!" I said, "I have some news!"

"Let's have it," Matumbo said.

I pointed to Broussard.

"He's with me," Matumbo said, "he can stay."

I said, "Hey, it's your call!" I was surprised to see the two of them together.

Matumbo gave me a chilling look. "Get to it, Percy."

"Your just gonna' love this," I said. I moved in behind Broussard, put my hands on his shoulders, and leaned on him.

He turned his head and asked, "What in the hell are you doing boy?"

"Boy my ass!" I whispered, "Turn your head back!" I kept pressure on his shoulders and said, "Vanderlip traded all his uncut diamonds and gold for cut diamonds. And what's important is he never leaves his diamonds anywhere."

"Then where are they?" Matumbo asked.

"*In* him," I said.

"*In* him?" Broussard chipped in.

"He swallowed them during our raid. I figure he thinks we won't kill him until we find them."

"Holy shit!" Broussard tried to jump up, but I held him down. "Let go of me Percy!"

I let him get up. He looked at me and said, "What's wrong with you?"

"More that you'll ever know," I laughed.

Matumbo slowly stood up. He towered over the short, stocky Broussard. He said, "Hold everything!" He patted him on the top of his head. "I'll handle this *my* way." He pointed at me. "Good work, my brother!" He left the hut. I knew it was my job to keep Broussard there while he was gone.

While we waited together, Broussard told me what had happened in the village after I left to go on the raid. He said he had been awakened at dawn by a commotion in front of his hut caused by a group of young boys beating the ground with spears, and shouting for him to come out. Word of an Afrikaner raid on a Zulu village near Nhlangomo had reached the village, and the boys had worked themselves into a wild frenzy over it. They were shouting that he was a white man and should die.

He had slipped out the back of his hut, before a couple of the boys got into it. Then he hid behind some large baskets at the side of his hut where they couldn't find him. The boys left his hut and went toward the center of the village where the warriors had gathered.

Broussard followed the crowd at a distance. He watched as the men and boys milled around pounding their spears on the ground and chanting. An elder motioned for everyone to follow him, and he led them to a hill near the edge of the village. From there you could see the savannah that spread out to the north. Another elder of the tribe, replete with ceremonial battle attire, had already climbed to a lookout point on a mound and was pointing north with his stabbing spear and pounding the ground with his shield. He shouted, "The Dream Maker has spoken. His prophecy is fulfilled and Matumbo returns!" All the villagers cheered. The elder held up his hands to still the crowd. He shouted a praise song to Matumbo; singing of his many successes, and of the brave men who served under him.

Broussard stayed out of sight until he saw Matumbo. He came forward and pushed through the crowd to get to him. He bumped against several men as he tried to move them out of his way. They grabbed him. He yelled for Matumbo, but he was quickly overpowered by the men. They dragged him to a hut, and pushed him in. They left him there, tightly bound, laying on the floor. Half an hour later, the Afrikaner prisoners were brought to the hut. Broussard asked the warriors who brought the prisoners in, to tell Matumbo he was there.

The warriors didn't answer him. Two stationed themselves in the doorway to guard the prisoners; the others left. Vanderlip had overheard him and squirmed over to where he was. Vanderlip asked him if he was an American. Broussard told him he was, and asked Vanderlip where he had come from. Vanderlip forced a laugh, and told him he had been in South Africa all his life. Broussard said he had meant how long had he been in the village. Vanderlip told him that he had just been brought there, and asked what an American like him was doing there. Broussard went into his cover story and told him that he was a biologist.

Vanderlip asked him what he was doing with the Zulu. He said he was on his way to Durban from Kenya. Vanderlip laughed and said, "I thought so! You're one of them erudite types."

Broussard asked him what he meant by erudite. Vanderlip said he meant the kind of man that goes to the Serengeti to examine the pustules on the hind parts of the great apes, and then make a big fuss about what he finds.

Broussard ignored him and asked him how the Zulu got him. Vanderlip said, "The bastards raided my trading post last night."

Broussard figured the prisoners in the hut were all from the raid. He asked if his trading post was near the village. Vanderlip told him that it was near the Rhodesian border. Then, he went on to tell him that the Zulu had a way of dealing with prisoners and it was going to get messy around the village.

Broussard asked, "What do you mean, 'messy'?"

He said matter-of-factly, "Just that we're all dead men!" When Broussard didn't answer, Vanderlip lost his temper and shouted, "Didn't you hear what I said?"

Broussard fought with his ropes and said, "Yeah, I heard you! How're they going to do it?"

"The fuckers are going to take us out, one by one, and kill us. And I'll be the last one they kill. You can bet on that."

"Matumbo isn't like that." As soon as he said it, Broussard realized he'd said too much. He looked away.

"I figured you knew Matumbo," Vanderlip said. "You're a fucking spy!" Vanderlip shouted, "How do you know him?"

Broussard didn't answer him anymore after that. Vanderlip kept talking, but Broussard pretended not to hear him. It was several hours before Matumbo's men came for him.

Vanderlip called out, "Don't forget our deal. You promised," as the Zulu took Broussard away.

One of the guards asked Broussard about Vanderlip. Broussard told the guard that he didn't know him, and had no involvement with him. The guard left Broussard in the hut and went to tell Matumbo what he had heard.

Matumbo had Vanderlip brought to him. Vanderlip had concocted a story so incredible that Matumbo knew that, on the face of it, it couldn't be true. Matumbo sent Vanderlip back, and had Broussard brought to him. That was the first time the two men had any interaction with each other without me there.

Broussard had picked up bits and pieces of information about my raiding party after I left the village, but he didn't know the details. I was in the middle of filling him in when Matumbo sent for me. I went to his wife's hut where he was waiting for Vanderlip to be brought in. When Vanderlip got there, Matumbo had him stripped naked and tied in a woven chair with the seat removed. Under the chair, Matumbo put five layers of finely woven cloth. Matumbo held a cup up to Vanderlip's mouth and offered him a drink of warm tea. He refused it. Matumbo had two guards administer it to him forcibly. It was an herbal tea laced with a strong laxative. Matumbo asked me to leave the hut. He would call if he needed me.

I waited with Broussard to hear from him. It was six hours until he sent for me. He told me that Vanderlip had had a lot of tea. He was force-fed the tea every fifteen minutes. During that time, he excreted 271 of the finest brilliant cut diamonds in Africa. Vanderlip seemed resigned to his fate. He sat quietly and watched as Matumbo's wife washed and weighed the diamonds right in front of him. When Matumbo was satisfied that he had all the diamonds, he gagged Vanderlip. Then he sorted the diamonds and laid them out on a table in front of me.

"Nice haul," I said.

"What would all the fine ladies in Europe and America think if they knew where these diamonds had been stored?" He laughed.

"They'll never know, and truth be known, I don't think they'd care if they did know."

"Well, to the victors, Percy," Matumbo said. "To the victors!" He put his hand on my shoulder and pulled me toward him. He embraced me.

"To the victors!" I said.

"How do you like that? We're the victors."

"Good feeling."

"It is, and I've got an idea that will make it even better," he said.

"What's that?"

"A full share for you," he said, "and that means half the diamonds."

"The way of the buccaneer!"

"Aye, aye, Captain Hays."

He had come full circle. The principled Headman of the Zulu had become a mercenary. I was happy. "Couldn't ask for more than that," I said.

"Are you sure about that?"

"Well, I could always use a ration of rum," I laughed.

We chose the diamonds by picking in turn, one at a time. Matumbo offered to let me go first, but I deferred to him. When we were done, I had 135 of some of the best diamonds ever to come out of Africa.

I left it up to Matumbo to reunite Vanderlip with his father. It had to be done, but I didn't want to be a part of it anymore. I went with Broussard, and we took a sojourn in Durban, to avoid the bloody spectacle that was to follow in the village.

By the time Broussard and I returned to the village, the carnage was done and things were already back to a relative calm there. The weapons Matumbo needed from the British took several more weeks to get there. I asked for leave to go back to America to be with my granddaughter. Broussard contacted the United States War Department and had my amnesty finalized. I was issued a valid American passport.

Broussard stayed on with Matumbo. He arranged with the Allies to stay and fight alongside the Zulu.

Broussard and Matumbo had given me my life back. I once again felt the euphoria that only a warrior can know from victory. I loved the feeling I got and it made me realize I hadn't done it for what I could make from the deal. I had enough saved in my Swiss account that Pearl would never have to worry about money. I did it for my brother Matumbo, and I couldn't keep any of the diamonds; they were tainted with the blood of my brothers. I gave my share to Matumbo with the hope it would help buy freedom for my adopted people.

During the last of my stay in the village, Broussard became a zealous advocate for a Zulu homeland. With the help of the American Ambassador, he wrestled a commitment out of the British to help the Zulu gain a homeland of their own after the war. He also became involved with a Zulu girl and married her. My first instinct was to tell him he was crazy. I just couldn't see how a good old boy from Louisiana could find happiness with an African woman, but I wished him well.

Broussard imposed upon the Allied commander to arrange safe passage for me. I headed to the United States on a freighter, compliments of the British government. A group of young warriors serenaded me the day I left, singing my praise song. I tried to hide the tears that welled up inside me, but I did a poor job of it. I would miss my adopted brothers, but I have never regretted going back to Baltimore, and to Pearl.

Michael Shure

Chapter 31

The war was going well for the United States, by the time I arrived back in Baltimore in the summer of 1944. Unfortunately, a lot of boys would die before Germany and Japan surrendered.

I decided on the trip home that it was the right time for me to start living the life of a retired man. All I would need to accomplish my goal was a library card, a supply of Cuban cigars, and a lot of good island rum. I should have known better, because I wasn't home three days when Little Willie Jonson's black Buick sedan pulled up and parked in front of Helga's house. I got to the door and opened it before he could knock. As soon as he saw me, he blurted out, "I need your help!"

"Don't I rate a 'hello,' boy?" I feigned indignation.

"Yes, sir, you do, I'm sorry 'bout that." He cleared his throat, "Hello Percy, I missed you. I've been looking for you."

"I see. Well, I've been away, boy."

"No one 'round here would tell me when you was coming back. I need your help, bad." He tried to get by me into the house. I blocked the door with my body. "Can't I come in?"

"Sounds like you want to talk some business. So we'd best be talking out here." I took hold of his arm and led him out to the sidewalk. Pearl was home, and she had a bad habit of listening in on my conversations.

"I'd rather not talk out here," Willie said. "Please, can I come in?"

"I'll meet you somewhere tomorrow," I said.

"It can't wait! Can we go in my car?"

I nodded. In the car he gave me a pained look. "They're moving in on my territory, Percy!"

"Who are 'they'?"

"Some Jews are rolling my runners for cash!"

"Jews?"

"Yeah, I think they're working for Goldstein."

"All of Goldstein's boys are Jewish!"

"No! Not like that! They speak Jewish."

"You mean foreigners, right?"

"Yeah! From Poland and places like that."

"Where'd you hear that?"

"Doc Allen!"

"What did he say?"

"He said they were refugees from Europe."

"You have a deal with Goldstein, don't you?"

"I thought I did."

"What do you mean, 'you thought you did'? You either do or you don't, boy."

"It's not that easy."

"It is. You just walk your own self down to his place and tell him to cut the shit."

"Percy, I tried that. That's the first thing I did."

"What happened?"

"He said he had nothing to do with them men."

"Do you believe him?"

"I don't know. In the last year or so, everything's changed. They's new guys there now. Refugees is coming here in droves. Morty said he's got enough to do protecting his own ground."

"Then they're not working for Morty, right?"

"He says not."

"But they're not bothering him?"

"Right. He said as long as they leave him alone, it's not his problem."

"So just what do you think I can do about it?"

"Straighten it out with Morty for me."

"What's an old man like me going to do, that you can't?"

"Don't give me that!"

"Well, I am an old man, boy. I'm old, and I'm tired, too. You need to hire yourself some muscle. Plenty of boys out there would be willing to visit Goldstein for you. One visit is all it would take."

"Ain't so, Percy. He's got boys of his own, and there'd be trouble."

"There's nothing I can do."

"Yeah, there is. I know about you, Percy."

"And what do you know, boy?"

"That you was a soldier of fortune."

"A soldier of fortune, huh? And for how long have you been carrying the burden of that information around with you?"

"I've known since I was a boy. My grandfather told me all about you. He told Helga, too. When you first came and took care of them Muelly boys, we never said nothing."

"You'd best be careful what you say now!"

"Hell, Percy, the whole damn city knows what you done to them Muelly boys."

"I don't like this talk, Willie."

"But it's true. Pappy was always telling stories about you. I wasn't a hundred percent sure the stories were all true 'til the day them Muelly boys died. And then here recently, I talked to Doc Allen when I was looking for you. He told me all about what you was doing. He's got a big mouth, you know!"

I heard Willie out. I loved the boy like he was my own son. He reminded me a lot of Pappy. He was small like Pappy was and scrappy, too. I put my hand on his shoulders. "It's going to be all right. Don't you be worried none; I'll handle it."

I invited him into the house, but cautioned him not to talk business. Helga was waiting for us in the hall, and greeted Willie, and offered him something to eat.

"No, thanks," he said.

"You sure, Willie? It looks to me like no one's feeding you." Helga laughed.

Pearl was on the steps watching everything. She giggled. I looked at her, and she flashed a big smile and winked at me. "Grandpa, you going to get dinner from Leon's Pig Pen, like you promised?"

"Sure, sugar. I'll go as soon as I finish up here with Willie."

"Willie, Grandpa's going to get some pulled pork for supper. Want some?"

"I don't know, 'cause ..."

"Stay! I'll only be a couple minutes getting the food."

"If you're sure it's okay, Percy."

"I want you to stay." I knew Pearl wanted him there.

"Yeah, then I'll stay."

I wasted no time. I made plans to set myself up in the drugstore again, and run everything from there. My first order of business was to break the news to Doc Allen that I was back. The next morning my first stop was the prescription counter. "I'm back, Boss," I said enthusiastically.

He was startled, "I .... ca...can see that. I'm, glad you sta...stopped in to say hello. I wa...was worried something ma...might have happened to you."

"I didn't stop in to say hello. I'm reporting for work, Doc."

"Ba...but Broussard told me you were ga...going to be working with him."

"I am, Doc. That's why I'm here."

He was upset. "But Percy...."

I interrupted, "It will be things as usual!"

"Where's Broussard? Wha...why isn't he with you?"

"I can't tell you, Doc. It's top secret."

"I...da...don't know, Pa...Percy."

"Doc, I have a job to do for Broussard. He's at risk, and so am I. This is going to be my safe-house." I was making the story up as I went along. "I have to work from here. I'm going to need a couple of phones downstairs, and I have to build a reinforced office for myself down there, too."

"I...dow...don't know. I don't na...need the ha...help, Percy. I got Ja...Jimmy doing the clean up, and he's ha...helping at the soda fountain." Doc was sweating.

"Listen! Broussard needs me, and I'm going to help him." I got right up in his face. "I need your cooperation, and I'm going to get it."

He didn't respond.

"I'll be back in the morning."

Doc was shaking. "I don't know! What about Jimmy?"

Jimmy heard what was going on through the vents and ran up to Doc. "Call me, Boss?" He was ducking and dodging like he was a boxer. He kept looking up at the ceiling.

"Na...no!" Doc said.

"What's the problem, James?" I asked.

"You not going to try and put me out!" He shadowboxed as he spoke. "I'm ready for you!" He kept looking up.

"We're going to work together, boy. Don't you worry none!" I said.

"Yeah! Okay!" He looked up again.

259

"What's troubling you, boy?" I asked.

"There's a goofus on the roofus," he said. He scurried to the cellar door and ran down the steps.

I looked to Doc for his reaction. He just shook his head. James' behavior wasn't my problem. I didn't have time to mess with Doc, and I didn't want him calling the FBI. I refocused. "The government is paying me, so you don't have to put me on the payroll. They said it would be all right for me to pay some rent too. Not a lot, Doc, but something. Oh! And it'll have to be cash. We can't leave an audit trail."

His ears perked up. "Cash?"

"Yeah, it has to be in cash. And you can't tell anyone about it, either!"

"Ha...how ma...much?"

"I can get you seventy-five dollars a month." I'd be working for nothing, and he could pocket the rent money. He loved the deal. I had rolled him over for pocket money.

By the time I got set up, the pressure on Willie had come close to the boiling point. His men were being strong-armed and rolled for their money almost daily. I figured some of the hits were real, but others were Willie's own men capitalizing on the situation. I needed some controls on my business, and more proof that Goldstein was directly involved before I confronted him.

I started making my runners make their drops three times a day at the drugstore. I had them eat their lunches at the drugstore fountain, and buy their cigarettes, beer, and liquor at the store, too.

There was some rough stuff on the street, but our losses were minimal. Willie's boys couldn't understand the refugees when they spoke, but they found out soon enough that I spoke their language. The boys were more scared of me than they were of them.

One of my tougher boys, an enforcer, was given a Kodak camera that I borrowed from Doc. He followed the runners and took pictures of the men who were mugging them. I sent copies to Goldstein, and asked if he knew any of the men in the pictures.

In response, Goldstein warned Willie that there was going to be trouble. Willie was more worried, and wanted us to give it all up. He owned a liquor store in downtown Baltimore, and wanted me to work with him there. I made him get out of the rackets and go to work in his store. I wanted him clear of trouble, but I couldn't tolerate being run out of business by the likes of Goldstein. I was going to finish what I started.

By March 1945, I had the numbers racket going full blast, and the diamond trade picked up, so a lot of chocolate found its way to me. But I made sure all the contraband was in and out of the store the same day it came in. I didn't want any diamonds around the store with the threat of a raid from Goldstein's men. I should have ended the numbers racket and walked away, because the money was pennies next to the diamond trade. But there was always something inside me that wouldn't let me be driven out of anything – *ever*.

One day, out of the blue, I got a threatening phone call suggesting that my family could get hurt if I didn't close up Willie's numbers business. At that moment, I became a very dangerous man, as far as Mr. Morton Goldstein and his friends were concerned. They knew Willie was out of the business, and they seemed emboldened by the prospect of dealing with an old man like me. No one had been killed in our little turf war, but there was always the possibility it could happen. I decided to be the first one to raise things up a notch, and bring everything to a head.

I made a call to Goldstein. I told him I would be at the streetcar stop at Liberty Heights and Garrison Boulevard at noon. I said I was taking the streetcar over to come see him.

"Why are you telling me that?" he asked.

"It gives you a chance to get to me before I get there and get to you," I laughed.

"What the fuck's wrong with you, Hays?"

"I'll be there at noon. You'll find out when I get there." I hung up.

At Goldstein's building, two large men with handguns were waiting for me. They frisked me, and then led me into his office. They found a razor I'd planted for them to find in my shoe. But they didn't find my throwing dagger and my Derringer. They put me in a chair facing Morty Goldstein's desk. After a minute, I heard a toilet flush, and then Morty came out of the head. He sat down facing me.

"Well, you called this meeting."

"I sure did. I came here to make you an offer."

"What kind of offer?"

"You see, Mr. Goldstein, I have a problem."

"And that is, Mr. Hays?"

"You can call me Percy, Mr. Goldstein."

"And you can call me Morty."

"Okay, Morty. See, we're making progress already."

"Get on with it, Percy."

"Well, here's the problem in a nutshell, Morty. If you don't stop your bagel-bending, motherfucking, Jew refugee bastards from robbing my boys, there's going to be a lot of trouble!"

"I wish I could help you, but I have no control over those men."

"Uh huh, I see. But they aren't bothering you. Right?"

"I've been lucky," he chuckled, "real lucky."

"It's not a laughing matter, Morty."

"Maybe not, but I can't help you. Now, I want you to go on about your business, and we'll forget you made this little visit."

"Is that so?"

"Yeah, that's so. And I don't want to ever see your high-tone, jaundice-looking, uptown nigger ass anywhere around here again. Hear me, boy?" He looked at his bodyguards, and they laughed.

I smiled. "I hear you, but I don't think you heard me, Morty. I want you to agree right now to call off your boys."

"You're one fucking crazy nigger."

"Morty, listen to me. I am not asking you. I'm telling you."

"And if I don't?" He and his men laughed again.

"If you don't agree, I'll throw you head first out that window over there." I pointed to a window behind his desk.

He snickered. "And how do you expect to do that?"

"By grabbing you by your collar and your belt, and then heaving your fat ass out the window. That's how!"

"In case you forgot, there's Manny and Nathan." He pointed to them. "They're here to see that things like that don't happen."

"I'll handle them. That's no problem."

They all laughed.

I paused for a second. "Do you mind if I stand up?"

"Don't move, Schwarze," Nathan said.

"That's all right. Let him stand. I'm curious. But watch him, boys," he said. Then he stood and said to me, "Okay, stand up. But do it slow."

I stood and looked around the room. I turned to Manny and said, "I noticed when I came in you were holding your pistol in your left hand."

"So?"

I put my right hand in my right pocket. Nathan was behind me. He said in his broken English, "Watch yourself."

"I have an itch. Don't panic!" and I put my hands up.

263

"Percy, you got an itch, you scratch it." He laughed. He looked at the men and said, "Keep an eye on him, so he doesn't do anything funny."

I put my hands in my pockets, and then through the holes I had cut in them to get to my backside. I got the dagger in my right hand and the Derringer in my left. I kept my hands in my pockets. "I was getting ready to tell you how I was going to deal with these men here. Here's what I plan to do. First, I'm going to stick a knife in Manny's left arm. Then I'm going to hope that Nathan doesn't move for his own goddamn sake."

"How do you plan to do all that?" Morty asked.

"I won't have to do it, if we have a deal. "

"We don't have a deal. There's not going to be a deal. So you get your high-tone ass out of my office, and don't ever come back. Do you understand that?"

"Then you leave me no choice, Morty. You're going head-first out the window!"

He stood up and grimaced. "Throw the nigger out!"

They came at me. I stepped to the side. I pulled out the knife and the gun. I stuck the knife, to the hilt, into Manny's left forearm. Nathan pulled a gun. I shot him in the hand, and the gun fell to the floor. I motioned them into the bathroom.

"Oh shit! Don't kill me!" Morty pleaded.

"Do I have to?"

Morty wet himself. "What the fuck do you want from me?"

"Here's the deal. The first time someone bothers one of my crew, and I find out it was one of your boys, I am going to cut your little finger off. Then, if it happens again, I'm going to cut your hand off. You use your imagination to decide what'll happen if there's a third time. Now, I want you to open the window and jump out head first."

"What for?" He was shaking.

"As a show of good faith. To seal the deal."

"You're fucking crazy."

"Maybe so. But here's the final part of the deal. You see that none of your people ever threaten me or my family again, and in return, I'll guarantee that you won't be found face-up in a landfill with your own dick in your mouth."

Morty was scared. "I can't control those guys."

"You're going to have to *find* a way to control them. If any of them gives you trouble, you let me know which one. If any of them get out of line and you don't call and tell me, then I'll have to assume you broke the deal."

"You son of a bitch!"

"Sticks and stones...." Morty just looked at me. "I take it the answer is 'yes'?"

He walked to the window and opened it, then turned and looked back at me. I waved my pistol at him. He turned to face the window and then slid out headfirst. I heard a thump and a scream. I looked out. He was lying on the sidewalk, holding his shoulder. I called the boys out of the bathroom and sent them out to help him.

We had no trouble between the factions after that day. Morty kept his end of the bargain, and everyone stuck to his own territory. After a few months, I turned the operation back over to Willie, and he ran it from his liquor store.

I decided to help ensure a lasting peace with a friendly gesture. I had a good-quality diamond made into a pinkie ring. I took the ring with me on my second visit to Goldstein's office. He was frightened when he saw me at first.

"Don't worry, Morty. It's a social call."

"I'm doing everything right," he said.

"I know you are."

"I'm going to honor our deal, Percy." He was breathing heavily.

"Look, Morty, I told you it was a social call. I'm glad things have worked so well."

He forced a smiled. "Is that all you came for?"

"I came to thank you for your cooperation and to give you a token of my appreciation." I held out the pinkie ring.

He looked at the ring, and it confused him. "What? I don't understand."

"I want you to have this as a token of my appreciation, Morty."

"What are you up to?"

"Building goodwill! I want you to wear the ring, and every time you look at it, think about how well everyone is doing."

He looked at me funny. "Okay."

"I want you to wear it in good health, you understand?"

He was nervous.

"By the way, how's your shoulder?"

"It's okay," he said, patting his shoulder softly. "It hurts sometimes when it rains."

"Sorry about that. I don't want anything like that happening to you again. I worry about you, sometimes."

"Don't worry. Everything's fine. Yeah. It's really okay."

"I'm glad of that. You take care of yourself, Morty, you hear me?"

"I do hear you!"

Willie and I never again had a problem with our good friend and competitor, Mr. Morton Goldstein.

Chapter 32

It was on a cold, dreary day in January 1950 when I cleared all my personal effects from Doc Allen's drugstore, and left for good without so much as a "fare thee well." I had retired from the diamond trade and there was precious little left for me to do that was of any interest for me. I began spending most all of my time at home reading, listening to records, and watching television. When the Korean War started, I read everything I could about it, and watched the news reports on the television every night. I liked TV, although I never really understood how they got the pictures into the box.

I liked my new life and didn't give much thought to my past – that is, until the war ended in the summer of 1953, and I felt sad. I found the peace treaty very disquieting, because I felt that a limited war kept a much larger conflict from developing. I worried for Pearl and her generation, and what the future would hold for them.

Helga died in January 1954, and I felt my time was nearing, too. I needed to think of a guardian for Pearl – someone I could trust. I had learned over the years that most people wanted not only what was theirs, but also what was yours. There was only one man who would fit the bill: Willie Jonson.

I talked to Pearl about Willie taking care of her, but she had a crush on him and she didn't want to have to deal with him as her guardian. She asked me to meet with her preacher, Daddy Grace. She wanted me to get to know him. She said he could be her guardian. At her insistence, I agreed to meet with him. But I was dead set on Willie, and told her it would take a miracle to make me to change my mind.

Daddy Grace was a disciple of Father Divine, a colored evangelist who recruited his followers by traveling up and down the eastern seaboard. Almost all of their followers were women, and both men lived off the generosity of their followers.

Daddy Grace held his Sunday services in a rundown storefront sanctuary, on a busy street near the city streetcar terminal. It was in a bad part of town, and a lot of derelicts hung around the neighborhood. I tried to convince Pearl not to go there, but she didn't listen to me. So unbeknownst to her, I had Willie send some boys to keep an eye on her every time she went there. I didn't like her leaving our neighborhood, because I felt she was safe there.

Daddy Grace was known to be a busybody who was always putting himself into other people's affairs. He was full of what I call Holy Roller bullshit. I likened him to the Hottentots that I had to deal with in South Africa – but I knew that if I made a big deal of my feelings, it would only strengthen Pearl's resolve. She was like my mother in that way.

I finally had to level with Pearl and tell her that my health was failing. She didn't want to discuss it, so I forced the issue. She said if I was going to talk to her about it, I should consider her feelings and keep an open mind when I met with Daddy Grace. I figured that she wanted to get her hands directly on her inheritance by having me name him her guardian.

I knew Daddy Grace would have his agenda set when he came to see me, but I had mine. To me, he was nothing more than a damn clown. But to humor her, I took the meeting.

Pearl led Reverend Grace into the living room. I stood up and greeted her with a kiss on her cheek. He was five foot five and weighed well over two hundred and fifty pounds. He was wearing a baby blue suit that made him look as wide as he was tall.

"Reverend, this is my grandfather, Percy Hays."

"We've had the pleasure before," he said. He walked over and held out his hand. "It's nice to see you once again, Mr. Hays." He stood in front of me, smiling.

"That was a long time ago, Reverend." I ignored the hand.

He withdrew his hand and folded his arms across his chest. "Oh my, yes, Mr. Hays, it was. But I remember you."

"Do you? And what do you remember?"

"All about you."

"You know all about me?"

"Oh my, yes, Mr. Hays," he said.

"Well, isn't that something!"

"Grandpa!" She signaled me by putting her finger over her lips. I winked at Pearl and sat down. She smiled.

"We're all glad you chose Baltimore for your home," Daddy Grace said. He never missed a beat.

"Let me tell you something." I looked at him for a moment. "There's never been a time in my life when I had the luxury of enjoying even one moment without worrying about my very existence. Do you understand what I'm saying?"

"Oh, yes. Yes, I do. I understand." He picked up on my tone. "You see...."

I interrupted. "What do you think you understand?"

"Well, you see..." He paused, turned and gave Pearl a toothy smile. "I understand that a man has to take care of himself. I think everyone admires a man who can take care of himself."

"That's it, Daddy," I said. "Do you and everybody else around here admire me for the way I've lived?"

"Oh, yes!" he said. "And the good Lord loves you too, Brother Percy."

"Call me Mr. Hays!"

"Reverend," Pearl interrupted, "Everyone calls my grandfather *Percy*." She gave me one of her patented looks.

"I'm Mr. Percy to the kids in the neighborhood!"

"Grandpa!"

"Pearl, I like the kids in the neighborhood," I laughed.

"I apologize for my grandfather, Reverend. He thinks he's funny," she glared at me, "but I don't think he's being funny at all."

"Don't fret girl, I understand," he said. "You know, Percy," he said with a shit-eating grin that annoyed the hell out of me, "I believe God makes room for all of us in one way or another."

"And that means *He* has a place for me, right?"

"Of course *He* does."

"It pleases me that a man of God, like yourself, knows there's a place in heaven for a no-count sinner such as me," I said. "And the good Lord has to know I really want to believe you. To be honest, you've given me some cause to believe. Do you want to know why?"

"Why?"

"Because, even though I've never given you a cent, you still want my friendship, and you told Pearl that you'd do anything for me – anything I ask. Isn't that right, Reverend Grace?"

"That's right." He pumped up his chest, took hold of his lapels, and cleared his throat. "That's the kind of man I am," he said, turning his head and looking directly at Pearl.

"It's hard for me to understand why you're so good to me. How can I ever repay you?"

270

"Oh my goodness! That's easy! You can give a little financial help to my ministry."

"No! That's not what I meant. I meant, you prayed for me, and I should pray for you."

"That would be nice. But you see, the church is in dire need of money. Without some big donations, I may not be unable to continue with my ministry."

"Then it's money that brings you here today?"

"I thought a man of your means...."

Pearl was uneasy. She shook her head.

I reacted, partly for her benefit. "My means?" I raised my voice, "What do you know about my means?"

"It's common knowledge, Brother Percy."

"Common knowledge, my ass!"

"Grandpa!"

"Excuse me, Reverend," I said politely. "I meant to ask, what common knowledge are you speaking of?"

"That you're a very wealthy man."

"Been counting my money, Daddy Grace?" I glared at him.

"Not your money, Percy."

"Not my money?" *That son of a bitch*, I thought. "What money are you talking about?"

"The money Helga left to Pearl," he said. He fidgeted with four gold rings that were on fingers of his left hand with his thumb.

"What!" I shouted. He was treading on dangerous ground.

"Grandpa!"

"Be still, girl!" I stood up and got in Daddy Grace's face.

Daddy Grace backed away and stood by Pearl's chair. "I'm talking about the house and everything," he said nervously.

"The house!"

"It's hers!" He turned his head and stuck his chin out and up as far as he could. He looked down his nose at me.

"So that's it?" I wondered how far he would go.

"Yes! And then there's the money Pearl was to get when Muelly's Tavern was sold." Daddy Grace gave me a strange smile.

Money from Muelly's Tavern, I thought. *All these years, and now there's talk of the Muelly money again.* I didn't react the way he expected. Instead, I smiled. I said quietly, "I think you should be careful about what you say."

He hedged. "It's not me saying that. It's other people saying those things. I'm repeating it, is all I'm doing."

"You take no responsibility for your own self, do you, Reverend Grace?"

"Oh no, I do. And the Lord works in mysterious ways, and I'm blessed, because he watches over me."

"He watches over you?" I said. "Is that why you think you can say things and then take no responsibility for your words?"

"What are you saying, Brother Percy?"

"I'm saying that I think you believe that you have some special rights."

"That's the truth. I do."

"The truth? I'll tell you the truth!" I took a step toward him. He backed up.

Pearl got up and put herself between us. "Please, Grandpa." She was upset.

"Alright, girl!" I backed away and sat down.

"You have to know that I would never offend you, Mr. Hays." He was shaken. "I will say a special prayer for you this Sunday."

"I thought you included everyone in your prayers?"

"Oh, my Lord, yes, I do!"

"Then you have already included me in your prayers, right?"

"Of course, but in a general way, you understand. I'm going to say a special prayer for you this Sunday. I'm going to ask God to protect you and keep you safe."

"You shouldn't go around telling people you can protect them with your prayers!"

He became indignant. "I call on the Lord, and *He* provides." He pointed his finger at me and shouted, "Let me tell you something, old man! You ain't what you was no more." He moved back behind Pearl.

"Tell me, Reverend, what was I?"

"I'm not afraid of you!"

"You're a damn fool. Don't you have any pride at all?"

"And what does pride have to do with anything?"

"I don't know much about you, and how you've lived, but you'd better know this about me: a man like me has to live proud. That's what a man has to do. It's a man's pride that drives him. That's how a man has to live – and die. A real man can't live without it, and that's a plain fact."

He turned to face Pearl. "You know I'm a real man," he said. "Don't you?"

She shook her head in disgust and left the room without saying a word.

I didn't care what Daddy Grace, or anyone for that matter, thought of me. My only concern was for Pearl. It worried me that I'd be leaving her soon.

I needed a man to watch over her and protect her from the likes of Reverend Daddy Grace, now more than ever. It had to be Willie.

I dismissed Daddy Grace with a wave of my hand.

"You'll be sorry for treating me this way! You'll be very sorry!"

He waited for my response.

I stood up. "Is that a threat?" He didn't answer me, and he quickly left the room.

Chapter 33

I called Willie and told him to come over to the house. I sat watching out of the window, and saw him pull up in a brand new 1954 Buick Roadmaster sedan. He got out, and moved quickly to my door. I didn't move from my chair when I heard him. "It's open!" I shouted.

He rushed into the living room and offered me his hand. I ignored it and told him to sit himself down. He cast his eyes down and asked me, "Why don't you never take my hand?"

"Listen boy, a Zulu never gives up the use of his right hand in dealing with anyone. In greeting a stranger, a Zulu holds the palm of his left hand under the right forearm to show there's no hidden weapon."

"What's that got to do with taking my hand?"

"I know you don't mean me harm."

"What are you talking about?"

"I don't need to see if you are carrying a weapon – like a knife up your sleeve, understand?"

"No!"

"Don't worry about it. Come on over here and give me a hug!"

He shook his head *no*, but he leaned over anyway to hug me. I grabbed him and used him to pull myself up. I patted his sides and then probed his groin while holding him tight. He wiggled away and glared at me. "What the hell you doing?"

"Making sure you don't have no weapon shoved up your skinny ass!" I laughed. "If Morty Goldstein did to me what I just did to you, we would've been out of the numbers business a long time ago."

"I'm beginning to worry 'bout you. You're doing some strange things lately."

"You'd best not be worrying about me. You'd best worry about your own self. You've got a lot to learn."

"Why you always saying I got a lot to learn?"

"Because you do! But we all do. Don't worry yourself about it."

"Okay. I won't. But why'd you call me over here?"

"Because I need your help, boy."

"Anything for you, Percy."

"I want you to take care of Pearl when I pass over."

He laughed. "If I'm not too old at the time, I will."

"I'm serious. I want you to be responsible for her." He sat down on an ottoman at the foot of my chair. I leaned forward and put my hand on his shoulder. "I need your help. I want you to be her guardian."

"Okay. Whatta I hafta do?"

"Handle her money."

"How do I do that?"

"I tell you where the money is, and you dole it out to her until she's ready to manage it herself." I handed him a Mercantile Bank book.

He looked in the book. There was one hundred ten thousand dollars in it. He shook his head. "She'll be fine with this money!"

"Think so, Willie?"

"Yes."

I took my Swiss bank deposit book out of my pocket and flipped through the pages to the last entry. I held it out to Willie. "Willie, look here." I pointed to the balance and waited for his reaction.

He looked at it and shook his head. He was confused. I asked him what he thought. He looked again and asked about the numbers. I told him it was a numbered account. He still didn't understand. I explained that it was written in German, French, and Italian, and pointed to the balance.

He said, "The last numbers here are in your hand."

"The bank's entries end in 1943." I pointed to the entry. "That was the last time I was in the bank."

"That was eleven years ago."

"In Lisbon, in 1943. It's stamped 'Lisbon' right there."

"Yeah."

"These papers correspond to the entries I made." I handed him the credit and debit forms.

He looked at the numbers on the forms and matched them up with the entries, like any good bookie would. "I understand that now." He stared at the numbers. "What currency is it in?"

"Dollars!"

"No way! That can't be dollars."

"Can and is! Fifteen million, nine hundred thirty-seven thousand, four hundred and fifty-two American greenback dollars," I said in a prideful fashion.

"Holy shit!"

"But listen to me. Having this book isn't good enough. To get the money out of the account, you have to have the book and the secret code."

"A code?"

"A password."

"Makes sense." He paused. "Percy, you've had all this money, all this time?"

"You see it, don't you, boy?"

"That's one hell of a lot of money!"

"It is, and I want you to transfer four million dollars of it into her name in the trust department of The Savings Bank of Baltimore, with you as the trustee." I handed him the wire information with the references and the password.

Willie was uneasy. "We should get a lawyer."

"No! I don't trust lawyers!" I pointed at him.

"You told me you trusted Santini!"

He was right, but it didn't matter. I said, "You take care of Pearl's money at the Savings Bank. And then we'll figure out the rest."

He couldn't control himself, "Okay, but after I do it, there's still a God-awful lot of money left!" He looked at the bankbook again, and shook his head. "And to think, you didn't ever spend any on yourself!"

"Don't you be worrying yourself about it, I got all I ever needed or ever wanted."

"Then what was the good of having it?"

"Plenty good, boy. And when I'm gone, I won't need it anymore."

"What's you going to do with it?"

"It will go to the Zulu."

"You're giving it to the Zulu?"

"Most of it, and maybe, just maybe, it'll buy them some freedom. Now go do what I told you."

He reached down and took my hand in his hands and said, "I'll take care of everything. But first I'm going to take charge. I'm going to get us a lawyer."

"No. Don't need a lawyer!" I stood up and grabbed his shoulder.

"Yes, you do. You need a last will and testament, and some legal documents, things such as that. If you don't have proper papers, anyone can claim what's yours."

"You do like I told you!"

"It don't work that way. If you want me to be in charge, I got to be in charge. I'm telling you, if you don't have a will, the court takes your stuff and then decides who gets what. Now, most likely Pearl will get it, but you don't know that. People can come out of the woodwork. And then there's the court costs and all. They've been known to rip people off."

"Shit!"

"Percy, we need a lawyer to help with this."

"I trust you! If you say I need Santini, then I need him. But I need him right away."

"I'll get it done for you."

"Today, Willie, you understand? I need it done today."

"It's after four already."

"Right away!"

"I'll get on it right away, but it'll have to be tomorrow morning. I want to go over everything with you and write it down."

After he finished his notes, I said as an after-thought, "Willie I want you to leave some spaces in the part where I'm giving people the money, so I can fill in some more names. Oh, and leave a place for the amounts they're to get, too."

When we finished, I said to him, "This is for you." I pulled my talisman from around my neck. I took out the vial of potion the Dreamhouse had put in the talisman. I retied the talisman, and handed it to Willie.

It had a musty smell, and Willie made a face. "What am I going to do with this old thing?"

"Pull it on over your head, and don't take it off."

"What is it?"

"It could be a key to a kingdom."

"What kingdom? I don't understand, Percy."

"Put it on, boy. And don't ever take it off!"

He pulled the talisman over his head and hid it under his shirt. "I still don't understand, but I'll do what you say."

"You'll understand when you're supposed to. Go call Santini. You promised it would be done by tomorrow morning."

"Okay." He pulled the talisman from under his shirt. "What does this thing have to do with a kingdom?"

"When you get everything done, I'll tell you about it. Don't ever take it off. Now make it quick, understand?"

"Yes, sir."

Things were in motion. I was tired. I was glad that I could soon get on with the business of my dying.

Chapter 34

Pearl was on her annual shopping trip to New York City. It was a trip she took in the spring with a friend and her friend's parents. The girls liked that they could try on clothes in the stores there, something coloreds couldn't do in the Baltimore department stores. She talked a lot about moving to New York. She thought it was more civilized there.

During Pearl's absence, my health suddenly began to fail. I became too sick to even make the effort to get up the stairs to bed. Because of that, I was still asleep in my chair at eleven-thirty the next morning, when Willie arrived. I was awakened by the sound of his car door closing. I looked up and saw him, and then saw Thomas Santini pull up behind him.

He let himself in. "What kept you, boy?" I said, feigning impatience.

"Nothing! I went to Santini's office first thing this morning. He went to work on your stuff right away."

I got up from my chair. "I'm sorry, boys. Please let me start over. Morning to you all."

"Morning, Percy," Willie said.

"Good morning, Mr. Hays," Santini said.

"Call me Percy, Tommy. Did you get my papers done?"

"Yes." Santini walked to the dining room and put his briefcase on the table. He took a folder out and brought it to me. "I think you'll find it's the way you wanted."

I took my glasses out and opened the file. I said, "Besides the money, Pearl gets the house and all the rest of my belongings, right?"

"Everything, Mr. Hays. But..."

"Percy. Call me Percy, Tommy."

"Percy, do you realize how much will be left in the Swiss account after Pearl's money is transferred."

"I do," I said

"And you want all that money to go to this Matumbo?"

"What's left at the end."

"Then I'll need his bank information to get him the money."

"Don't worry about that. Willie will take care of it."

"I can do it quick and safe with wiring instructions."

"Willie will take care of it and he'll take care of Pearl's stuff, too."

"Yes. That's the way it's set up," he said.

I thought about what Santini said about getting the money to Matumbo, but I wanted to do it my own way. I took the wire authorization forms out of my bankbook and filled out three of them. I had Willie leave me alone in the room with Santini. I motioned him closer to me. "Santini, I want to make some changes to what Willie told you. Here's what I want to do. Take this signed draft and get the four million dollars from my Swiss account for Pearl. I want it transferred to the Mercantile Bank today. Also, here's a form to send another four million dollars, to be transferred to an account I want you to open for Willie Jonson. And the last thing I want you figure out how to do is send one million dollars to Miss Thelma Jackson of Monterrey, Mexico. The rest of the money you leave be."

"I can do it, if it's what you want?"

"It is!"

"I'll take care of it right away, Mr. Hays."

"Percy. Call me Percy. How you going to remember all this stuff if you can't even remember to call me Percy?"

"Force of habit," he laughed. "I'll always call you Percy from now on, Mr. Hays."

I laughed. I pointed my finger at him and said, "Tommy, I want it done today, and I want a receipt in my hand, too!"

"I can get it done if I go right now."

"Yeah, do that. That way I can sign the rest of the money in the account over to Matumbo, and that'll take the account out of my will completely, right?"

"Right."

"Okay. I want you to make the changes to the will and set up the trust account for Pearl. And I want you to get right back here, understand? It's important to me."

"Okay Percy," Santini said.

"Good. Then what are you waiting for? Before you can get back here and get paid, you have to get going."

"No problem, Percy, I'll be right back. But you don't have to pay me today. I'll send you a bill."

"No, I want to pay today. I don't want to leave any loose ends."

"I'm on my way," Santini said.

"I'll go along with him just in case he needs me," Willie said.

"Okay, but you come back here when Santini comes, you understand me, Willie?"

I was tired from all the excitement and I fell asleep. I was still sleeping when Willie and Santini returned.

Willie woke me. "You okay, Percy?"

"I'm fine. Is everything ready for me, Thomas?"

"It is. All you have to do is sign here. Then Willie and I will witness it." Santini pointed to a line at the bottom of the page.

"I'm going to sign, you understand. But it may be hard to read my handwriting. My hands are very unsteady."

"That'll be alright. We'll witness it."

I signed my name on the paper. My hand was unsteady, and my signature was barely legible. They both witnessed the signature. "That's good. I feel very relieved," I said to Santini. "What do I owe you?"

"I charge by the hour. I have five hours in it and the travel time. Including everything, a hundred and seventy-five should cover it."

"And what if there are some loose ends down the road?"

"We'll worry about that then," he said.

"No, I want to pay you now." I took twenty-five hundred-dollar bills out of my pocket and held them out for Santini.

He took the money and counted it. "This is way too much. There's twenty-five hundred dollars here."

"That's so there's no loose ends."

"Percy, I..."

"You take the money. I don't want any loose ends. If Pearl or Willie need anything, you do it right away. You charge for whatever you do, you understand. But you do it right away. Consider the extra money a permanent retainer. I want no loose ends, you understand?"

"Percy, I can't take your money like that."

"It's the way I want it," I snapped.

"I'll take care of things. Don't you worry about anything."

"I won't, Tommy."

"You take care of yourself, I want to see you up and around soon," he said. He closed his case and picked up his hat and waited for Willie at the door.

"I'll check on you later, Percy," Willie said.

"No! Stay here." I waved to Santini. "Thanks again."

After he left, I told Willie to get me some rum. While he was in the kitchen, I called out to him, "You might as well bring me the bottle and get me the phone too, while you're at it."

I called the overseas operator and made a person-to-person call to Roger Broussard in Durban, South Africa. When I got him, he was surprised to hear from me. "How the hell are you?" he screamed into the phone.

"Been better. How you doing?"

"What's wrong with you, boy?"

"Getting old is all." Willie was listening to my end of the conversation.

"Yeah, I'm getting there, too. But to what do I owe the pleasure?"

"I want to get some money to Matumbo."

"Why not send it the usual way?"

"No. Can't do that. I need to get some papers to him too. I want to send someone over there with them."

Willie realized I was talking about him. He started to squirm in his chair. I put my hand over the receiver. "Pour me another one, Willie."

"Yes, sir. But what..."

I held up a hand to silence him. "Just pour the drink, and easy on the Coca-Cola this time."

"Is something wrong?" Broussard asked.

"No, nothing's wrong."

"Tell me what's going on there."

"There's nothing going on. I thought I'd get an old Cajun to help me out, is all." I took a drink of rum.

"Anything for you," Broussard said.

"I need you to meet my man at the airport in Durban and take him to see Matumbo."

"That's going to be hard to do."

"Why's that?"

"He's in Russia looking for help."

"What kind of trouble is it this time?"

"The British reneged on their promise, and things are bad here for the Zulu. There are only two kinds of Africans under the new law: Bantus and Coloureds. The Zulu are being moved off their land."

"What happened?"

"They passed the Population Registration Act. Matumbo didn't think it would affect him like it is. Things are really bad for tribes."

"What's he want with the Russians?"

"He plans to go to war!"

"It will never be over for him," I said.

"You're right, Percy."

"He always needs money, and I want to get some to him."

"That won't be a problem," Broussard said. "I still do work for some friends in Washington."

"That won't work for this. The money's in Switzerland."

"Just tell me what to do."

"I'll get you the bank book. You'll be contacted by a man wearing my talisman."

"Okay."

"And I need you to get a message to Matumbo!"

"What's that?"

"Tell him I am going to drink from the talisman."

"You're going to drink from the talisman. What's that?"

"He'll understand."

"Okay, but I don't."

"It's not for you to understand. Just tell him. I got to go now," I said.
He said, "Goodbye."

I sat for a minute with the receiver to my ear. I had finished the rum while I spoke to Broussard. I gave Willie the phone. "While you're up, pour me another one. We have to celebrate."

"You shouldn't drink any more."

"I'm fine, boy." I looked at Willie and smiled. "Boy, you got something on your mind?"

"Yeah, I'm going to Africa. I've never been out of the country."

"There's nothing to worry about."

"There is! I don't have no passport."

"You have Santini take care of that. He knows people. Now, get that picture off the table over there."

I showed him a picture of Broussard with me and Matumbo that was taken right before I left Africa for the last time. I handed him an envelope and said, "You go there and show Broussard the talisman when he meets you in Durban. That's all you have to do. When he asks for the package, you give him the envelope. That's all there is to it."

I felt a sharp pain in my chest. I closed my eyes and tried to catch my breath. Willie helped me sit up in the chair. I could hardly breathe. The pain was bad for a minute, but then it let up. I heard him calling me, but I couldn't answer him.

I was drawn back when I heard him say, "I should take you to the hospital, Percy."

I caught my breath and told him I was okay. He insisted that I go to the hospital. I told him I wasn't going. I expected Pearl would be coming home in the evening, and I told him she would take care of me. I said for him to go on about his business.

He wanted to stay, but I insisted that he leave. He helped me to the sofa, and I lay my head on the arm and fell right to sleep. When I opened my eyes, Willie was still beside me. "Go on about your business Willie, I'll be alright," I said.

"I'm fine here 'til Pearl gets home."

"You're a good boy." My breathing was labored and I coughed. "I'd best not have a cigar," I joked, "but you could pour me a fresh glass of rum?"

"I don't know..."

"Mind me, Willie. I need it." He filled the glass, and I took a long swig. "Know something, boy?"

"What?"

"I'm feeling a whole lot better now, so don't hold yourself up. I'll be fine."

"No, I'll wait."

I rested my head again. "You're a good boy, Willie."

"Why do you keep saying that, Percy?"

"'Cause it's true. You're a good boy."

I drifted off to sleep, thinking I had only one wish: to see Pearl, to hold her, and to tell her I love her. Her love gave me hope that there was life eternal. I remembered what my mother had told me about the *here after*. I was sad to be leaving Pearl, but I was happy I would soon be with my mother, my wife, and my son. I felt the presence of God in my heart. *He* had been my protector, and while I often drifted from *Him*, *He* never denied me *His* Grace.

I was tired, but I wasn't afraid. I was losing feeling in my legs, and my left arm was tingling. Soon it would be my time to pass over. I knew I could have done better in my life, but I never really had a choice to live any other way then I did. I was born to oppression, but I would not be oppressed.

Chapter 35

'Willie tells me you were sick while I was gone," Pearl said, as she shook me to awaken me. "He says you told him you've been working."

"I don't understand, girl."

"Willie says you're coming out of retirement or something silly like that."

"Willie seems to say a lot of things to you, girl."

"What do you mean, Grandpa?"

"We all know he's a lot older than you," I laughed.

"What are you getting at?"

"You're too young," I paused and waited for her to speak. When she didn't say anything, I said, "And he's too short for you, too!"

"So!" She shook her head, "What does that have to do with anything?"

"You're too young and he's too short."

"Okay, I'm too young and he's too short!"

"Exactly!"

"What are you getting at?"

"If you stick with him, you're going to have short kids."

"Grandpa!" She frowned. "Stop it! He doesn't even know I'm alive."

"Oh, he knows you're alive, all right."

"Well maybe, but he treats me like a child."

"For goodness sake, girl, you *are* a child!"

"No I'm not, and one day I'll show him."

"I hope you wait 'til you finish high school."

"Why are you saying that? You know I graduated last year." She was agitated, and snapped at me, "You wait and see, Grandpa. You just wait. One day Willie will notice me!"

"Imagine that, a young girl like you wanting a man twice her age."

"Is that so? Then what about you and Grandma?"

"That was different!"

"It was? You were more than twice her age, weren't you?"

"Back then people were thrown together," I said.

"Is that why you married her, because you were 'thrown together'?"

"No!"

"Then why?"

"I loved her."

"You loved her and she loved you. Age didn't mean anything to you."

"Yeah, but Willie's still too short for you."

"No he's not!"

"Yes he is! And then you're still growing too. Get yourself a young man. A tall one, too!"

"To make Willie jealous?"

"No, so you'll have tall kids. I want your kids to be big and strong."

"I'm not going to talk to you about it!"

"Fine with me!"

"Fine with me, too!" She turned and stopped in her tracks. "You changed the subject on me. Why'd you say you were going back to work?"

"I have to."

"And when do you plan to do that?"

"Tomorrow?" I felt another pain in the chest – a dull pain, not like the sharp pain before. I felt myself drifting away.

"Grandpa...."

I refocused. "What, girl?"

"Grandpa, you should stay retired."

"I'm not retired?"

"You're kidding, right?"

I was tired. "What are you talking about, girl?" I fought to stay awake.

"Grandpa, you haven't worked in four years."

"A man has to earn his way."

"You don't have to work anymore, Grandpa."

"Maybe. Maybe, I'll see. I'm tired now. Leave me be."

"Okay, but don't you think about that work anymore!"

"Why you say it like that, girl?"

"Grandpa, the work was degrading!"

"You don't understand, girl. How many times do I have to tell you that I have a good business going on there? I'm making my own deals."

"Grandpa, you're retired. And when you were there, all you did was sweep the floors," she said angrily.

"I lean on a broom just enough to keep up appearances. I have my own thing going there. You worry too much about appearances. You haven't been paying attention to what I've been telling you all these years."

"I have too!"

"You have not." I reached into my pocket and pulled out a diamond necklace I had made for her. I planned to give it to her on her birthday, but I felt was as good a time as any. I opened my hand and showed her the necklace.

"Grandpa!" she said, "What's that for?"

"For you, to prove I love you, or maybe just to prove that you weren't paying attention to your old Grandpa," I said. I held out the necklace for her to take.

She looked at it, and then reached out to give it back to me. She said, "I *have* paid attention to you. More than you know. But that doesn't change anything. You never should have pushed a broom. Not a man like you. You could have quit anytime you wanted to."

"Girl! The necklace is for you."

"For me?"

"Yeah! I thought, since you liked New York so much, you could take this there to the jewelry district if you ever needed money."

"Oh my God, it's beautiful," she held it up to the light. "But why would I want to sell a gift that you give me?"

"Because it's not for casual wearing, little darlin'. It's an eighteen-carat flawless diamond, and it's worth a king's ransom."

"If you had this diamond all the time, why didn't you sell it and quit that job?" she snapped at me.

"A man like me doesn't quit. He never quits!"

"I see! A man like you never quits. No matter how well he has done, he keeps working a menial job."

"Let me tell you something, girl: that's what I let people see, but it wasn't me. All they saw was an old man pushing a broom. There were those who didn't believe I was a colored, but in the end I think most people knew I was of the colored race. But in any case, it kept me safe from prying eyes.

"Now, you know, you've become my world, and I live for you. I love you, Pearl. Soon I'll be leaving you, but not because I want to, only because it's my time. I need another hug, girl." I felt my tears running down my cheeks.

"Stop talking like that, Grandpa!"

I felt a sudden overwhelming urge; it was time to drink the Dreamhouse's potion. I was ready to test the promise that I would spend eternity looking down on the world with all the other Zulu warriors who had died with honor. I drank the potion down in one gulp. The pain eased right away. I thought, *maybe I've used it too soon.* It was supposed to be for my deathbed. I straightened up on the couch and said to Pearl, "Get me some more rum, girl! You let my glass get almost empty."

"Almost empty isn't empty. The only thing I'm going to get you is a doctor."

A strange feeling came over me. "Did you know in some towns in Germany they'd never seen people like your grandma and me?"

"What?"

"I said there were towns I went to in Germany, and all over Europe for that matter, where they'd never seen anyone like me. When I was in the sun and got some color, people stared at me. I stared right back at them. In one town, most all of them had six fingers on their right hand. Would you believe those freaks stared at me?" I laughed.

"What are you talking about?"

"Freaks with six fingers! They could have been in a sideshow."

"And what's that got to do with anything?"

"You see, they never had any new blood in some of the towns. They drove strangers off. They had no use for them. They wanted it that way."

"I don't understand."

"You should find a man…." I had a shooting pain in my chest. "You have beautiful eyes, Pearl."

She shook her head and gave me one of her looks. I finished the last swig of rum. I lit one of my Cuban cigars and leaned back on the sofa. I smiled at Pearl. "You know, girl, I loved that damn parrot."

"What are you talking about now?"

I sang. "Percy the Pirate needs a new parrot. His last one died at sea."

"Are you okay, Grandpa?"

"Yeah! Bring me the shirt hanging there next to the door."

"What shirt?"

"The one I keep in the hall, for lounging around."

"That old thing hasn't been there for years," she laughed.

"Old thing! It wasn't an old thing until Benny Chu ruined it in his laundry."

"He did not. It just wore out. It was threadbare when you took it there. And anyway, that was years ago."

"I want it."

"Sorry Grandpa. I threw it away."

"Can't trust them!"

"Who?"

"Benny and his family; they're looking at you cockeyed all the time."

"Stop talking like that, Grandpa!"

"We should have listened to MacArthur and wiped them all out."

"Grandpa, I'll get you another shirt."

"That's not the point. That was my favorite shirt. I got it in the Congo thirty-five years ago."

"Grandpa! *I* got you that shirt."

"That shirt was a gift from a fellow who was from New Orleans."

"No, I got you the shirt."

"You're mistaken, girl. I got the shirt from a man I met in the Congo."

"No! *I* gave you that shirt! And you should stop taking your shirts down to Benny's laundry if you don't like the way he cleans them. Don't do business with him!"

"You're right. You can't do business with them. They're all communists. That Mao fellow has messed with all their minds."

"They left China long before the Second World War. Remember that war, the one you always get worked up over?"

"Yeah, I remember."

"Grandpa, they're not communists."

"Yeah, they are."

"I think we should call it a night."

"You go to bed. I want to sit up a while longer."

"Don't fall asleep on the sofa again." She took my arm and tried to get me to go upstairs.

"Let me be." I pulled away and fell onto the sofa.

"Grandpa! Are you okay?"

"Let me be," I gasped.

I tried to sit up, but couldn't. I felt a presence and looked up. The image of a man began to take form right in front of me. I struggled to make him out. Then I saw him as an albino, with a chiseled white face and piercing red eyes. His suit glowed white, and there was an iridescence emanating from him. He stood in front of a tunnel that was as black as pitch.

I tried to see what was behind him. I stood and made myself as tall as I could, hoping to see over him. His aura grew and it cast a shadow that I couldn't see through. He spoke, "I say it is so good to see you again. I missed you." He moved out of the shadow.

Missed me? Why would he say that? He didn't know me, I thought. "Who are you?" I said.

"I came to you in New Orleans."

"I haven't been to New Orleans since I was a boy."

The man didn't reply.

"You! You're an explorer, right?"

He stood motionless; his eyes were glowing embers. He didn't answer.

"Sure, that's it!" I slapped my hands together. "You're from Africa!"

The albino answered in an eerie drone. "No, now think back. Remember back to when your mother passed."

295

"I don't remember that. I don't remember."

"Think, Percy. I told you to run away."

"I guess."

"I told you to trust no one."

"That came to me in a dream. But you looked different!"

The man slowly faded and reappeared as a black man in a dark suit. His eyes were black circles with bright, white light streaming out of them.

I was scared and wanted to run, but couldn't move. "You coming for me now, aren't you?"

"No, Percy! I'm not coming for you. I have always been with you."

"Been with me?"

"In all your dreams," he answered.

I closed my eyes.

"I was with you in New Orleans when you were born, and I'll be with you when you pass over. I'll be with you forever."

I was barely able to speak. "I'm tired," I said.

"You can stop running now, Percy."

"I want to!" I said, "The good Lord knows I need rest."

The black man disappeared. In his place, a white man with a full beard materialized. He had a sword in one hand and a pistol in the other.

He looked familiar, but I couldn't place him. "Do I know you?"

There was no answer.

"I must know you," I said. "I know you."

The man started toward me. I backed away and reached into my pocket for my pistol as I had done so many times before. But my hand went through my leg as though it wasn't there. I held up my hand and looked at it. I was terrified.

The man laughed. He held his gun out for me to take. I reached for it, but my hand passed right through it. He let it go. It dissolved and disappeared as it fell from his hand.

The man spoke. "I was with you the night you were born. I was with you the night your mother passed. I will be with you tonight."

"How do I know you?" I pleaded. "Tell me! Tell me how I know you!"

"As you know yourself, Percy."

"'As I know myself'? What about the other man? What about him?"

He ignored my questions.

"For God's sake, tell me why you're here!" I shouted.

He slowly faded to nothing right in front of me, and mirrors appeared where the tunnel had been. I saw my reflection in the mirrors. I saw myself, but wasn't sure how. It wasn't like looking into a mirror. The image didn't move when I moved. It moved on its own. My image disappeared, and then it reappeared, only to disappear again.

I sensed a presence. I turned and saw an image of myself as a young man. I held my hands out and said, "I'm dreaming. Lord help me, if I'm not dreaming. Someone please tell me I'm dreaming."

There was no reply.

I spoke to the image. "What can you tell me? Please, what can you tell me?"

There was no reply.

I started to speak, but stopped when I felt Pearl shaking me. She was there and so was Willie.

"What should we do?" she asked Willie. She was crying.

"I'm not sure. He's been like this for a while," he said. "He didn't want to go to the hospital when I was here before."

Pearl tried to right me. She tugged at me. I didn't move.

"I'm calling for help, Pearl," Willie said.

I struggled to speak. "Look at the color of my skin. Here, I'll roll back my sleeve. Look at the color."

Through her tears, Pearl asked, "Willie, what is he saying?"

"I don't know. I can't understand him. How long has he been going on like this?"

"For a short while before I called you."

"What color am I?" I cried. There was still no answer. No one would answer me. Willie and Pearl were acting as though they couldn't hear me. "Will there be time for me? Do I have any time?"

An image of a young boy appeared. I felt relieved. The boy walked over to me and spoke slowly. "It is your choice. No one would blame you if you decided to sleep now. If you want to wake up, you can. It's up to you."

I turned away quickly and found myself sitting straight up. Pearl had helped me up. She was standing next to the sofa, holding me.

I heard Willie say to Pearl, "He doesn't look good."

I felt hot flashes go right through me, and was covered with sweat. I called out to Pearl, "I need some rum, girl."

"What, Grandpa?"

"I want my Mount Gay Rum! There's a bottle I've been saving under the credenza. Get it girl! Please!"

She brought me the bottle. I held it out and looked at it; I thought of when James was drinking his last. I asked her to open it for me.

"No, I'll save it for later," she said.

"No! I want it now!"

"I don't think you should have any more!"

"Open the bottle," I shouted.

She handed the bottle to Willie and he opened it and poured a glass. He added a splash of Coca-Cola and handed it to me. I drank it down in one long gulp. I tried to ask for another glass, but couldn't get the words to come out.

"What is it, Percy?" Willie asked.

I tried, but couldn't answer.

"I'm worried about him, Willie. What do you think is wrong with him?" Pearl came over to me and took my hand. She put it to her lips, but I couldn't feel anything.

"I don't know, Pearl," Willie said. He came over and sat next to me. He put his hand on my shoulder and gently shook me. "Percy, will you explain why you gave me all that money?"

I didn't try to answer him. Pearl rushed over to us, and confronted him, "What are you talking about Willie. What money?"

"It's not up to me to say."

"You'd better say! And you'd better say right now, Mr. William Jonson."

"I guess there's no real reason why I can't tell you. Percy put four million dollars in an account for me. I found out about it from Santini today."

"You've got to be kidding me!"

"No. He set it up, and he set one up for you, too."

"For how much?"

"The same as mine."

"Four million?"

"Yes."

"Oh my God!" Pearl said. She came over to me and gave me a hug. "You never stop surprising me Grandpa." She gave me another hug. "Is there anything I can do for you?"

I didn't answer her. I grabbed for the bottle Willie was holding, and it fell from his hand, landed on the floor and spilled.

Willie picked up the bottle. "Pearl, I'm going to call for help," he said

They're calling for help, I thought. Yes, that's good. I was tired. I closed my eyes for a second and drifted off. I woke with a start. *Where am I*, I wondered. *Where have I been?* I didn't know how much time had passed.

I saw Pearl at the front door with Willie. I heard him say, "You know, Pearl, I feel bad about taking the money. It should be all yours, and besides, I really don't need it. My grandfather left me a lot of money."

"Where'd your grandfather get a lot of money from?"

"He told me before he died that he got the money from New Orleans, and that I could thank his friend, Percy Hays, for my good fortune."

"Don't feel that way; my grandfather wanted you to have it. Think about it now, he gave us both the same amount of money. I think he was trying to tell us that he loved us both the same. That's a good thing, Willie; it's a real good thing."

"Yeah, I guess you're right."

"Of course I am."

There was a knock on the door. He looked over to me and said, "They're coming to take you to the hospital, Percy."

I didn't even try to answer.

Pearl opened the door. She said to the ambulance crew, "He's on the sofa."

"He needs to go to the hospital right away," Willie said.

"You'll have to make him go," Pearl added.

An attendant said, "He'll be fine with us."

"Okay." She looked at me. "Grandpa, the men are here."

I tried to tell her I didn't want to go, but I couldn't speak.

"Grandpa, are you alright?"

Pearl shook me. "Grandpa!" Pearl hugged me and cried. "Grandpa. Oh, no! Grandpa!"

Willie put his hands on Pearl's shoulders. "It'll be okay."

"He's...."

"Shush," Willie hugged Pearl.

A feeling of calm overtook me. Things that were hazy became clear and bright. The pain in my body left me. I couldn't move; yet I could hear, and I could see everything. Willie and Pearl were crying. *They shouldn't be crying*, I thought. Not now, when I feel so good.

Chapter 36

I sensed the nearness to my mother, my wife, and my son. I closed my eyes and prayed for the warmth of their embrace. But when I opened them, I was looking down on myself in a coffin. I saw Daddy Grace push his way through the door into the viewing room. He shoved people out of his way, waving and smiling as he went.

"Bless you, Reverend Grace," an elderly woman seated near the rear of the room cried out.

"Bless you, sister," he said without breaking stride, or taking his eyes off Pearl. She was sitting next to Willie in the first row, in front of my coffin. He made his way to her. "Sister Pearl," he said quietly, "we all gone ta' be missing your granddaddy." Then he called out loudly, so "I say, we all gone ta' be missing Brother Percy 'round here now!"

Willie stood up and placed himself between Daddy Grace and Pearl. Daddy Grace backed off and stood at the head of my coffin. He held his chin up in the aggravating, exaggerated way he would do, and moved his head back and forth and from side to side. He was all full of himself, and he hadn't given up on the chance he could get his hands on some of my money.

Willie took a couple of steps toward him and he moved away from my coffin. He was nervous and he hummed for a moment;

then he sang under his breath,

When you die, you best try Daddy Grace

He's the best lay preacher any place

He's got prayers by the dozens

For husbands, wives, and cousins

So, when you die, you'd best try Daddy Grace.

Willie got up from his seat to talk to the funeral director; Daddy Grace moved right in and sat down next to Pearl, "If you had made your decision to have me here sooner, we could have gotten a larger room and had a bigger turnout."

"It's fine as it is."

"But you have to know that I'm a preacher who can fill the big tents!" He saw Willie returning to his seat. He got up and moved to the front of the room, and stood at the open end of my coffin. He raised his head and stared up at the ceiling. Then he raised his hands over his head and opened his arms as though he were reaching out to God. He looked down into my coffin. "Good Lord, it is still hard for me to believe that Brother Percy was a man of the colored race!"

Pearl cleared her throat loudly and glared at him. He moved off to the side and stood quietly with his hands folded. At 2:00 PM sharp, the funeral director walked to the lectern behind my coffin. By then, the room was filled to overflowing. He motioned for Daddy Grace. "Can I have your attention, please?" he said. When the crowd settled down, he said, "Reverend, if you please."

"Thank you sir," Daddy Grace said. He slowly looked over the gathering. "I came here today...." he paused. "I say! I came here today to say goodbye to Brother Percy."

There was a muffled, "Amen," from the crowd.

"There are those who would have left me out." He looked at Willie and made eye contact. "That hurt," he said.

Willie stared right back at him.

Daddy Grace looked back at the crowd, "Yes, I say it hurts!"

"Amen," came from the crowd.

Daddy Grace held up his hands. "But I have learned to turn the other cheek." He turned his head and struck his obnoxious pose.

"Turn the cheek," was heard.

"I have...I say, I have turned that other cheek."

"The other cheek...." echoed.

"That's right. I have turned the other cheek. And because of that, Daddy is here to say goodbye to Brother Percy. Daddy always says goodbye."

There was an echo, "Goodbye," and after a pause, an "Amen."

"Sometimes it is very hard, I say, hard. Very, very, very hard." Daddy Grace put his head in his hands.

"Hard," came from around the room.

He looked up and responded to the congregation, "But hard as it is, Daddy is here to say goodbye." He held out his hand. "But why am I here?"

"The other cheek," resonated loudly.

"That's right. So no matter what, Daddy always says goodbye."

As if by one voice, was heard, "Amen!"

"God knows Daddy loves everyone!"

Again, "Amen!"

"And you all must know Percy was...." Daddy Grace heard the door opening as he started to speak; he stopped in mid-sentence and looked up. Roger Broussard led Matumbo, his son Mzilikazi, and his twenty-year-old grandson, Shaka, into the room. The Zulu were dressed in their royal robes and carried battle shields and stabbing spears. Broussard wore a dark suit, giving him the look of the FBI agent he once was. All eyes in the room were fixed on the men as they moved toward my coffin.

Broussard looked in my coffin and crossed himself. He said a silent prayer, then walked to the back of the room and stood with his back against the wall.

Mzilikazi and Shaka stood by Matumbo as he knelt over my coffin. He laid a leather pouch across my chest, then he stood at the head of the coffin. Mzilikazi moved to the foot of the coffin, and Shaka moved the lectern aside and stood behind the coffin where the lectern had been. They stood there, motionless, with their spears raised. I saw a tear roll down Matumbo's cheek.

Willie whispered to Pearl, "Your granddad showed me a picture of these guys. The old Zulu is Matumbo, and the white one is Roger Broussard. I don't know who the others are."

"He told me that Matumbo is one of the headmen of the Zulu."

"He told me that too, and he also said he was the Inkosi of his Klan."

"What's that?"

"It has something to do with foreseeing the future, and magic," he pulled the talisman I gave him from under his shirt and showed it to her. "That's where this came from."

"Daddy Grace doesn't have a clue who these men are."

"No, not a clue," Willie laughed. He got up and went to the back of the room to Broussard. He showed him the talisman, and handed him the envelope I had given him. Broussard patted him on the shoulder and motioned for him to go back to his seat.

Daddy Grace leaned over to the funeral director and asked, "Who are these fools with the costumes?"

"Some friends of the deceased. I got a call from the State Department, telling me to expect them."

"The State Department, huh?" Daddy Grace muttered under his breath. There were rumblings among the congregants. He moved

306

back to the lectern and began, "I want you all to understand that I'm here to say goodbye to Brother Percy. And I'm here because I loved him."

"Loved him," was heard.

"There are others that are here too. Some of them are strangers in our midst!" He thrust both of his hands into the air, palms up. "But we welcome them." He put his arms out and then closed them as if he were hugging the air. "And you know why?"

"Why?" was heard.

Daddy Grace pulled out a handkerchief. "Because we love everyone," he said as he wiped his brow.

"Everyone," echoed.

"Yes we have learned to love everyone. And I would have taught Percy how to turn the other cheek, if Almighty God hadn't called him home before I could," he paused. He looked over the mourners, "All praise to the Lord!"

They responded, "Praise the Lord."

He looked at Pearl, "Sometimes a loved one goes to their reward and we are left alone. We feel lost. But you don't have to feel lost, Pearl, not as long as you have Daddy Grace on your side."

"Amen," from the congregation.

Little Willie stood up. "Reverend Grace, I want to say a few words."

"Wait 'til I'm finished, Mr. Jonson! Now, sit yourself down!"

Matumbo told his grandson to move Daddy Grace away from my coffin. The boy, a muscular six-foot, seven-inch behemoth, grabbed Daddy Grace's arm and easily moved him aside.

Daddy Grace pulled away. "What do you think you're doing?"

Shaka put the point of his stabbing spear under Daddy Grace's chin and prodded him further to the side. Matumbo joined his son and grandson at my coffin, and they all chanted my praise song. When they were finished, Willie came forward and spoke. He spoke quietly of how he missed me, and of his grandfather, Pappy Smathers', love for me. When he finished, he motioned for Matumbo to come forward. He showed him the talisman. Matumbo gave him an embrace. Willie introduced him to the mourners as the Headman of the Zulu, who had come to honor me.

Daddy Grace made an effort to move next to Willie, but Shaka intervened and pushed him back. Daddy Grace tried to put on a good face. "They're here with the blessings of the State Department," he said. He looked around the room and smiled. He took hold of his lapels and fixed his gaze on my coffin. He shook his head from side to side. "You ain't heard the end of this, Willie Jonson." He pointed at Pearl and said, "Pearl, we should go now."

Pearl didn't answer.

"Well?" Daddy Grace asked.

She waved her hand, signaling him to leave. There were some snickers from the congregation as he beat a hasty retreat. He motioned to his entourage to follow him, and then pointed toward Pearl. She shook her head no. She turned around and looked at Broussard still standing in the back of the room, and smiled. She remembered him, even though she hadn't seen him since she was a little girl. She mouthed the words, "Who is *he?*" as she pointed to Shaka.

"A Zulu prince," he said loud enough for her and the rest of the people to hear, including Daddy Grace.

Daddy Grace stormed out of the room. He gathered his followers outside, next to the cars that were lined up in front of the funeral parlor. He signaled his driver to pull out of line and come over to him. He opened his car door and climbed up on the running board. He cleared his throat, "I tried, Lord knows I tried," he paused, feigning tears. "It was hard for me, when Percy rejected me and my ministry. But I guess you all can now see what I had to deal with. It's time for me to face the facts, and realize the stories that I heard about Percy were true."

"What stories?" A man called out.

"I'm talking here about the death of the Muelly brothers. And I am sad to say, that it appears to me that not only Percy, but Willie Jonson, was involved in those murders too. There'll have to be some looking into it all." With that Daddy Grace got into the car and slammed the door and the car drove off.

Willie knelt at my coffin and spoke quietly, as if he knew I could hear him. "I will keep my promise, Percy. Sleep well, my old friend."

Willie sat down, and Broussard came forward. He stood in front of my African honor guard, who towered over everyone as they stood their posts. Broussard looked at Pearl. "You know, your grandfather was a man who faced every challenge in life without ever taking a backward step. He was a man who played hard at the game of life, and he won.

"Percy once told me that he knew the earth turned, but not from lessons taught him as a child. He knew the earth turned when a breeze would touch his face. He knew the earth turned when he saw the sun travel across the sky each day. He said he could feel the movement of the earth beneath his feet.

"He spoke of the cruel fates, and how he would challenge them at every turn. He believed it was no accident that put him in his place and to his trials. But he never complained, and he survived.

"Jean Perceval Hays was born to a freed woman, in New Orleans, Louisiana in 1874, and he died a free man in Baltimore, Maryland eighty years later. He lived a full life; he was loved, and he will be missed!" Broussard stepped aside.

Matumbo placed his spear and shield inside my coffin. He said in Swahili that he would see me again when it was the time for the

309

great warriors to assemble.

I hoped that it was time for me to join the assembly. I closed my eyes, believing I would open them in paradise, but instead I was looking at Broussard and Matumbo driving to the cemetery. With them, in the back seat of the car, were Mzilikazi and Shaka. Broussard was driving and telling stories of my time in Baltimore. Matumbo wasn't listening; he was staring straight ahead, looking stone-faced. Being able to see everything the way I was, but not being there with my friends, gave me a strange, uneasy feeling. Broussard reached over and pushed on Matumbo's arm. He said, "Percy always talked of Juju magic. You know, maybe we should get him to Haiti to one of those voodoo priests?"

"Voodoo! What made you think of that?" Matumbo laughed.

"He talked about it when he was being held by the FBI in Washington."

"He was putting you guys on. He didn't practice voodoo; he was by his very nature a Catholic. But, that notwithstanding, I think he would like to be buried in a simple rock and thorn tree enclosure back in Africa with his adopted brothers. That's where I think he belongs."

"God damn, boy, what do you know about Catholics?"

"I read about them when I was on a ship in the Caribbean. Percy had all kinds of books on religion. He could cite chapter and verse from both the Old and the New Testaments."

"You talk awful pretty for being a heathen like you are."

"I'll heathen you! You damn illiterate Cajun!"

"Damn it all to hell! One thing for sure, Percy deserves better than he got today." Broussard pounded his fist on the dashboard.

Matumbo sat straight up. "I'm taking Percy back to Africa," he said. "I'm going to see to it that he has the warrior's funeral he deserves. You know that he's still in the thoughts of every Zulu who enters battle. The Zulu will chant his praise song until the spirits return."

"But is that where he would want to be?" Broussard asked.

"Where else would he want to be, but with his brothers?"

"He would want to go home," Broussard said.

Matumbo furrowed his brow and was deep in thought. He looked in the back seat at his son and grandson.

Shaka asked, "Where's his home, grandfather?"

"A place called New Orleans, Shaka," Matumbo said. He closed his eyes for a moment, and then he opened them and leaned into the back seat of the car. He spoke softly, so only Shaka could hear him, "And soon we will be taking our brother home."

Broussard followed the procession to the gravesite. Matumbo waited for his son and grandson, and they walked together to the grave, carrying shields and spears.

The funeral director conducted a short service before a small gathering. I was surprised by the number of people who came to the cemetery, especially by Morty Goldstein. He had shown his respects to Willie and Pearl by going to the funeral home, but then he went the extra mile by going to the graveside. I had never been completely convinced that the deal with him would perpetuate, but he turned out to be an honorable man.

After the mourners had paid their condolences to Pearl and left, the gravediggers took hold of ropes under the coffin and prepared to lower it. Before they could remove the boards under the coffin, Matumbo stopped them. Broussard walked with Willie toward the cars, and he told him they were taking me home to New Orleans. Broussard went to the hearse and had the driver get out. They got in, and Willie drove him across the lawn to the gravesite.

"What 'ta yah you think you is doing?" the funeral director hollered as he ran after the hearse. Shaka grabbed him before he reached it. He lifted him off the ground and held him in midair, a few feet from the grave. The funeral director yelled for help.

Broussard told him to hold down the noise, and had Shaka let him go. "We can get this done," he said, pointing to my coffin. Broussard and Willie joined Matumbo and his son, and they lifted my coffin into the hearse.

Pearl realized what was happening. She smiled. "We're going to take my grandfather back to his family," she called out in a voice loud enough to wake the dead. I felt a strange warmth inside me. It was the first time I had felt anything since I had passed over.

"You can't do that!" The funeral director shouted.

"Yeah, I can," Broussard shouted back. "I want your hearse. What will you take for it?"

"It's not for sale!" He put his hand on the hood. "It's a '46 in perfect condition. I bought it new."

"That would make it eight years old. Now, how much do you want for it?"

"It's worth at least a thousand dollars!"

"Eight hundred!" Broussard came right back.

"Nine hundred!"

Broussard counted out nine one-hundred-dollar bills and handed them to the man.

"I'll get you the papers," he said.

"Don't bother, you can give them to Willie later," Broussard said.

"Okay, then – you bought yourself a hearse, but you still can't take the body!"

"We can and we will," Broussard said. "And what's more, you'll have your men close the grave, and as far as anyone will ever know, Percy is in there." He took out three more one-hundred dollar bills and handed them to the funeral director.

"And may Mr. Hays rest in peace," the man said as he put the money in his pocket.

"Let's go!" Matumbo said.

"I'm coming, too," Pearl shouted, and ran over to Shaka and took hold of his arm.

Willie rushed over to Pearl and slipped his arm through her arm, and put himself between her and Shaka. "It's a long way to New Orleans!" he said.

Shaka laughed and moved to the side. Willie stood as tall as he could, but was still over a foot shorter than Shaka. Pearl put her arm around Willie's waist and said, "Are you jealous?"

"Nah...I'm not...." He put his arm around Pearl's waist. "Maybe a little."

"That's a good thing, Willie. Oh, and it doesn't matter how far we are from New Orleans. You're going with me, and we are taking Grandpa home. I'm looking forward to the trip."

As I watched them walk away, they faded into a mist that was coming from a colorless void. Everything grew dim; I struggled, but I was unable to see what was going on. There was an explosion of bright light that blinded me. Then, after what seemed like an eternity of nothingness, my eyes adjusted to the light. When they did, I was looking at my mother.

The End